Very slowly, Jordan brought the unsuspecting fly down low so Belinda could see it. The fly perched among the hairs on the back of Jordan's hand, working its way down to his skin. Belinda saw large yellow-green pupilless eyes looking at her or perhaps at the hand it was about to bite, she couldn't tell which.

"The fly takes time to ready its bite," he said. "If you are lucky, you will kill it before it bites the back of your hand. The fly must never suspect that any treachery is afoot!"

She never saw Jordan's right hand move. She heard the smack and the fly disappeared beneath his palm. When he lifted it, the fly rolled off onto the ground. Belinda squatted on her haunches. The deer fly didn't look as big now as it lay in the dust. The eyes hadn't changed, but she could tell there was no life in them.

"You took its life," she said.

"Yes, child." He took his hat from her and replaced it on his head. "You can't always reason with the one who will harm you."

Book One of the Fadó series

The Senchai Mosaic

Joseph A. Callan

Jigsaw Press
Sun River Valley, Montana

ISBN: 9781934340615 (paperback)
ISBN: 9781934340622 (eBook)
LCCN: 2010942021

Back cover photo of Mr. Callan by David Harris

Proudly published in the USA

For the missing pieces of your reading puzzle…

Jigsaw Press
www.jigsawpress.com

To Paul Bagdon,
writer, friend,
and the meanest teacher I ever had.

Cathy - for a little fantasy in your life.
Love Joe Joe

Acknowledgments

For me, writing this book, was a mixture of very hard work and tons of fun. There were times I felt brilliant and times I felt intimidated and inadequate. It was at those difficult times especially, that I was (and am) thankful to my wife, Mary Eileen, who encouraged me and kept me going. She remained resolute when I felt like quitting. She is my "Verdor." Every man should be so lucky.

It was my great fortune to have a father who loved literature and words. I have never met a man who had as extensive a vocabulary. It is because of him that I write and enjoy doing so. Unfortunately he didn't live to see this book come to print, but he is in here. He is my beloved "Pater Nos."

I acknowledge my children, all grown now, Meghan, Brendan, Sean and especially Devin, our youngest who inspired my story telling when she was a young child. I can still hear her saying: "And then what happened?" after the bed time story I was making up and thought I had finished.

Brendan, thanks for your edits and suggestions and encouragement.

Thanks to Meghan, who now has two "wee wanes" of her own, (future writers, I hope) and Sean, you were both very kind and tolerant of my reading to you, trying out new chapters and plots at the dinner table.

Thanks to my sister, Teresa Valentine.

Writing is an art, rarely perfected. Writers seek that magical turn of a phrase like the word addicts they really are. For me, it took help and I had the best. I belong to two writing groups who gave me the most valuable of gifts: their time and honesty and their skill. The first group was known as "Paul's Group." (Paul Bagdon to whom this book is dedicated) I will always cherish the time spent with these wonderful people, all great writers: Emily Altman, our POV police, brilliant with her comments, if she said she "loved it," you knew you done good; Bonnie Frankenberger, who kept us organized and set the standard for writing natural dialogue; Blanca Mastbaum Kane, our fact checker, (outstanding cook too, her snacks kept us all feeling loved); John Karp and Louise Whitney have writing humor down to a tee; Willow Kirchner, who has a most insightful mind and an edgy and always interesting perspective on all things; Art Maurer, calm, methodical, and spot on with his criticisms; Peter Maurer, who brought the fresh young voice and insight this genre needs; Linda Pepe who told me in my early miserable attempts that I had imagination and the rest would come, thanks for that; and last but not least, Roz Pullara, who showed me the power of great imagery and metaphor, and who never wrote a dull scene.

And my second group called "Writing Pals": Larry Belle, Cathy Salibian, Sue Vinocour, and Neil Frankel—Your exceeding generosity of valuable time and talent is humbling. Your intelligence was a boon to me and even though not one of you would purchase or take a fantasy book from the library, you gave me your best. I hope that I made you proud.

There is no substitute for a skillful editor. Because of the scheduling format of both these writing groups, it was impossible for either group to critique this book in a contiguous time frame. Therefore I would like to thank Mari L. Bushman of Jigsaw Press. She put the important finishing touches, strengthened the weaknesses, trimmed the fat, evened out the jagged places, and simply made this novel so much better.

—*Joseph A. Callan*

Prologue

"To become a Senchai is a lifetime of study. What does that mean, Thomar? *Reprose ne nihi ta!* Respond to me!" Pater Nos' dark eyes peered out from under bushy white brows. With his right hand, he stroked his long white beard. In what he considered his most playful, imperious mood, he raised one eyebrow in mock parody of himself, as he had seen the students do when they thought he wouldn't notice.

Thomar was on his feet, rigid as a candlestick. A bright lad of eight years, he was now in his fourth year of training, ahead of some of the others present, although it was not uncommon to mix the academic levels, especially for story time. A shock of brown hair fell over freckles that blended into one on a pug nose. He was the smallest of his class. Pater Nos enjoyed him and picked on him regularly. The girls in the class favored him also.

"It means that," the words poured from Thomar in his haste to please, "it means you keep learning, but you are never learned; you can be grand, but never humble enough; that when you think you are wise, then you are a fool."

Thomar studied his teacher with eyes so intense that no one could tell if he were about to burst out laughing or crying.

Pater Nos kept him in suspense for a few seconds with his arched brow, then said, "Good, Thomar. It is my hope that some day you will come to believe your words. For that, you may bring me my drogha, as hot as you can carry. There's a lad, and put it on my chair. Now then, as for some of you, soon, perhaps tomorrow, you will begin your education in the divining arts."

A ripple of excitement flowed around the room with the creaking of chairs and the turning of smiling faces.

"All of you please me," Pater Nos said. "I see in your bright, young, faces, many rewarding tomorrows. But for today, I will sit with you a while longer and finish my story, as you wish, if you promise to return to your studies straight away when I am done. Kinlein, be dear and fetch my cloak. There is a chill in the air that wants to get the better of me."

Pater Nos studied the young faces in front of him wistfully. Only he knew what lay ahead of them. He wrapped his cloak about him, then slowly lowered his ancient frame into his chair. With cup in hand, he continued the story the students had begged of him.

"Yes, Onnie, to answer you, I did send a mouse to Darkin's lair, poor thing. It suffered because of my arrogance. So mind that you are careful about such things, when you become Grand. It is not a badge to do what you wish, I assure you."

He again tightened his cloak about his old shoulders, then sipped the steaming drogha. The hot liquid, made from the leaves of the Moo plant, always soothed him.

"It is cruel," he continued, "to enlist the innocent to fight evil, yet at times the pure are the only ones who can. The mouse's death bruised my soul, but nature, as you know, seeks a balance, and as for Putris Darkin, well, you will learn what happened to him, but all in good time."

The new girl sat on the floor furthest from Pater Nos, her legs crossed in front of her, her hands supporting her chin the way four-year-olds sit. She stared up at him, soaking in every word, every movement he made. She was a captivating child of surpassing beauty. Her blue eyes penetrated rather than looked; her composure hinted at one who takes interest in all things, yet hides her pain well. Her father had recently been killed. Pater Nos had been expecting her.

"But first, you must introduce me to your new friend."

All the young heads turned toward the girl. Thomar stood. "Her name is—."

The blond child cut short Thomar's introduction.

"My name is Belinda, Grand Lord Pater Nos, and I want to go to school here."

Pater Nos studied the child over the rim of his steaming cup. A quickening of hope stirred within him, his hands tightened their grip on the mug of tea.

Finally, he thought. *Finally.*

One

FLEN THE EXECUTIONER eased his large hand inside the leather bag that hung on a wall hook above his bed. He worked his fingers over the smooth surfaces of the spheres inside until he found the one he wanted, then withdrew it, massaging the obsidian orb in his palm, thrilled with the luster, the response to his touch.

He would kill her with this one.

Flen rubbed the globe along the outside of his nostril, imparting an oily sheen. The cleft at the end of his nose showed clearly on the stone. He grinned at his ugliness.

"You're a handsome one, you are."

He sneered, exposing corrupt teeth. "It is your turn, Bortal. The rest of you will have to wait and I'll abide no jealousy among the lot of you."

He shook the bag as if to discipline the remaining orbs, listening to them click against each other.

"I'll wager it's been a long time since you tasted the blood of a woman," he teased the orb he called Bortal. "Let's see if you are up to it. If not, I have a willing replacement in Testo or even Vord. Aha! And the nasty little Tro awaits to show all of you,"

He shook the bag again, then returned Bortal to its home. In his mind, he pitted one against the other, whipping them, he fancied, to a fever of envy. Finally, he tied the bag by its leather drawstring to his belt and strode from his bedroom through a solitary house, out the back door where his executioner's block waited.

The execution block was no more than a great stump of cedar, three hands high and twenty across, with a hollow depression carved in its center. He had not covered the block of late, so scarce was the rain. If the others discovered his negligence, there would be reproach.

"The depths of Nye claim them all," he swore loudly. He hated them all and they, in turn, had little to do with him.

The young children of the city were terrified of him and cried out, so their mothers hid their faces until Flen's hulking form was well past. Older children dared taunt him, sometimes throwing stones from behind the safety of a wall, but he never gave chase. He wasn't stupid; he would never risk his office for a loutish child.

A poor example of the Giant's race, Flen was the kingdom's wart.

Again, he removed Bortal from the bag, placed it gently in a nest of dead grass on the ground next to the stump, and grabbed a battered seed sack full of sand that slouched over the top of a nearby fence post. On the sack he had painted a crude pair of eyes, a nose and mouth.

"Come along," he scolded the face. "Let's not bring shame to yourself by cowering like a hairless rat."

He roughly placed the sack down in the hollow of the stump, then knelt beside it.

"That's just so," he coaxed. "Put your head down and keep your eyes on the block. If you do, I'll be kind to you."

Flen began to caress the sack, gently stroking the makeshift cheeks, pretending to move hair or braids away from its neck. The trembling he imagined beneath his touch excited him.

"There you are, you witch," he murmured. "What do you have to say for yourself now? Not so high and mighty without your purple hat then, are you?"

He rose up to pace about the stump, lecturing the sandbag that was now, in his imagination, the person of Governor Lorca. He fell silent for a time, strutting about as one preoccupied with some detail of office, then began to chastise her again. With a swift kick to her side, as if she lay a prone supplicant, her head resting on the stump, he punctuated his remonstrance.

"Let this be a lesson to all of you," he bellowed angrily at the dry air. He knelt again, plucking the orb from its nest.

"Do your job, Bortal my love."

His excitement grew, engorging him.

Flen rested the orb gently on what would be the nape of Lorca's neck. He gained his feet and strolled leisurely toward the fence post, where his hammer leaned. Looking down at his arms and legs he watched the swell and give of his muscles, admiring the tone of them. His sweat made them glisten like newly tanned leather. He opened and closed his palms, watching the play of tension along his forearms, fascinated with his protruding veins.

He would sweep her legs with his great hammer. When she lay crippled and moaning, he would drag her to the block and give her to Bortal. The swelling in his loincloth pinched, demanding to break free.

In a tremulous whisper, he said, "I tried to tell you now, didn't I, Lorca? But you would never hearken to me, would you? He's just an ox, isn't he? No one asks me. And now you've invited a foreigner, a Senchai. You are a fool and you will pay the fool's price."

Flen grasped the long-handled hammer, then returned to hover over the sandbag that lay unaware. Some of its threads had detached themselves and lay awkwardly frazzled. The sight of them, for some reason, caused him the irksome disappointment of not seeing the head of Lorca any more. The victim of his virulence was only a sandbag.

His thoughts turned sour, the excitement deserted him. Deflated, the disappointment hung on his face. Feeling weak, he bent and retrieved the sphere, returning it to the bag.

Flen had never executed anyone.

He tossed the hammer and it slid across the barren ground toward the fence post from whence he had retrieved it. Before it rested in place, Flen turned and shuffled, head down, back into his house. He returned the leather pouch of globes to their hook above his bed and threw himself across the tick. He would try to sleep.

The house shook with a pounding at his front door.

A visitor?

Flen quickly came to his feet, immediately suspicious. He glanced at the bag to see that his treasured orbs were safe. It struck him that whoever was at his door might see the block uncovered in his back yard and his hammer poorly regarded. He would say he was earnestly practicing and had just now come inside for refreshment.

I'll have to be more careful, he rebuked himself, *but who would think that I would ever have a guest?*

"Peace to this house."

He recognized the voice of the assistant governor. He knew what she wanted.

Flen opened the door and replied, "And peace to those who enter it. Welcome, Hisash. Come in. You find me unprepared for visitors, as I was working my trade out back."

He made a show of wiping his brow with the back of his forearm. *Hisash—in my home? Her plans must be more urgent than I thought.*

She had been attending him of late. Twice within this month, she had "run into" him by the town's deep well on his way back from the Library of Tomes. She had been flattering and conversational.

"I have noggin, but no wine," he lied. "Will you partake?"

"Joyfully," she lied in return. "There is nothing like the drink of the commoner to remove the dust from the parched throat of even the highest born."

Flen eyed her momentarily. Had he just been insulted? He pointed to the only table through a doorway into his scullery.

"Sit there," he said before retreating to the basement for a flask of the bitter drink.

"High-born, my red round bottom," he grumbled, out of Hisash's hearing. "Who does she think she is? I know you, you vixen. You are the daughter of Dep the Soaper, as lowborn as a toad."

Flen pushed bottles of good wine aside on the dusty shelves to lay his hand on a flask of noggin. Satisfied that it wasn't his most recent, he returned to the kitchen.

Hisash sitting in his chair needled him. He would have none of it. *The darkness take bad manners.* "You are in my chair," he said, scowling at her.

"Your pardon, good friend, I meant no insult." She removed herself to a seat on a bench opposite the table.

"None taken."

He took two mugs from a cupboard shelf, blew the dust from inside them and placed them on the table.

"To what do I owe the honor of this visit, good Hisash? Are you lonely for the company of a good man?" He snorted derisively. What could she do to him, anyway? *In one month she'll be laboring at the soap works.*

It wasn't romance, he was sure. He knew, as did anyone, that she was Lorca's lover, at least up until last season's pitiful harvest. She would have little to do with men. Flen, being a quiet listener, relied on gossip to glean his knowledge. His position as executioner gave him not only voting rights at the council, but access to the Governor's hall as well. It was there by the shadowed door that he overheard the whispers.

The last council meeting was of particular interest. Governor Lorca had decided to invite the Senchai wizard to the valley. The decision was not well met--with some, including Hisash, openly hostile toward it.

Six days ago, a pigeon had brought the news from the Mosaic. A female wizard called Verdor would be sent. Flen was sure she was due any day now.

Hisash grabbed one of the mugs just as Flen filled it, and had it to her lips before the blessing. She grimaced at the taste of it.

Flen sensed the urgency in her. He liked it better. *Get to it and state your mind.* He was no good at the social protocols anyway, having little opportunity to practice them.

"You know the law of Troca, good Flen?"

"And if I do?"

"Then I can make you governor if you have the hair for it."

Flen noticed a glint of fear in her eyes. She had crossed a line and knew it. Hisash had goods to sell now and, if refused, her fate in the soap works would be assured. She had come too far and was too accustomed to the life of an assistant governor. She was ready to die rather than go back to being a commoner.

"I have been thinking about Troca lately," Flen said. Hisash, herself, had germinated this seedling in his head at their last meeting by the well in a conversation that had stimulated his avid rash of practice sessions of late. "What is it that you could offer me?"

"Power." She let the word linger in the air as if she had spilled perfume on the table before him.

"I am quite satisfied with my humble office. I have no needs. Besides, how could you, who in one month will be swabbing soap scum for your daily bread, help me, already an officer of the council?"

Hisash winced, recovered herself swiftly, and said, "Think, Flen, you could be governor. Think what that will mean to you. You will be powerful beyond your wildest dreams; you will be an emissary to the Mosaic. The name Flen will be respected. And, with my help, you will turn our valley back to prosperity. Your name will be scrolled in the Tome of Governors. You will be forever revered as the one who saved us."

"If I challenge Lorca and kill her, why should I need you?" Flen poured the noggin again, carelessly spilling some on the table. He liked what he was hearing.

"You will need me for very important reasons," she said, retrieving her filled mug. "You will need an assistant with experience, since you know nothing about the legalities of governing, or how to approach the Mosaic. You cannot look the fool to them or they will shun our kingdom. Look around you, Flen. The drought is drying us to slow extinction. The oxen, even our most hale lines, are about to collapse. The women in the valley are barren. A child has not been born in more than twenty moons. You could change that with my help, Flen. You could be our Deddimus." Her voice barely above a whisper, she breathed the god's name.

The two conspirators bowed their heads, more from habit than any reverence.

Hisash slurped her noggin. Flen looked about him with feigned indifference as she continued.

"I could gain support for you. Already Entwas is angry. He believes nothing but a change of governor will save his precious animals. Several others are incensed that Lorca has asked for the wizard. What can the wizard do that we haven't done for ourselves these many centuries? And the people of the valley need someone to blame for their hardships. I can place the blame right in the lap of Lorca, where it belongs. At the same time, I can make you a hero. They will be hungry for her blood. I can do this for you, Flen, and no one else can, or will."

"Why not just poison her and relieve us, wouldn't that be easier?"

"Easier, yes, but why risk an election when the Troca has given us a means to kill her legally and establish a rightful successor, namely you? Think, Flen, when will this opportunity come again for you? The time is right. You will challenge her, kill her and then you will be in her mansion before this month is over."

Flen traced the rim of his cup with his thumb. He regarded Hisash, who was now leaning toward him, awaiting his reply, a reply that could save or condemn her. She was correct. He had no expertise in matters of the Mosaic or the inner workings of councils. He sat at the same table with all of the Burba Council, pretending aloofness by his silence. His votes were often cast on the basis of which buttock he scratched or which way his feather quill would fall from vertical.

He couldn't seem to follow the complexities of kinship or oxen lineage or the economics of the soap works. Taking his cues from some of the other members, he timed his grunts of approval or disapproval on his best guess of the mood of the rest of the council. He never volunteered an opinion or argument. His contribution was to sit and await the vote, which he would then scribe boldly with head shaking or loud sighing as he folded the ballot. He might deposit it in the box with emphasis added by bold arm movements or a sound thumping on the lid after the vote disappeared into the slot. The burdens of government always showed heavily on his face, but in his head were thoughts of which of the members present he would like to mount or how one might look prostrate before his executioner's block. That he fooled no one rarely entered his mind.

"What of the wizard, the Senchai?" Flen said. "She may be here tomorrow. What if she sides with Lorca and invokes some magic or trick on Lorca's behalf?"

"Like what? What could she do to you?"

"I know not what," he replied. "Perhaps some spell or potion to befuddle me. What say you to that?"

"Impossible! She can never harm you. She is sworn to that. A Senchai is mandated to never interfere with the government of any kingdom. All was discussed at the council meeting, surely you remember that."

Flen didn't remember.

"She comes here as an advisor only," Hisash said. "She can do nothing to you. She cannot hurt you or she violates her oath."

"What's an oath but so many words," Flen said with a sneer.

"True, Flen, true, to mortals such as we, but through all of time, never has a Senchai foresworn. You are safe from her, be assured of that."

Save for the momentary silences that punctuated their earnest conversation, the two might have missed the noise. Not a thump exactly, more like a rubbing sound, as if an intruder listening at the door had lost balance and moved more heavily than prudence would allow.

Flen put a finger to his lips, but the warning was wasted on Hisash, who sat frozen in silence, her mug part way to her lips. He moved quietly to the door and, with a quick movement, opened it to no one there.

He raced into the yard, moving to his right, across the path to his house, then around to the back where his executioner's block remained undisturbed. He hurried to his hammer and stood it against the fence post. Turning back, he nearly bumped into Hisash.

"See anyone?" she whispered

"No one. If someone was here, he is very fast, or just disappeared. Mayhap the Senchai, arrived early?" A chill spread across Flen's broad shoulders. "They can disappear, mind you. They dart about unseen."

"Mayhap, but I am doubtful."

"Why?"

"A Senchai would not have been heard. If it were someone, it was like to be one of Lorca's spies."

"One thing is sure, this meeting is over. Go and come here no more."

Hisash hesitated. "I will go, good friend. But I would go with certain information."

"Like what? Woman, you wear my patience."

"Like if you are disposed to my plan."

Hisash leaned toward him, poised on the balls of her feet. Perspiration had bloomed just above her upper lip, betraying her. She must have invested everything into this meeting, her future as she saw it, and, indeed, her life.

Flen nursed the silence that hung between them. He knew what he wanted to do, yet enjoyed seeing her squirm. These plans were best started and once governor he would deal with Hisash at his leisure. He would control many things then.

"I am agreed," he said finally. "I will kill Lorca and be governor and you will be my assistant. Now go."

A comely woman, Flen thought, *a stretch too broad in the hips for my liking and with ears too big for her face.* But in Hisash's smile he saw what Lorca must have seen at one time.

"To us then, good friend," Hisash said, "and may Deddimus bless this plan. I will contact you soon about when and how to make your challenge under the laws of The Troca."

The afternoon was fading. She would finish her journey home in the dark but she left him with a buoyant step.

Flen turned toward his door and was about to enter when a movement startled him. A crippled bird lay next to his stoop. If it hadn't moved he might have missed it completely; its brown color blended with the dust.

"Ah little one," he said, "so you are the intruder. And why would you come knocking at my door?"

Flen looked around again considering the lack of breeze. The bird couldn't have been blown into the door. He gently picked the creature up. In his great hand, it looked no larger than a brown nut. It stared at him through black, cabochon-like eyes. He felt the trembling life beneath its brown feathers, the warmth of it in his hand. He stroked the bird softly under its beak with his thumb.

"Were you sent, then? Or did you just lose your way?"

He continued to stroke the bird's chest until the trembling began to subside.

"There, there," his voice was low and mild, "nothing to fear. Did the Senchai send you? They can be tricky like that. And what did you see? Just two friends gossiping, verily. Nothing more, neh?"

He pushed his thumbnail into the throat of the bird and popped its head off as if it were the hat of an acorn he was about to eat.

The bird's head thudded against the doorframe and fell into the dust next to the stoop. He threw the carcass up on the arched roof over his doorway and went inside. He didn't give the bird another thought, but as he headed for his wine cellar, the Senchai was very much on his mind.

Two

WHEN VERDOR FIRST crossed the Mohr Mountains into the Valley of the Giants, she was a six-year old child and Lord Pater Nos had carried her most of the way on his shoulders. Her energy and excitement, enough to sustain both of them during the long walk and difficult climbing, quickly surrendered to quiet trepidation when she saw how large, in every way, the Giants were.

"I'm afraid, Master."

"What do you fear, child?"

The Giants' eyes seemed gentle, but their big noses and large hands and the way they towered over her teacher intimidated the girl.

She was Pater Nos' apprentice back then, starting her second year at the Mosaic School. Her name was Belinda—Belinda with the golden hair. Already she knew more science and numbers than her parents ever would, had they lived. Much of that first visit to the Giants, she now recalled, had been spent peering out from behind Pater Nos' black cloak.

Today, she would see the Giants again, not as a young child, but thirty-three-years old and with a new name. A thread of fear from her earlier visit still tugged at her, challenging her courage. Still, a Senchai wizard goes wherever he or she is needed. Since the Giants had summoned such help—although her honor would have remained unblemished in declining—she, Verdor, wizard of the Senchai, Grand by all accounts, would never allow considerations for her safety to hinder a mission.

"They may be a doomed race," Pater Nos had told her on that first journey.

"Why, Master?"

"None of the other five kingdoms will associate with them, except in commerce."

"Why?"

"They are too large physically. Intermingling would be impossible."

Pater Nos had spoken to her like this always, as if she was an adult student, and she loved him for it. He was ever tender with her and patient, never condescending, other than perhaps with her name, which he shortened.

"You see, Bell…" They were sitting on a fallen tree to rest. Pater Nos was waxing pompous as he would when he thought there was something important for her to grasp. He pointed his forefinger at the canopy of leafy trees overhead. "There are fewer than ten thousand living giants. They persist in applying to our Mosaic for changes in kinship laws. But that, I think, will prove futile. They are, my love, running out of breeding stock. Even now they are almost all blood related. That's not good."

"Why, Master?"

"That answer will come later in your education. For now, do you remember what I told you happened to the Cauldea in the time of the Wolf?"

"Why, yes, Master. They were all swept away by a plague."

Pater Nos had waved his hand in front of him as if in dismissal. "It could be a matter of time before a similar fate befalls the Giants."

So today, in the time of the Stag, Belinda, now called Verdor, crossed the last mountain of Mohr to begin the long descent to the valley below, the valley of the Giants. She had grown to a svelte six feet tall. Her hair still golden blond, she was not only very beautiful, but also possessed of a quiet self-assurance. She was poised, and not in a studied way; her gifts were as natural as the petals of a flower.

The rising sun cast magenta daggers across the distant peaks of the Saget Mountains that defined the Valley's eastern boundary. The brilliant sky might have portended a weather change, but she knew there would be no rain. The valley had been in drought for two years.

Verdor found a large, smooth rock at the apex of the mountain on which to place her mantle and, sitting on it, she lay her Cept— a willow staff as tall as she—over her right shoulder so that its length crossed in front of her, the worn tip touching the ground to her left. She removed the strap of her bag from about her neck, made obeisance to the new sun, then placed the brown, leather sack in the cradle of her crossed legs.

She sat for two reasons: one, to drink in through her very pores the beauty that Deddimus had surrounded her with this morning; and two, because a Senchai should never bolt into any territory, be it the Giants', or Catsyu, or even the peaceful Dardyea.

"Remember that," Pater Nos had once told her. "Hover like the falcon before you alight. Learn all that your six senses can teach you before you approach, for as you know, the Senchai are not loved or respected equally in all kingdoms."

Verdor's delay also afforded her the warmth and comfort of the new sun, having the spent the night in a deep and drafty cave with only her cloak to cover her.

Already the air was drying, yet there was a hint of tincture, which she couldn't name. It smelled at first like foul spue or chide or sassafore, very faint, just touching the edges of the air. She concentrated on the odor, as she knew it would soon be lost to her once she became accustomed.

Before her, and to a far distance, stretched the Giants' valley, a desolate scene, and not as she remembered it.

The Grune River, just a trickle now, sparkled like a chain of diamonds under the already bright sun, winding through brown grasses and leafless trees as if searching for a reason to exist. The shrunken river, Verdor assumed, could offer little to the Giants.

Even the evergreens had only new growth, as if the sawfly had infested them. The bright green tips on their bare branches seemed a valiant effort to greet the new season despite the odds. The tilled fields that bordered the blanched woods were barren and dust blown. Planting had been postponed or given up altogether. No animals grazed the blighted pastures or firebreaks.

Verdor had not heard of famine here, but from what she could see it wouldn't be far off. The valley was ill and she sent to heal it, but where to start?

A noisy flock of ravens that suddenly jabbed and darted above the trees an arrow's flight below her interrupted her deliberations. *I have been seen. Remarkable how well the Giants hide, despite their size.* She sat a while longer, giving the sentry time to inform the others.

Preparations would be made, a table set in a home vacated for her or likely one of their libraries. On this table, a feast of cured meats and dried fruits and other delicacies cut in portions to fit her hands, but in quantities sufficient to gorge a Giant's appetite. The sacrifice they would make to feed her, when their own may soon go hungry, was not lost on her. But to refuse the largess would be an insufferable insult to the Giants.

Verdor was hungry, eating little in the five days, but the biscuits and wine she carried, and occasionally a handful of early mountain berries, since leaving her home, the Mosaic School.

The sun was higher and smaller, the brazen colors of the early sky blended to a bright blue. She gathered her mantle and slung the strap of her bag around her neck. She left her seat on the rock, tapped her Cept on the ground before her to warn insects of her footfalls, and set out to meet the Giants.

The path was sometimes steep, causing her to lean heavily on her staff as an old woman might, and, at times, gently sloping, but ever downward, straining her knees. She stopped often. The mysterious smell she had noticed upon cresting the mountains gave way to dust and pine pollen, and the odor of the city below: cooking fires and the manure of their beasts of burden called oxen. Her nose detected bee's wax, compost mold, and new cut lumber. There was a rendering fire, no doubt cooking lard to make their prized soap.

Verdor could easily detect the stink of their bodies. They were by now, she suspected, grudgingly unaccustomed to bathing, because of the drought.

There were aromas missing—the fragrance of spring flowers such as trillium and myrtle and hyacinth. But most disturbing wasn't the smells or lack of them, it was the silence. Except for the bark of one of their great dogs or the cackling of ravens, the valley was quiet. She had no fond memory of the music of the Giants, the thumping drums and shrill lute, but its lack echoed deeply within her.

They should have sent for me sooner.

By the time the sun was at its peak, Verdor was approaching the gate of their city called Burba. She had stopped to make water in the privacy of the woods. She suspected the introductions might take a while and her modesty would prohibit her from taking care of that matter in the open, as the Giants were accustomed to doing.

The gate was only a swinging pine pole before a bridge spanning a nearly waterless gully, the bed of the River Grune in better times. The barrier was of little more use than to keep the oxen out of the town. Giants had little to fear from invaders, for although their city was rumored to store great treasure—a rumor Verdor doubted—no army had any interest in challenging them. The practice of war had disappeared from their lives, but no one doubted that they could do more damage with a hay hook, if so inclined, than any aggressor might accomplish with a sword. They were big, many nine feet in height or better, and very strong.

The Giants were content to stay in their valley. No one dared change that. Verdor wondered how much longer that would be.

She ducked under the gate, crossed the bridge and continued along a cobblestone street toward the city center.

Twelve adult giants had gathered in a small group to watch her approach, some shielding their eyes from the sun's glare. Young children, too, milled about, many of these youngsters likely had never seen an outsider before. It amused Verdor to think what they might have expected.

I look only a stripling adolescent to them. What have they been told by elders, or exaggerated amongst themselves in their child-like ways, concerning me?

The city of Burba looked more like a town with a circle rather than a typical town square. Streets fanned outward from a round well, like spokes of a wagon wheel. The twelve, apparently of some civil rank or other, stood with their backs to the stone wellhead that, more than the houses, whispered of antiquity. Each Giant, male and female, assumed a benign posture with their prodigious hands at their sides, showing her their palms in welcome, as if preparing to embrace, though she knew they would not touch her.

They were dressed in the earth tones of their tribe, olive-green sleeveless jerkins and sand-colored, baggy pantaloons, girded by great straps knotted in the front of their bellies, not nearly as ponderous as Verdor remembered them to be. Their pantaloons extended down to their knees, leaving thickset, sinuous legs exposed to the tops of their ankle-high leather boots. There was little variation in dress among them, which accentuated the strong familial appearance.

Each shared features that seemed to distort the symmetry of their face—brown hair and eyes, and overly large ears, tumid noses over thickened lips that pouted, making them appear dull of wit. They were an ugly lot at first look, and frightening to a novitiate outsider, but as with all races, what beauty they must possess cannot always be seen with eyes.

Verdor studied each face as she approached. Some appeared compliant. Some sulked. In the eyes of others burned a quiet hostility. *I must be cautious.*

The female governor was foremost and took to one knee, bowing deeply so that the brim of her purple hat, the distinguishing symbol of her office, dusted the ground. Verdor too, knelt briefly on one knee and bowed, though not as deeply in deference to her own station. Excessive humility by a Senchai would be embarrassing to them.

The governor, still on her knee, said, "I am Lorca, governor of Burba, chief counsel and keeper of the tomes of the Green Tribe. I am principle emissary to the Mosaic. There is none higher." She stated this not as a boast, but to assure Verdor of their regard for her. "All inhabitants of this blessed valley, the high, the middle, and the low, welcome you."

So, there had been a change in governors. *Did old Maysi die or was it the turmoil of the times that replaced him?*

Lorca rose to her feet, awaiting a formal reply. Though no taller than the others, Verdor divined from the aura of competence that the governor ruled by a strong presence of will. She had her charges' respect, though it appeared given only grudgingly by some.

"I am Verdor, Grand Wizard of the Senchai Order. I accept your welcome and, in return, offer you fond greetings from Pater Nos, Grand Lord of the Mosaic, who wishes you prosperity."

Verdor had omitted that she was summoned, which had the desired effect—a general grunting of approval. Lorca had referred to the Green Tribe, but once in the Giants' history, Verdor knew from her studies, there had been many tribes. Kinship lines had blurred over the centuries. Only the Green Tribe was mentioned now, though the name had little meaning. History was very important to them and well recorded. Belonging to a tribe placed the Giants solidly within the scrolls of their storied past.

Lorca introduced the others one by one: the Counselors—Chops, Osah, Osish, and Piash; Duron, keeper of the water; Hisash, assistant governor, historian and minder of the lineage. Hisash avoided Verdor's gaze. Next, Lorca introduced the keeper of the soap works, Noish; Entwas, the herder, and Pusah, the grainer. Finally, Lorca acquainted her with the woods keeper, Telf and the scribe, Nakus, who doubled as Lorca's cook.

All bowed deeply and offered blessings, most with sincerity, some with pride, a few with cold formality. *It appears that not all are of one mind regarding my summons.*

The formalities behind them, Lorca dismissed everyone except the scribe, Nakus, whom Lorca had instructed to accompany both her and Verdor from the wellhead along one of the broad streets. Verdor lengthened her stride so as to not encumber them.

"You are tired," Lorca stated, as if Verdor had no opinion of the matter. "I will take you to your home where you shall eat and rest. Tomorrow is soon enough for us to solve the problems of the world." She grinned, contorting her lips to a sneer, yet the humor was clearly in her eyes; intense eyes, though locked in a permanent squint from the weight of flaccid lids, sparkled with wisdom. In them, Verdor could see the burdens of leadership, of holding together the multiplied opinions, denunciations, while reaping the few rewards of public office in troubled times. Verdor judged Lorca to be at least ten years older and there was power in her. She could feel it and the comfort of it. *Would that we become friends.*

After a short walk, they stopped outside a library.

"Before you leave," Verdor asked, "can you say if you have noticed any new smells in the valley of late?"

Lorca studied Verdor with interest. "Smells like what?" she asked.

"Like a hint of sassafore or spue. I can't say for sure, but I noticed it as I crossed the Mohrs, when my nose was new to your valley."

Lorca's keen gaze intensified. She knew the question wasn't asked to make conversation. "No," she answered and turned to her scribe. "You have a good nose on that face of yours, Nakus, what do you say?"

Nakus sniffed and said, "None."

"I am alerted," Lorca said to Verdor. "I will find out what I can. Enjoy your house and I will see you tomorrow. Nakus will stay with you, to reach you things, or help you with the records, as you may need them. You can trust her."

She departed without a backward glance, leaving Nakus and Verdor at the threshold of the library, Verdor's home for the near future anyway.

Three

HISASH WAS IN FULL STRIDE now, heading back to her home. She was enjoying the twilight air as the setting sun relinquished its hold on the earth. Her mind went back to the meeting with Flen, the evening before the wizard's arrival. Flen had not been at the city center to greet the wizard. Hisash smirked. *What might Lorca say to that insult?*

Her plan was going well, she thought, even if she was now partners with an oaf.

What a beast Flen is, as ignorant as dirt.

She could handle the dolt with ease. Yet, for the briefest of moments in facing the wizard, she had lost control.

Had my fear shown?

She had plotted the course of her life quite satisfactorily up until now. Hisash was determined to never go back to the soap works. She shivered just thinking about her years there, about her father, Dep, another beast. Since her mother died when she was small, her most vivid memories were of the late evenings when Dep came from work, stinking of lard or dried oxen blood. Hisash had learned one thing from Lorca—one either worked or governed and governors never smelled like her father.

Now twenty years old, Hisash had labored in the soap works for much of her young life. Her last job, before what she referred to as her liberation, was tending the scum boiled to the top of the great clods in the massive iron caldrons. She would scoop the scum, called brack, from the top of the hot lard, an important job, in order to keep the evaporation going smoothly.

"This way, flip, then over and flip, then dump here. Then again, so you see." That was all the instruction she had received from the Seer teaching her to brack, but that was all that was really needed.

If the brack—hence her title as Bracker—became too deep, the evaporation of the water would slow. This slowing would have a ripple effect, eventually stalling the entire system.

Each clod was large enough to fit the remains of ten oxen. After the oxen were butchered and the meat salted for food or for shipment, the fat, the blood, the skin and bones, were carted to the clodding basins. These were partially filled by the water carriers who tied large vessels to the backs of oxen and transported water in an unceasing chain from the Grune River to the soap works. During the process of clodding, the rendered lard would be changed from one caldron to the next in sequence, purifying the lard under the constant care of the Bracker. There were seven changes in all. More ingredients were added toward the end: bees wax, liver oils and in some, the fragrant oil derived from the Sweet Nule flower. Finally, the end product was poured into molds.

The brack was not wasted. Once cooled, it was carried to the fields to be spread on the ground as fertilizer for the next season's hay crop, which, because of the drought, was in danger. Hisash didn't need to be a farmer, to know that dry soil and sparse grass didn't bode well for the oxen.

Tending the fires, called fiercing, was left to the men. A Fiercer could be deep in the forest one day chopping wood or, on another day, working in the drying house, a vast structure where the wood was stacked and dated for curing before being transported to the fire pits beneath the clodding cauldrons.

The fires could never go out, so a Fiercer's life was tied to the flames. It would be hard to say if the Fiercer controlled the fire's life or the other way around.

It fell to the Fiercer to plan which sections to cut from the surrounding forest. He would do this in a way as to not exhaust the nearby trees, forcing him to go deeper and farther away for his load.

Hisash loved to hear the men talk about their job. She strained to understand their peculiar language:

"Menshun, will mine cut the high or the nay, th-morn?" A Fiercer was questioning his boss.

"The nay it is, Jon, to the breaks. Then the high on the high. Twain the aixen, in the blithers. The ruffs be neken."

Theirs was a fascinating speech that few other than a Fiercer born to the woods would understand.

Hisash had asked, "What are they saying, Seer?"

"I don't know much of it, but Jon wants to know should he cut close or deep into the woods in the morning. Menshun told him to cut close in the cool of the day then deeper in when it gets hot. He told Jon to take a team only. He said that stumps have yet to be cleared by the firebreak and to take more than a two-up could risk injury to the animals."

"He said all that?"

"Sure he did, girl. A Fiercer's life is about the work, not the talkin'."

A Fiercer's job also included planting and pruning to ensure a constant supply of fuel for the coming generations. Hisash envied them. They were outdoors under the open sky and smelled like, well, like they should, and not like boiled fat.

Once she had begged for a job collecting the petals of the Sweet Nule. She had to get away from the clods.

"Please, Seer. If I walk this ring any longer, you'll be makin' soap of me by week's end."

She would be outside, like the Fiercers, in the sunlight, gathering the sweet smelling petals. What could be easier?

It didn't work out as she had thought. The Sweet Nule grows only in the bogs. Gathering these petals was brutal work. Her feet were wet from morning 'till night. She was constantly prying off giant leeches.

The water beetles, though not as prevalent as the leeches, were nasty biters and the clothing that she needed to wear to keep the biting flies at bay made her life under the sun as hot as her feet when walking the ring of planks around the clodding cauldrons. After three days she was begging for her old job back. The Seer quickly relented, because he liked her, he said.

"You were my best bracker, Hizy. I'll see what I can do for yer."

The Seer had worked her job as bracker in her short absence, and was thankful to have her back. No job in the soap works, it seemed, was any more or less pleasant.

Scaffolds were built to surround the caldrons at the top to enable the water carrier to add, or the Bracker to take away. The job was dangerous work, made more so by its unvarying tedium.

Hisash's mother had been a Bracker. None could say why, but she fell in one sad afternoon and became part of that week's pouring. Seer had watched her go in, but she never made a sound, he said.

The night was closing down over Hisash and she quickened her pace. She remembered walking the ring , as it was called, scooping and dumping incessantly, arms aching, perspiring from the heat and steam that rose all around her, burning her feet if the water carriers weren't timely in soaking the walkways. The constant play of heat and high humidity in the factory caused the supporting planks beneath her to warp and twist. The lumber was changed on a regular schedule. Hisash had dared to think that perhaps her mother's death was no accident. Maybe her mother just let go and fell in, unable any longer to put one foot in front of the other.

Hisash had caught herself several times mesmerized by the churning and bubbling just below her feet. At times, woozy from dehydration and stiff with sore arms that could hardly carry her bracking scoop, she had considered how easy it would be to just step out and drop. But she hung on to a life of grueling days and, after her mother's death, frightening nights when her father would come to her room stinking of smoke and boiled blood to demand favors of her, which she was neither prepared to give nor able to refuse. The darkness still made her fearful.

Hisash spat on the ground, thinking of her father. She stamped her feet on the road for several paces. She had crushed his skull one night while he slept with her bracking scoop and, that same night, unseen, dumped his body in the bog to be claimed by the water beetles. She told the others that in his grief he had followed his wife into the clods. Since he was no friend to anyone, and because she put up such a show of grief, no one cared to question the orphan on the sad matter.

Being seventeen then, and employed, she was allowed to keep her home and though her days were no less a drudgery, her nights were her own. She taught herself to read. The letters were difficult at first, but she possessed a quick mind and never had to be shown anything twice. She was stunned by her first visit to the libraries. The books there and the knowledge in them were intimidating. But once discovered, the library was where, when not bracking, Hisash spent her free time.

She'd flirted with one of the young foppish keepers, promising with her eyes and smile what she would never deliver with her body. He'd helped her eagerly through difficult words or passages and let her take volumes home. At times like these, while isolated in her home with a book and a tallow, she could relegate walking the ring to a distant tomorrow. Through the magic of reading, she could go outside the valley, over the mountains, and into strange lands where even stranger inhabitants lived. Her father would have never let her do this, just one more reason she was happily rid of him.

A waxing moon was already high. She hadn't noticed its rising, but was grateful for the light. It silvered everything around her, the road before her, the trees that rose up some distance back from the road on each side. She couldn't distinguish individual trees exactly, but she knew the woods. She was now where, this week, the Fiercers had gone to trim and harvest. Occasionally there was a break in the wall of trees for a cart path or a lesser access road.

Hisash's home was just outside the city, not far from the soap works. An easy walk, but one she rarely made after dark. Moon shadows cast by the tree trunks began to take shapes, one a wolf, another a bear. Her mother had told her stories of the deep woods when she was younger, and although she knew they were just fables, she couldn't deny the prickly bumps rising on her arms and neck.

She had left home this morning with a cloak over her arm, and was now glad she had thought to bring it. She hadn't intended to return in darkness. Hisash redoubled her pace.

Behind her now was the black skyline of the houses of Burba. Ahead of her, Hisash could see the dark peak of her home against the wind born sparks and glow of the soap work fires.

Night fears began to weigh on her spirit. Loneliness reached out to her. She fought the sad grip by turning her thoughts to anger. "You'll pay, you hag." Tears welled to the edges of her eyes. She wiped them away viciously with her sleeve.

Even the night was once tolerable when Lorca loved her. How beautiful everything seemed to her then. At days end, Lorca set aside her never ending work and the two of them would sit close together sipping wine and not talking, gazing up to the night sky, absorbing its twinkling mysteries.

Sometimes the night air awakened a deep ache in her left leg, the vestige of an injury years before at the soap works. She thought that day to be the luckiest of her life. She had fallen from her scaffold and, by rare good luck, she didn't fry in the fires under the clods. When she fell, her leg struck a standing plank, a replacement due to be installed. The lumber was there only because the Fiercer who carried it had stopped to view a crowd of visitors to the soap works and had rested the board against the scaffolding on which Hisash stood. The plank broke her leg and the bone jutted from her thigh like a boar's tooth, but had the board not been where it was, she would have dropped to her death in the fire.

Governor's Day in Burba, the one day each year Lorca visited the soap works. Hisash was walking the ring as usual, bracking scoop in hand, when she heard the entourage approaching below her. She leaned out to watch the nobles pass, and fell. The pain was horrible, worse than any whipping at the hand of her father. She was so embarrassed to fall in the midst of these royals that she held her tongue, a marvel as much to her as the crowd that quickly gathered about her.

She never heard what Lorca said, but she remembered seeing her lips move as Lorca bent over her. Mostly, Hisash remembered Lorca's eyes. They seemed to flow gentleness toward her like a river. She stared back into them as long as she could. The current washed over her. Hisash gave herself to it, falling upon it, as if she were a leaf being carried along in a tender rivulet.

She awoke two days later in Lorca's home. There was a dull throbbing in her leg, but no real pain. She had never known such comfort. Lorca didn't sleep on a tick stuffed with straw, but a feather mattress cornered by the four posts of a real bed. Covering Hisash were luxurious quilts, a solace unknown to her.

She stayed with Lorca three years. At first she was to stay only while she recuperated, but then one afternoon, Lorca found her reading in the library on the second floor of her home. The governor was surprised at her youthful exuberance and probing questions. They found themselves locked in conversations that, as time went on and Hisash healed, became mutually challenging and beneficial. As Hisash had nothing but idle time, she read from Lorca's books on government, law and agriculture. Soon Lorca began to rely on her for details and finer points of the law. Lorca arranged for her to be a full time paid assistant, which stunned Hisash. *You can make a living by reading and talking?*

Later, Lorca put Hisash's name up for assistant governor. With Lorca's endorsement, there was no contest. Within that third year, Hisash learned to write. It was also in their year together that they became lovers.

At first, Hisash was a reluctant partner in the joys and mysteries of physical love. Lorca taught her with gentle skill to take delight in her body and give pleasure in return. Their bodies and minds melded in physical and emotional release; Hisash discovered fulfillment beyond imagining; her life was perfect. Until Lorca brought Nakus into their home and everything changed.

Four

VERDOR AND NAKUS WERE ABOUT to enter one of the newer but smaller libraries that also served as home to a bachelor custodian named Dair. He would stay with relatives for the duration of Verdor's visit.

The Giants lived in timber-frame houses, two story structures with gabled eaves, stone chimneys and split cedar shingle or thatched roofs. Main beams were left exposed and the in-fill was a stucco made from clay mined from the banks of the Grune and imported lime mixed with the hair of oxen. There was little variation in design or color. The only requirements were that their homes be sturdy and dry. The houses were well maintained, however; the stucco was regularly white-washed. The streets were clean. Verdor thought how newly built the ancient city appeared.

There were five libraries throughout the city of Burba. The oldest and largest was called the Library of Tomes. Every bit of the Giants' history was stored in them, including their laws. Even the accounts of timber harvests, of trade and tradable goods, and yearly food pro-duction, could be viewed by anyone interested. All of them housed records of the Giant's kinship lines, marriages and deaths, animal husbandry, and soap recipes.

The Giants were a clever people and their soap trade to many areas enabled them to import all manner of interesting things from beyond their valley. One of these was the glass that they used in their doors and windows. The glass allowed them, without shutters, to keep out the rain and wind, yet allow a very pleasant brightness within. Verdor noticed that they framed the glass in the manner of gates, which they could open and close at will. Few of the other kingdoms used glass, a cause of envy and, Verdor suspected, the basis of the rumors of their great wealth.

"You see that we don't lock doors here," Nakus commented to Verdor

In fact, Verdor had noticed that none of the doors had locks. Theirs was the only Kingdom where such security was considered unnecessary. Thievery was rare in the valley and dealt with harshly when discovered. With no clasps or fasteners to enforce privacy, the respect for discretion was valued and expected.

"If you wish to visit a home, you just call out to the house. 'How the house?' you will say, or 'Bless the house,' will do," Nakus instructed the wizard on this custom. "Just entering a home with no call is not done."

Within a fortnight, Verdor would have reason to break this rule twice.

The front door of the library opened into a grand foyer against an adjacent wall with clothes hooks. Immediately facing them was a stairway up to the second floor. To the left of the stairway was a large room with a fireplace by which was stacked a good supply of dried oxen dung and seasoned wood. On the opposite wall, the Giants had attached a table of suitable height, stacked with plates, and cups also made for Verdor. Here was the food as well, bowls of dried meats and fruits and the expected flasks of wine.

The scullery behind the staircase was half the size of the fireplace room. There was a convenient indoor water pump by a steel tub, large enough that Verdor could bathe.

To the side of the washbasin was a door overlooking a withered garden, bordered by a weathered stockade fence. In all other spaces in the Library were shelves stocked with books, carefully preserved and attended, some new or rebound, some worn with use.

"Eat with me, good Nakus," Verdor said. "And tell me what Lorca meant when she mentioned that you can be trusted."

They sat, the wizard at the table and Nakus on a chair she'd dragged over from the fireplace. The chair Nakus chose was large but even so, her great bottom smothered the seat. She broke wind as she lowered herself and without comment waved a big hand to disperse the foulness. The table too low for her, she situated herself to one end, still within easy reach of any food that interested her. Nakus poured wine for the two, mumbled a blessing, and drank greedily. Verdor filled a plate, then pushed the bowls toward her guide.

"There has been trouble," Nakus said. "Many are unhappy, some are angry."

"How angry?"

"There have been threats."

"Against whom?"

"Lorca, though there is little she can do about this drought."

"Yes, a drought is a hardship."

"There is more."

"Tell me," Verdor reached for the wine flask and filled Nakus' cup also.

"I will tell you, as I have been charged, all you wish to know. The drought is only part of Lorca's problems. There have been many stillbirths, many fertile woman never come to term. Even the Oxen have not calved as they should."

"Throughout the Valley or just in Burba?"

"Most of us live within the city but the problems are throughout. No one has seen any young of the year from the wild animals. Some claim there is a curse on the land. Some want Lorca to give over her leadership."

"Is Hisash the historian one of them?"

"You could see that, then?"

"Hisash wears her anger on her face. I would expect a historian to be more, shall I say, balanced."

"Yes, Hisash is the main instigator and as for balanced, even the high and mighty have their jealousies." Nakus did not explain further. "But there are others. Noish the herder is very unhappy. His oxen are not doing well and he is frustrated."

"Is Lorca in danger?"

"Perhaps. She can resign her post, which she won't do, or she can be challenged for it."

"Challenged in what way?"

"Her term has two marks left. She can be killed for it."

"By Hisash?"

Nakus snorted. "Hisash hasn't the core for such a challenge. Lorca would kill her."

"Who then?"

"Flen the executioner could kill Lorca, readily. Hisash has been talking to him."

"Could Flen lead?"

Another snort. "Flen couldn't find his buttocks with both hands. Lorca thinks he would be a mouth for Hisash."

A rat edged into view by the chimney, its nose up, nostrils working as if touching and sorting strands of air. The rodent trotted along the wall in the direction of the table.

"Is this killing legal in your Kingdom?" Verdor asked, keeping one eye on the rat's progress.

"It is, an old law called The Troca. It hasn't been used since well before my father's time, but it is still the law."

"So anyone can challenge to mortal combat an elected leader and take the leader's job? Why have elections then?"

Nakus shrugged off the question, filling her mouth with more wine instead. "It has been many years, if ever, since this valley has had such problems as it has now and many years since the Troca has been spoken of. If anyone ever thought to change the old ways, few are inclined to do so now."

The rat loitered under Nakus' chair.

"Will Lorca fight Flen?" Verdor asked.

Nakus again filled her cup, draining the flask. She drank noisily and wiped her lips on the back of her wrist. She studied the floor as if the answer were written on the boards there, then looked up at Verdor with sadness in her eyes.

"Lorca will fight," she said. "And she will lose."

"Perhaps I can help her, then."

Nakus spit the wine back into her cup, as if startled by the remark. She coughed boisterously as though choking, though to Verdor she seemed to be trying desperately to tame a sudden fit of laughter. She stared at Verdor's tender frame over the fleshy hand that stifled her cough. Her eyes belied a merriment that faded to terror. Nakus averted her eyes, studying the floor and finally noticed the rat, now between her great feet.

Verdor realized that Giants being terrified of rats was no myth. Instantly, Nakus was standing on her chair. She wrung her hands into her apron.

Nakus stared as the rat abruptly rose into the air as if an invisible hand had caught it by the tail. There it hung, suspended, jerking like a hooked fish. Slowly, the hapless rodent drifted past Nakus' gaping face toward a window by the fireplace. The window bolt slid back from its latch, seemingly of its own accord, and the window swung wide. The rodent sailed through the open window where it dropped out of sight into the shadows of the alley.

"I can't abide rats indoors," Verdor said with a wink.

The Senchai was not enjoying the moment at the expense of poor Nakus. Her demonstration was clumsy, she thought, and perhaps unnecessary, but the Giant with her would now understand that the diminutive wizard was not without resources. It may be a while before she grasped the extent of the problems in the Valley, but a change in leadership now, for good or not, could hamper her work here. Work that was, Verdor felt in her bones, perhaps too late in beginning.

Red-faced, Nakus huffed and blew her way back from the seat of the chair to the solid floor, one foot at a time.

"Lorca would be grateful for your help," she said to Verdor.

Five

VERDOR AND LORCA DID NOT MEET the day after her arrival as planned. Once Verdor sent word through Nakus that she would need additional time in the library, they met on the fourth day at Lorca's home.

Verdor had studied the Giants' bloodlines with the able assistance of Nakus. There were no clear reasons within the tomes of kinship as to why the women were not coming to full term and bearing children. Nor did Verdor expect there to be. The oxen, which the Giants so prized, suffered similarly, leading Verdor to think that what she looked for was not to be found in the books.

Governor Lorca was as courteous a host as she was curious. She insisted on learning about Verdor, and her rise to Grand, before she would discuss anything else. As big and strong as she was, Lorca had very feminine interests, wanting to know from Verdor what the latest fashions in the other kingdoms were. "What are the Dardyea women wearing?" she asked.

Lorca said she was tired of her garb. "Drab," she called it, adding, too, that the clothing of other kingdoms excited her. She desired to know many things: about Verdor's golden hair; if Verdor could change giants into mice; did she have a lover, and was her lover a male or female; did she think the Giants were ugly?

Lorca wondered aloud about the diminutive stature of other races, and no offense to Verdor, she said, but it was a curiosity how anyone could find such delicate features attractive.

"Too brittle for my liking," she commented, then laughed.

Lorca displayed a good sense of humor, never missing a chance to laugh at herself, in her looks, or dress, or even her high office. Verdor discovered she liked the Governor very much. Well into the afternoon and deep into their third cup of tea, they finally began to discuss the Valley's troubles.

"I attempted to find out about the smell you noticed as you came across the Mohrs," Lorca said. "The odor of spue or sassafore or chide, you said."

"And?"

"You were right, there seems to be such a smell, though unidentified."

"Who discovered it?"

"Telf, the woods keeper. Only once, he said, but it made an impression. He was coming back from a deep foray into the woods to check on next seasons' cuttings when he smelled it."

"Could he say from where?"

"He couldn't, but he noticed it, as did you, when his nose was fresh to the open air, out from the woods. For him, also, it quickly faded."

"I would speak to Telf with your permission."

"Telf is an odd one. He spends his time talking to the trees and yanks the ears of young Fiercers for cutting a limb wrong or tromping on new sprouts, but there is none wiser about the woodlands. As for my permission, you need none of that. Our whole kingdom is at your service and everyone knows it." Lorca gazed intently at the Senchai. "Do you think we're being poisoned? Is that what concerns you about this smell?"

"It's possible. The oxen are having similar gestation problems. Drought alone could not cause such maladies."

Lorca, who had been sitting opposite Verdor at the table, stood and walked over to a window. She looked out on the street below. After several long moments, she returned. Verdor sensed fear in her as well as something else.

"The oxen do not know of drought," Lorca said. "Entwas, whom you met when you arrived, is a curmudgeon, but he would die himself before he let his precious animals go thirsty. The river is low, but he manages enough water for them."

Lorca hesitated again, yet in that pause, only a broken intake of breath, Verdor felt certain Lorca was hiding something.

The Governor pushed on. "Entwas wants to dam the river as does Pusah the grainer. It's their concerns for the beasts and the crops that they want me out of office. I will not allow the river to be harnessed. It is nothing between us and, in truth, they are both good men for the jobs they have."

Verdor decided to chance confronting Lorca about her feelings. "You are in pain," Verdor said gently. "How can I help you?"

Lorca gave her a guarded look, then smiled. "So, Senchai, you seek to work your magic on me?"

"There's no magic here. Is it the idea of poison that upsets you so, or is there something you withhold from me?"

"I withhold nothing," she protested.

Verdor waited.

"But yes," Lorca admitted in a subdued voice, "I am alarmed by poison. I have a recent experience that makes the word echo painfully within me."

"If the strange smell is poison," Verdor said, "I wonder who in this kingdom could gain such an exotic substance that I would not know of?" Then, as if her tongue were charting its own course, she spoke aloud a thought her mind had yet to grasp. "Unless it were from another world."

In the next instant, Verdor rebuked herself for the lack of discipline. But the spoken words were there now, responsible for the haze of fear that seemed to follow them. Silence hung heavily, daring who should next speak.

"Putris Darken?" Lorca's dark eyes were fixed on the wizard's face, as if searching for an answer she did not want.

Verdor gave no reply.

"Deddimus be with us," Lorca whispered. "Who would invite the blackness to our valley? And why?"

She stood again, walking slowly back to her window. This time, instead of looking out on Burba, she drew on a cord, which loosed a richly embroidered tapestry that fell over the window, shutting out not only the daylight, but whatever else might be lurking. For a long time she stood staring at the cloth, as if seeing the figures depicted there for the first time.

Finally Verdor rose to stand beside her, looking up at her care-worn face.

"Lorca, be at peace. There is nothing certain yet. Give me two of your pigeons and I will seek the wisdom of Pater Nos. But first tell me of your experience with poison."

Lorca sighed deeply, then wove her fingers through her long hair, entwining them at the back of her head. She closed her eyes as if to conjure a memory that lay on the back of her eyelids.

"It's Hisash," she said finally.

"What about her?" Verdor said.

Another long sigh. "She attempted to poison Nakus."

"Why would she do a thing like that?"

"Hisash was jealous of her, and for no reason. I took Nakus in as a personal scribe and cook. Nakus had been working in the libraries, a very intelligent woman, though a trifle callus. Hisash thought we were lovers. For all the world I don't know why."

"So Hisash tried to poison her?"

"Yes, with larch sap in her wine. It was only by happenstance that I caught her mixing the deadly potion."

"What did Nakus do?"

"She knew nothing about it. I told Hisash that we were through as lovers and that she would not be invited to run again for lieutenant governor. I sent her home immediately."

"It was difficult for you."

"Very, I loved Hisash like none other, but I was blind to her faults."

"What will Hisash do now?"

"She will return to the soap works, which is an unfortunate waste for such a talented woman. But I could not turn her over to Flen the Executioner since no real harm was done. I hope I don't live to regret that also."

The sound of approaching feet on the oak floorboards interrupted their conversation.

Nakus appeared with much coughing and bluster, carrying a large parchment. Her face was as red as a chokeberry.

"What is it, my good Nakus?" Lorca said. "You look like death has you by the neck."

"This has just arrived for you, my Governor," she said, handing the parchment to Lorca.

Lorca studied the document briefly. "Now then, Nakus, we expected this, didn't we?" She handed the paper to Verdor.

"What is it?" Verdor asked.

"A notice of intent to challenge my office under the Law of Troca. Are you aware of this law, Senchai?"

"Nakus told me about it. She said you can be challenged by combat to death for your position as governor. It's a strange law for these modern times."

"Yes, Senchai, it's a terrible law, a vestige of olden times. But nevertheless, it's still the law. See there who signs it."

Verdor looked at the document. Hisash's name was on it with others.

Lorca walked back over to the tapestry, again studying the fabric. Her pain at the betrayal was palpable in the air.

Verdor rose to her feet, handing the paper to Nakus. "You have been overly gracious, Governor Lorca, but I must now leave you as I have work to do."

At first Lorca continued to stare at the tapestry, leaving Verdor uncertain if she had heard, until the Governor abruptly faced her.

"Yes, Senchai, as do I. You'll find pigeons on the roof. The Redbeaks are Pater Nos'. Choose from them. If there is anything you need, you will know where I am."

They bowed toward each other, Lorca's obeisance just lower than Verdor's. As Verdor was leaving, she overheard Lorca say to Nakus in a tired voice, "Bring your feather and good ink. We shall make reply to the challenge according to law."

A strange thing, the wizard thought. The Giants had a law of such barbarity, yet were otherwise peaceful, or so they seemed.

Verdor made her way up a narrow stairway to the roof. There she found a flat alcove cut into the angled rafters, large enough for a walkway and a pigeon cage, wherein perched twenty or so birds. She selected two of the plumpest. Examining their wings, she determined they were strong flyers. After accessing the message chest beside the cage, Verdor wrote identical notes hidden in a language known only to the Mosaic school.

She told of the smell and of her haunting suspicion concerning its origins. She also spoke, under the assumption that Pater Nos knew of the Troca, of the pending fight that may claim the Governor's life.

Rolling the messages into small cylinders, she tied one to each of the pigeons legs and set them free. They spiraled upward into the cloudless sky. It seemed to be an auspicious moment to her—a wizard of the Senchai placing the burden of hope for this valley on the wings of two fragile carriers. She watched them dwindle to small specks and disappear into the brightness of midday, praying that at least one would make it over the Mohrs, past the raptors, the arrows of poachers, and the dangerous winds, home to the Mosaic and Lord Pater Nos.

Six

THE TIME HAD COME to meet Hisash, the assistant governor. From her seat on the roof deck next to the pigeon's cage, Verdor drew her mantle about her and closed her eyes to focus on the house of Hisash. When she opened her eyes again, she was sitting on the path that led to Hisash's door.

The house was a modest one, not as large as most, but well built, sitting staunchly on its foundations as if proud of its independence. One of few houses outside the city proper, it stood alone in the fire-break, equally close to the city and the soap works factory. Poorly tended flower gardens surrounded the yard. The beds harbored a good variety of plants in need of urgent care as if the planter, ambitious at the first undertaking, had lost interest in them.

Verdor stood up, unsteady on her feet at first, because travel in this manner depleted her energy. But she chose this route because it was quick, and time, she felt, was against her.

"Blessings on this house," Verdor called out, to no reply from within.

The Senchai slowly approached the door, ajar about the width of her Cept. Emanating from the opening was the odor that had eluded identification. Here it was, bold now, oozing, weighting the air like the stink of a suppurating infection. Fear prickled Verdor's spine.

With her staff, she scribed a broad arc over her head touching the ground on either side of her feet while three times chanting a spell for her protection. *"Singtoe ee, Daiena."* She stepped forward, jabbing the point of her staff through the narrow opening. Touching nothing with her hands, she entered and, using her Cept, closed the door behind her.

Though still bright daylight without, the inside of the house was dimly lit by the soft glow of a taper that wavered, as if a light breeze played it, creating shadows that made the furniture seem to move of its own accord. Verdor carefully made her way across the room to another and there on the hearthstone of the fireplace burned the sinister candle.

Lumped on the hearth also was a Poker, squatting, its arms and legs so entwined Verdor couldn't tell at first which was what. Under a thin layer of hair, pale white skin glistened wet at elbows and knees and forehead. A single tooth in the Poker's pig-like snout glittered in the weak light, the round head darting feverishly side-to-side as if someone would blindside it at any moment.

Verdor guessed the Poker's height at only three feet, tall for its kind. Abruptly, the creature's mouth curved into an evil looking grin.

"Eh, eh, eh," it snickered. "Welcome, Senchai." What passed for a voice bore only the stridency of a rasping whisper on which it overlaid with exaggerated exactitude sibilant words, giving the effect of spitting its message, each sound an accusation, each lip movement a challenge. "It have expecting thee."

"Who invited you to this kingdom?" Verdor demanded, hiding her fear behind the force of her question.

The Poker grimaced in the effort to speak the unaccustomed language. "Thee twos hath me thee invite, eh, eh, eh."

The creature raised one finger from a hand that clenched its bony knees and pointed upward, lifting its head to expose the hole in its lone tooth through which it sucked its nourishment.

Verdor looked up and, though dim, the candle faintly illuminated the body of Hisash pinioned to the ceiling directly overhead, facing down. Perfectly cleaved, as if struck by a reaper's scythe across her middle, the two halves of her body were separated by the width of a fist. The blood boiling from her did not drop, but spread across the ceiling, seeking the four walls for a conduit to the floor.

Verdor steadied herself. It was no time to show weakness.

"*Singtoe ee dieena.*" She looked back to the Poker, gazing up at her through feral eyes the color of opals and blinking erratically. The round head was twitching back and forth, its posture insolent and challenging. Lifting one foot off the hearth, the Poker exposed its anus to Verdor, then defecated an olive green excrement on the hearthstone.

"They two hath invited it, eh, eh, eh," the Poker repeated like a macabre joke, its finger jabbing upwards.

"You will leave. This is innocent ground. You have no sway here."

"Nay, Senchai, Hisar nay the innoshent, eh, eh. Murder she maked here. Water beetles feast on father's eyes, eh, eh. Business here I hath. Thee no power to me thee hath. Eh eh eh. Thee leave now! Not it!"

The door through which Verdor had moments ago entered crashed open to smash the wall, shaking the timbers of the house, and daylight flooded the room.

Verdor turned toward the noise to Hisash's silhouette filling the doorway. Startled, Verdor turned back toward the hearth. The taper no longer lit, smoke wafted from its spent wick. The Poker and its offal had disappeared along with the odor, the ceiling as pristine as the day the house was built.

"So, Senchai," Hisash screeched, "you have taken to trespassing. By what right do you enter the home of a free-born Giant?"

Verdor, angry with herself for being deceived by the Poker, was in no mood to parley words. "Sit down, " she commanded, "or I will see you free no more."

The two glared at one another, eyes locked in challenge, until Hisash turned, closed the door, then took a chair a comfortable distance away, her bluster replaced by a fearful expression.

Verdor spoke first, but only after a protracted silence meant to heighten the discomfiture of Hisash.

"I know about your father, Hisash."

Hisash caught her breath, her body rigid, looking stunned as if slapped across her face. She continued to sit mute, but her eyes began to shift, fighting an obvious panic, looking for a place to run.

"Tell me, Hisash," Verdor said, "if I were to look around outside your home, what would I find?"

"You would not find my father's body if that's what you are thinking."

"Your father's body is not a concern to me. But you are, Hisash. Do you know what is happening here?"

Hisash pressed the palms of her hands together between her knees. Her shoulders sagging, she glowered at the Senchai.

"You are too young for such intrigue, Hisash," Verdor said, "and I assure you, you are in deeper trouble here than you can imagine."

"It's the Troca then, and how I press for it? It's the law, Senchai. There is no mystery here. It is my right."

"The Troca, my foolish child, is a distraction. Governors come and go. But what has been invited here will not leave so easily. One thing's certain, you will be powerless against it and even your new friend will be like a feather before a great wind."

"He is not my friend, if you refer to Flen. And I have never invited him here."

"Think, Hisash. When did you first notice the stones. Was your father still alive?"

Hisash shifted in her seat, locking her hands tighter between her knees. She searched the ceiling, then the floor. Her lower lip trembled. "You know about the stones? What do they mean?"

"I will tell you, but first tell me when you noticed them."

Tears welled up and Hisash stood abruptly. "I wish to be left alone, Senchai. You are not welcome here. I'll show you to the door."

She strode to her door and grasped the latch, and although she struggled powerfully, her heaving and pulling availed nothing. Pounding the door with her fists, then kicking the heavy wood, ramming it with her shoulder, until the sweat soaked her jerkin and she collapsed to the floor, breathless.

"Will you make me a prisoner in my own house?" Hisash whispered and covered her face with her hands.

Verdor approached, reached out and placed a hand on Hisash's broad shoulder. "There is a door within you that is locked tighter than this one you now try to open. It is this door that holds you prisoner." Verdor's voice echoed like quiet thunder. "Harken me well, Hisash, for I have seen your death. A lifetime of walking the ring at the soap works will seem a frolic in myrtle compared to what you face if you do not open that door."

Verdor fished inside her bag and extracted a small leather purse.

"When it comes again, as it soon will, this will protect you long enough for you to escape. Do not speak to it, just hold this in your hand and leave quickly. Find me. That is the best I can do for you."

Verdor walked around the slumped giant and casually lifted the latch on the front door.

"Wait!" Hisash cried. "When what comes again? What are you saying?"

Verdor turned back, appraising her. "You haven't seen it then, have you?"

"Seen what? You frighten me, Senchai"

"When I arrived at your door, Hisash, it was open a crack. I called out but no one answered. It was then that I noticed the same odor that I divined when first coming into your valley, five days past."

"What odor? This house is always clean, I see to that."

"Just listen now. When I entered, there, right there on your hearthstone, perched a lone Poker."

"A Poker? Here? In my house? May Deddimus help me!" All color drained from Hisash's face. "Woe to me. It's my sins will lay me at Darkin's cloven foot."

Hisash rocked back and forth, a low moan beginning deep within her.

"Hisash, Hisash," Verdor scolded, "bear yourself, you can't fall now. You must turn this around. It's your life you must attend."

Slowly Hisash looked up. "What do the stones mean?"

"Very little. I saw them when I arrived. It's a Poker's trick to terrify you. It could have been anything, stones, crossed sticks, any type of marker that you can't get rid of."

"Then why put them here at my house?"

"It knows you carry guilt and it won't let you forget it. The Poker, or rather the one who sent it, has plans for you, Hisash."

Eyes bulging, the giant stared at Verdor, her face parchment white.

Verdor continued in a soothing voice, "The stones will not harm you, Hisash. When did they appear?"

"The first stone appeared," she gulped for air as if she were drowning, "the morning after the first night he came to my bed. It was just a simple stone, by the path, and—."

"Hisash, you refer to your father? Is it he who raped you?"

"Yes."

"And then the stone appeared?"

"Yes. If I moved it, by the next sun it was back where first I found it. Once I threw it into the River, but it appeared again."

"One stone?"

"Then. Now there are three."

Verdor closed the door. "Rise up from there, Hisash, and we'll sit at your table. If you have a strong drink, this might be a good time for it."

Hisash found a large sack of clew nuts with which to build up the seat for Verdor and the two of them drew their chairs up to her scullery table. She poured from a wine flask, but would not meet the wizard's gaze. Instead, Hisash studied her cup, hands clasped between her knees.

"I can't fight this, Senchai," she said, shaking her head. "It terrifies me to stay in this house. I will burn it to the ground, is what I'll do."

"Can you burn the very ground too, Hisash?"

"How the ground? It is my fault."

"No, Hisash. The Poker follows your father's crime. It has been here since then. Your sin simply made it welcome."

"You know that I killed him then." She raised her eyes to search Verdor's face. "When the stone kept reappearing, I marked it as my shame. I thought only to rid myself..."

Hisash paused, then asked, "Will you turn me over to Flen?"

"I'll not judge you, Hisash, it is not what I came for. Your father's death is likely the second stone. The third is your attempt to murder Nakus."

"'Tis an evil woman you behold, Senchai. I was angered when Lorca took Nakus as her personal scribe and cook." Hisash's shoulders trembled. "I thought it the end of me. I am a fool."

Hisash pushed her wine away and let her head rest on her hands. "I don't understand," she mumbled. "My fear rules me." Deep heaving sobs racked her. Suddenly, she lifted her head. "Can you help me, can you drive the Poker out? I'll do anything you want." She stood up quickly. "I'll leave the valley, I'll leave this day."

Verdor showed the Giant her palms. "Sit down, Hisash."

The rapid breathing slowed, terror fell away from her. Once Hisash had re-taken her seat, considerably calmer,

Verdor lowered her hands. "Leaving the valley would be the death of you. None will accept a Giant. You will be forced to live in the forest with rogues. Is that what you want?"

"Tell me, Senchai, what to do."

"First you must understand that the original crime belongs to your father. You were a child. Fear was his gift to you. Fear belongs to the darkness. It is why the Poker left the stones in your yard. When you are always afraid, the darkness gains power over you.

"Second, this intrigue you undertake with Flen and the others, the Troca you bring against Lorca, plays into the claws of Putris Darken. It must be stopped. Surely you see that it is based on jealousy and revenge."

"I'll do that. I'll go see Flen before the sun sets."

"Leave Flen to me, Hisash. He will not countenance your change of heart. Go and find Lorca. Confess to her what it is you have told me. As for the Poker, speak of it to none other than Lorca. Tell her to ready pigeons to the Mosaic."

"Where should I stay, then? I won't stay here."

"Lorca will take you in. Carry what I have given you especially at dark. The Poker desires you for use by its master. It will stop at nothing to get what it wants."

46

***

Hisash left her house, carrying only the charm given to her by Senchai Verdor. It was a good distance to the governor's mansion for the Giant, but with fear prodding her, Hisash lengthened her strides to a clumsy jog. She was keen to arrive at her destination well before dark. Her lumbering gait quickly put ground behind her.

She wondered how she could have let her life turn as it had. She didn't regret killing her father, she would live with that. She shuddered to think of his hands on her, the filth of him filling her nostrils with the greasy stench of the soap works. Hisash remembered the grunting, pawing, inarticulate mewling of endearments while the lust was upon him, as well as the coldness afterward. His smell, as much as her defilement, had poisoned her so. Now, even going near the clods, smelling the boiling grease was like being under him again. *I can never return to brackering the clods.*

The wizard's words are the truth, Hisash thought. *The crime belongs to my father.* This was no small realization, and she rejoiced at it. She felt lighter on her feet. *Could this be the door that Verdor spoke of, the door within me that I must open?*

How could I betray Lorca ? Was that me who tried to poison Nakus? Thank Deddimus that I was discovered before any harm befell Nakus. And why, for the love of sunlight, would I let myself fall in league with that scoundrel Flen? I have much to answer for, and none too soon.

Darkness descended, simply dropped on her as if she had entered a tunnel. She tripped over a stone in the path into a flying, stunning, cartwheel that knocked the wind from her. She fell into the shrubbery, scraping skin from her palms and narrowly avoiding a solid thump to her head on the drought-hardened ground. She sat up, bewildered, not just at the abrupt turn of events, but by the sudden nightfall. It made no sense. She had been jogging in bright daylight just moments ago.

The fear that she had been subjugating with the promise of redemption washed over her again like a bracing tidal wave. She allowed time for her eyes to adjust, and then studied her palms. She could barely make out the dirt and small pebbles painfully embedded in her wet, torn skin. She brought her right hand to her mouth in an attempt to lick the wound clean. Her saliva stung, but she kept at it, first one, and then the other. The tension of fear worked into an ache in the small of her back, but she renewed focus on her hands, licking then spitting again and again until she was satisfied.

Please, please, please, she repeated to herself, as if begging some unseen evil to leave her alone.

Then her nose wrinkled.

No experience in her life could have prepared her for the odor. She had never smelled anything so vile before, but the stench reached out to her as if it were a hand, violently clutching her stomach with a wrenching twisting grasp. She knew before her eyes confirmed it that a Poker was near. *The evil thing brought the darkness!*

Hisash sat very still, moving only her eyes to their limits without daring to move her head.

The Poker's eyes, like tiny lantern flames, blinked, unmoving a while, gazing, blinking, then gazing, not a stone's throw down the path she had already walked. Hisash caught her breath. Her stomach constricted and warm urine wetted her inner thighs. The Poker began to move toward her and, closer now by half, it stopped. Hisash could see its form now, squatting in the middle of the path.

"Whither goest thee, Hisar?" the Poker rasped.

Hisash was mute.

"Thou ist mine, Hisar," it continued. The Poker acted afraid, perpetually on guard, like a sparrow in the granary.

"Leave me be!" Hisash screamed.

"Nay thee, Hisar, thou ist mine and I wouldst have thee. A choice thee hast maked"

"I made no such choice!" she bellowed.

The creature undaunted jerked its head back and forth, then back to her. Hisash could now discern the snout-like mouth, fleshy lips curled back to reveal a lone tooth.

"Evil thou art. Kilted thy father."

The Poker grew agitated, the head jerking increased, accompanied by snorting noises.

As if from the dark air, there appeared more sets of eyes, nearly identical to its own. Four, five, six, Hisash counted, approaching from further down the path, jostling and snorting and squealing at each other, like a pack of dogs closing on a kill.

***

Verdor searched within the house, then without, looking for sign. She found the three rocks, similar in size and shape, stacked atop one another just to the side of the path leading to Hisash's front door. Verdor considered how easily such common elements as stones could induce terror. Just one of a Poker's tricks that in themselves meant little. What they did indicate was that the Evil One had some designs on Hisash.

At this time, Verdor knew there was little she could do about the Poker, but make its stay less pleasant. From her bag she removed a fine red powder that she sprinkled over the three stones, reducing them immediately to a small pile of sand. It was not the Poker that worried her, nasty as it was, but the One who would follow with his army of Pokers and Mels, and sooner, perhaps, than she dared think about. She had been trained for such confrontations, but never tested. The possibilities frightened her.

Verdor sat on the ground, drew her cloak around her, and spent the rest of the late afternoon in chant and meditation. When she arose, she felt more at ease, ready to visit Flen the Executioner.

Seven

EVENING WAS DRAWING ITS MANTLE down slowly, allowing the world time to seek shelter from the coming night. Flen had just left his back yard, satisfied with a rigorous workout of his executioner's tools, where he had again, in his mind, grotesquely murdered Lorca while she begged pitifully for mercy.

Flen's was a meager plot five miles from the city. His ancestral home stood alone in the firebreak set about by unevenly spaced fence posts that supported nothing. The fence, when finished, would further isolate him and his possessions from the town's people whom he thought to be avaricious. The long neglected poles, some still leaning in unfilled holes, said as much about Flen's industry as the poor shape of the thatch on his roof or his dusty yard.

Living things did not thrive there. Not just because of the drought that plagued the Valley, but because the blood-soaked ground opposed life. Even beetles and crows avoided Flen's homestead. He would share nothing for food or drink, and many had been squashed under his careless feet or killed for merely getting too close. The dead ground on which his house stood was tainted generations ago during a time of bad governors, when there never was a shortage of the condemned. Still, the office gave him at least some standing and saved him from the prospect of earning a living which, for him, without any other skills, would reduce his lot in life to menial work like those employed in the soap works or, worse, those who tended the oxen.

Flen returned his treasures to their hook above his bed.

There were six spheres in the sack, each of a different size, the largest about the size of a small melon, the smallest no bigger than a calf's eyeball. With them he could accommodate any Giant, from child to the largest of the condemned.

The spheres of death were the trappings of his office. Ever he marveled at their exact roundness, carved and burnished from the hardest of wood called lignum vitae. Whoever made them had a great eye for symmetry. *How did they do it?* Flen had often wondered. Once he tried chipping into one with his knife, but the blade was useless.

Flen lived well on the public dole in a job no one else wanted. There had been mention, a time or two, of taking an apprentice. The thought of suffering the company of any of them, the idea of anyone else's groping hands on his precious possessions was insufferable. They were all fools, he determined, and none would be worthy. So, he and the disinterested city elders continually postponed the idea of any change to the established ways.

His office was never voted away by the elders and Flen was kept on at six Cindo each week, a generous stipend. "Thrice each day," he was to practice his blows. For years he was faithful to the law of his office, but no death sentences had been pronounced. In time he grew disinterested and weeks would pass before he would work.

His position as Executioner had another dubious benefit to the residents of the Valley. Mothers would threaten their naughty children with a visit to Flen or issue the warning that if they didn't mend their ways, they would certainly kneel to Flen's craft.

Only in Flen's mind had hundreds died at his hands, when in his dreams, the spheres he carried were bashed deeply into the backs of skulls with his hammer. Then he would be the center of the town's attention. Great throngs of his countrymen would gather in and around his yard. He would show them his skill. But in the daylight hours he complained: *I was born too late.*

He longed for the old times when the Executioner had greater status, and one's skills never dulled for lack of work. Flen could often be found, if ever wanted, pouring over the great tomes in the library. He could recite from memory the names of the condemned at the hands of past Executioners as far back as the time of the settlements: Genco of Burba, son of Back, whose crime was rape; Lon Lister of Koso, son of Stei: thievery; Morne Detch of Tule, daughter of Borst: murder.

For many there were notes in the margins in the very hand of his forebears, words of advice to future Executioners. The admonitions enthralled Flen. He read them over and again: "Needed five quaff of Hodge to sedate." Or, "defiant to the end, refused to quaff," or "should have been starved three days, evacuated her bowels at the block."

***

"I would tell you, Flen, there is evil on the Land."

Flen stared at Verdor, his contempt, thinly disguised, churning like lava within him. She had refused to drink with him, making it clear how she felt. She had never even made the customary greeting, but simply appeared in his scullery. He'd nearly jumped from his skin. The two were now sitting at his table.

Denied the courtesy to build up her seat, the wizard sat with her head just above the lip of the table making her, by his intention, as diminutive as possible. Somehow it failed to work and he struggled to attain dominance, glaring down at her like an irate father scolding a child.

"You wizards," he said, waving his hand in dismissal, "see trolls behind every tree and Mels behind every rock."

"You mock me to no avail, Flen, and you dismiss me at your peril. For I say to you plainly that before next growing season, there will be trolls behind every rock and this valley as you now see it will become anathema. You and the Giants will be gone and the very soil, like the death-soaked ground around your house, will be useless."

Flen's bushy eyelids began to twitch. *Does she threaten me?* He calculated the cost of knocking her head off her shoulders. One quick swipe of his bear paw fist should do it. *What then?*

The wizard's lips never moved, but in his head he clearly heard her calm reply: "It would cost you your hand in the attempt." *Did she really say that? Did I think to bash her aloud? What manner of sorcery is this?*

She held his gaze steadily.

He knit his brows. There was no denying that he'd heard her, even if she'd made no sound.

"What manner of witchery do you mumble?" He feigned innocence. "You come to my house and threaten me? Did you forget your mother's face? Have you no manners?"

He stood and walked away from the table. He bore the indignity he'd just suffered with heavy sighing and the exasperated upturning of his arms, as if begging for reason from the roof above. When he sat again, he chose another chair, a safer distance from her. He wished he had his hammer now, but it remained where he'd left it by the fence post. *Another time,* he comforted his slighted humor.

"What do you want of me, Senchai? To what do I owe the pleasure of your company?"

"Hisash has forsaken her claim to the Troca. The others, I am sure, will forsake theirs also."

"That's a lie!" Flen was again on his feet. He raised a pointed finger level with his waist, shaking it at her, careful to keep his hand near to his belt.

"I don't hold you in enough regard to lie to." She waved a hand in dismissal. "Hisash is, at this very moment, kneeling before Lorca, begging her forgiveness. Now you mark me well, Flen. I see you for what you are. The evil in you festers like a rancorous pustule, so I won't waste kind words on you. It is not for you that I come, but for this valley and its survival. The horror that will descend very soon will scorch the ground and kill all living things. So your presumed victory will be for nothing."

"Ha! So you admit that I shall kill her."

"I said presumed victory. It is you, not I, who presumes thus."

"I shall kill her and I shall rule, Wizard. This valley has been here under our control for many generations. You only need to see the tomes, which I read every day to attest to that. If there is any evil here, it lies with a weak governor who invites witches to solve problems that we and we alone will solve."

"Tell me, Flen, what would you do about the drought, about the river that dries up before our eyes? What will you do about the barren women? What will you tell Pusah when he asks why his fields produce nothing and what will you say to Entwas whose oxen wither like grass after a kill frost? And when your race is clawing the ground in hunger, what law will you pass to keep them from starvation? How now, Flen? What would you say to these things?"

"Your words are the drivel of wrought-up women. Our Valley has suffered drought. It will pass. The rains will come. Yes, mayhap a few will die, but that is our lot. It is no concern of yours or the Mosaic."

Flen approached the table to grasp the flask of wine he left there. Lifting it to his lips, he drank deeply, belched loudly, and drank again. The Senchai watched him closely. He returned, brooding, to his chair.

"In truth, Flen, the people of this valley will not starve."

"Ah, so…" He had caught her.

"They and the river and the trees, and the fields of hay, will have dried up and blown away long before that will happen."

"You speak nonsense, Witch!" He spun and punched the wall behind him for emphasis. A shower of fine dust filtered down from the rafters, catching the last of the sun's light that hung just above a window ledge.

For a moment the two watched the dust descend. Flen comforted himself that it would be impossible for so much to become so little. *Blown away? Our Kingdom? Bah!* He cared nothing for the wizard's predictions. Weren't they always seeing what wasn't there? Everything foreshadowed something to these witches.

When Verdor finally spoke, her voice heightened the silence like a water drop echoing in a sepulcher.

"Did you know that dust has no value in it, Flen? It is not Mother Earth, from which grows our life's sustenance. It is nothing."

"I weary of your prattle, Wizard."

"This very afternoon, I found a Poker within the house of Hisash. I spoke to it. It lays claim to her."

"Pokers and Mels," he waved his hand, "to scare vexing children to stay abed. If you wish to frighten me, then you waste yourself."

"I wish only to impart some sense into that empty melon you carry on your shoulders. You cannot win in what you seek"

The courage within the wine flask gave him the daring he needed. He bounded to his feet.

"I shall win," he bellowed. "Lorca will tremble before me, as will you and the rest." He hurled the bottle at the wizard's face.

He was neither sure then what he saw, nor could he say with any clarity when he awoke. He, of course, would supply a ready answer: he drank too much and passed out. But gnawing at the back of his head, repressed, but staunchly refusing to quit him, was the memory that the bottle he'd thrown at the wizard had reversed its trajectory and began, without assistance, thumping him repeatedly on his "empty melon" from every angle, easily defying his flailing arms. Eventually he gave up his futile defense and surrendered to the eager container, which seemed determined in doling out the most punishment possible before, and perhaps after, his head banged heavily on the floor.

Eight

"Gendau, there is a pigeon on its way from Verdor. Go up and wait for it, then bring me the news as soon as it arrives."

Gendau bowed and then raced on his young legs to the roof.

Pater Nos watched, amused, as the young apprentice—his latest and likely his last—disappeared up the attic stairs, his feet beating a staccato tattoo on the treads to the roof.

"Was I ever that young?" Pater Nos quizzed himself aloud, then immediately answered, "Of course you were, you bearded skeleton, but never that fast. Why, if I had his energy I would, what, what would I do? Nothing, get back to work. Where was I? Quickly now, before anyone should discover how useless you are. Here!" He waved his magic glass over the map spread amongst the clutter that threatened to overtake his desk. He drew the lens down close in order to focus, then away, and down on another grid to focus again.

He knew the depictions on the maps like the knuckles of his hand. What he didn't know and what he enjoyed searching for was the additional information that his looking glass could provide.

With his glass, he could simultaneously visit the physical landscape of the portion that came into focus. If the way was too steep or too snarled with brambles, or passed through any danger, he would pull the glass back and drop down into another, more promising, area. Pater Nos was determined to find a route to the spice regions for the Dardyea. He despised tariffs. But the five kingdoms were about business, not friendships, so the best he could hope to do was to find for the Dardyea a route of their own. He was resolved in his endeavor and had spent this and many other afternoons searching the ungoverned terrain surrounding the Dardyea's kingdom. It was just moments ago, during one of these "look-ins" that he glimpsed the pigeon, like a storm petrel, flying home with undeniable determination.

Pater Nos rolled the map and inserted it into its leather tube, then filed the tube with the others in one of many baskets that hung from the arched ceiling of his room. He ducked a large telescope, crossed the room, and began rummaging through other baskets, taking them down, then replacing them, all the while mumbling to himself until he found what he was looking for. "Here you are." He plucked the leather cylinder from its basket and spread the map out on his table.

"Gendau!" he squawked at the ceiling, "Where is that bird?"

No answer.

There is trouble, he knew, not by any intuition, but because he knew his former apprentice. Verdor would not send a pigeon for trifling reasons.

"Gendau, come you now!" Still, no response from the roof. "Ah, my dear Verdor, so independent. Your curiosity will be your undoing."

He smiled at a memory of the young Belinda and their special closeness. He had been her principal teacher throughout her apprenticeship and as such he glowed as if her intelligence were his own. What a delight she was then. He was still in awe of her. She had come to him as a small child.

See how she sits her mother's lap. What was her mother's name? Yes, Nordara, a beauty she was, too.

Verdor, whose name was Belinda then, would have a text in one hand, something she was rarely without, and on those days when Nordara would visit, Belinda would excitedly teach her mother whatever it was she happened to be learning. Belinda was the first female accepted into the school and the first woman to achieve the status of Grand Wizard. Pater Nos congratulated himself on his decision to enroll her into the Mosaic School. He couldn't say what it was about her that he loved more, her stubborn tenacity, or the curiosity that reminded him of his own beginnings.

***

"Belinda, were you in the Cloistral while I was away?"

Pater Nos called her Belinda only when cross with her. Otherwise he called her Bell. Being angry with her was difficult for the old Master, but she had broken an important rule, one that could have hurt her development as a wizard's apprentice.

Only Grand Wizards or students in Dotson were allowed in the Cloistral, Dotson being the period of training between a wizard's twentieth and thirtieth year.

"No, Master Pater Nos." The answer came too fast.

Pater Nos looked down on the child as she stood before him, her face was red, and she fidgeted with her hands. The two, master and apprentice, were in the study for the Cloistral, an antechamber of desks aligning both walls. The room was well lit by south facing windows.

At the far side of the antechamber hung the Cloistral door. It was no more remarkable than any door in the building except this door had "Trebasion", "forbidden," carved deeply across it at eye level. The word was well known and understood by even the youngest students. The door opened to a cavernous room that had been built into the double thick wall that surrounded the entire campus of the Mosaic school.

"I see," Pater Nos said. "Do you lie to me because you love me and have hurt me or because you are afraid that this will be your last day at this school?"

Pater Nos was aware of the rumors bandied about by the children concerning this most secret of rooms. One favorite story, which happened to be true, was that some of the books stored within this room could talk. Other rumors were wilder yet and most untrue, but he could understand why the room would overwhelm a girl with a mountain of curiosity stuffed in her small frame.

Belinda stammered, "I…I…" then fell to the floor, a puddle of linen and blond hair. Her skinny shoulders shook, her tears truly miserable.

Pater Nos would not allow her self-pity for long. "Did you find my key or did someone leave the door open?" he asked her.

"I searched for your key." Her face pressed against the floor, her arms covered her head. Pater Nos winced at her shame, but he knew that it was necessary. The girl had put herself in serious danger and left him with no choice.

"Get up off the floor, Belinda, and follow me."

Belinda pushed herself up and wiped her eyes, smearing her tears with her bare arms. She followed the wizard across the room toward the door.

"I will take you inside the Cloistral, Belinda. You will tell me exactly what you touched and what you looked at and what you read. If you lie to me now, or ever lie to me again, I will send for your mother to take you home. Your studies here will be ended. Do you understand?"

Belinda audibly caught her breath at his offer of a reprieve. Her "yes" was barely heard. Pater Nos pushed a heavy iron key into the lock and swung the door open. The hinges moaned at being disturbed. The entryway to this sepulcher for books was dark and foreboding. A cold mass of air smelling like mushrooms drifted out from the dark cavern, raising visible goose bumps on Belinda's bare arms. She picked up a candle from a nearby box and lighted it with a flint. Stepping in front of Pater Nos, she entered.

"I looked at all these." The candle made a sweeping gesture along the bookshelves as she walked. "But I didn't open any of them."

The walls were covered with books, encroaching the passage on the left and right. The candle flame seemed to give them motion, the way the shadows moved along the shelves. Some hadn't been disturbed since the school had been built. Others had been used, but none recently. She led him on, pushing away fresh cobwebs with her free hand. Pater Nos stayed close behind her.

From deep within the cavernous room, there sounded a cry, low and anguished, the soft wail of a feminine voice.

"Unger, Is that you? Can you help me?" The mournful sounds froze Belinda. She shivered, reaching back to grab Pater Nos' cloak.

"Ignore that," Pater Nos said.

"Who is Unger?" Belinda asked.

"The one to whom that voice belongs has been dead three thousand years." Pater Nos replied softly. "Unger was her husband. Her spirit is entombed in one of these books. She is safe here. It is all we can do for her. But talking to her only increases her despair which has no end."

"How terrible to be so lonely. I am sad for her," Belinda whispered, "Can't you free her, Master?"

"I cannot. And I, too, feel her pain. But she made a choice when she was alive."

Pater Nos and Belinda were standing in the passageway facing the darkness that lay ahead, beyond the reach of the candle flame. Again the voice cried out, this time higher in pitch like the notes of a flute. "Ungerrrrr."

Belinda rocked her weight to her toes as if ready to flee. Pater Nos placed a hand on her shoulder. He regretted that Belinda had to be in here, to hear what couldn't be explained to a child, but he had no choice. He had to find out for her own safety what book or books she had opened. He wouldn't be able to treat her until he knew the poison she had taken. He nudged her onward down the dark alley.

"Show me which books you opened," he said to her.

Her reply was tremulous. "It was just one book."

Belinda would not see the look of relief on Pater Nos. Perhaps all was not lost.

"Get it and bring it with you."

Holding the candle higher and closer to the bookbindings, Belinda quickly found the one she had opened. It was distinctly cleaner than its companions. She pulled it from the shelf, turned back toward Pater Nos, and they walked back toward the open door. They left the Cloistral. Pater Nos closed and locked the door while Belinda extinguished the taper and put it back in its box.

"Place the book on that desk, there," he said. "Show me the pages that you read."

Belinda flipped the leather cover over and perused with her index finger the table of contents which were listed by chapters. Her finger stopped at one line and then she quickly opened the pages to the middle of the book. She looked up at her master. "This one," she said.

"Only this one?"

"Yes."

Pater Nos looked down at the heading of the chapter. "Fantec-tuhea". The word meant "to separate." Pater Nos was familiar with the technique. It was never practiced here, but it wasn't lethal. There were other chapters in this very book that were far more dangerous.

"Show me what you learned." Pater Nos pulled a stool out from under the desk and sat. Belinda remained standing. She was being truthful; he would not dismiss her from the school.

"Now?" she asked.

"Yes, now."

"With you?"

"With me, right now."

Belinda took a step back. She closed her eyes. Pater Nos watched her lips move, then he was watching himself standing by the desk, pulling the stool out from under it and sitting down. The exact same action he had just done for himself moments ago. Every detail was there, even the sound of the stool scraping across the floor. "Enough."

With his command, the room went back to present time, to normal again. Belinda stood in front of her master and he gazed at her. He didn't speak for a long time.

"Since you learned this," he asked finally, "have you shown anyone else?"

"No, Master. It frightened me so I only did the spell once." She hesitated, "Oh and then just now with you."

"On who, then?"

"On Jodi," she said. Jodi was a red squirrel that she had been feeding outside her bedroom window.

Pater Nos took a deep breath. "Belinda," he said. "I will dismiss you from my service for one season. You will go to Master Singh and help him with his gardens, the planting and the harvest. You will not read anything or do any school work in that time."

As he spoke, Belinda began to blink tears that streamed down her smooth pink cheeks. This was hard on her and, he had to admit, would be sad for him. He already missed her. The next year would be diminished without her energy.

"But before you go to Master Singh, I will talk to you now. You will listen to my words and you will think about them when we are apart. You will work hard in the soil and learn patience from Mudria, the earth mother. When Master Singh feels that you are ready, he will send you back to me and we will continue with your training.

"Your willfulness has placed you in great danger. And I, too, am to blame for not being more careful with the key. That room was forbidden and you knew that.

"There is, Bell, a difference between an adult and a child. You are almost grown, but you are not ready for what lies behind that door. You know that no one ever goes in there before Dotson. Yet you thought those rules didn't apply to you. As it is you have already seen more than you should and it will haunt your dreams. So I will give you a chance to understand what you have heard up to now. After this you will speak to no one about what you have heard or seen in there. Not even to Master Singh."

Silence became a wall between them. He felt the pain of their distance, of her embarrassment, the weight of deep regret about doing what he must do.

Belinda wiped her eyes again with the heels of her hands. She took a deep breath and let it out slowly. It would be torture for her, to not have a book in her hands for a whole year nor study with him. Pater Nos could tell that she was sorry for what she had done, how she had hurt and betrayed him. Still, he was concerned about the effect her visit to the room had on her; would she be greatly disturbed by the tormented voice she had heard in there? He knew her, knew that despite the harsh punishment, her thoughts would be concern for the tormented woman she had heard.

Pater Nos broke the silence. "Putris Darkin has put a spell on her. She was once a queen who betrayed her race for immortality. What she didn't understand is that you cannot win when you bargain with the Evil One."

"Is there no hope for her?"

"Very little, I'm afraid. She got what she asked for, but not what she wanted. It is very sad. I can't break the spell. But I can keep her safe. She didn't cry out when you went into the room before?"

"No," Belinda said. "There was no noise at all."

"Hmm," Pater Nos stroked his beard. His eyes were tired. "Maybe someday," he said.

"Must she stay in there?"

"Yes, Bell, the light of day would be a torment to her."

"How horrible for her," she said after a short pause.

"She is in agony, yes. But she is still from the dark side, Bell. She has not been reconciled. She prefers the darkness and she might have been a real danger to you. We treat her kindly, but she cannot be trusted. In there, at least, she is safe from Putris Darkin."

"Are there others?"

"Yes."

"How many?"

"Legions," he said, his tone reflecting his sorrow. "Only some of them are in there. Others have not been found."

Belinda was again quiet for a while. Pater Nos waited. She looked around. Pater Nos watched her take it all in: the high arched ceiling; the brightly painted walls; windows through which a bright sun poured its gift. She wouldn't see this room for a time. Her eyes fell to the orange tile floor.

Without looking up, she asked, "Did what I learned from the book hurt me?"

Pater Nos might have been surprised at her vision in this regard. But he knew her to be precocious. She had mastered a magic spell on her own in one reading. She was now asking an important question that would affect her future as a wizard.

"I cannot say, Bell. Knowledge in itself is not good or bad. What you have learned may even help you some day. I don't know. I can tell you that most of the knowledge in those books favors the dark side of magic. That is the reason we do not teach it here in our school. We are not sorcerers, Belinda, we are wizards. We must be aware of it, but we don't practice necromancy or trickery. We cannot, as Senchai wizards, become known for such things. It would be the beginning of our downfall." Pater Nos clasped his hands together and rested them in his lap

The talking was done, for now. Both knew it.

"Go, Bell," he said. "Learn patience and then come back to me."

Belinda flew at him wrapping her arms around his neck. "I'm sorry," she said. "I have hurt you. I'm sorry."

She then tore away from him, and left the room. He listened until the last sounds of her shoes echoed away. He then picked up the book and walked toward the Forbidden door.

Pater Nos had told no one yet, but he had already decided to begin training her as his successor, starting one year from now.

***

Upon graduation, Belinda had asked Pater Nos to give her a Grand name. He had fulfilled this honor for others, but it was with exceptional ease that he decided upon Verdor. "The word derives form the old language and means one who verifies," he told her. "This is what you shall be called because the name belongs to your nature."

He had sent her to the Valley of the Giants because he believed that she would stand well among them and gain their trust.

"Let us see, my loved one, what is it that I have gotten you into." He lowered his glass over the map and soon he was exploring the valley, cruising like a falcon high above the Grune River, swooping and drifting right and left with the movement of his glass. He could see the city Burba just looming into view when his nose signaled an alarm that started ominously in the depth of his bowels and rumbled louder as he cleared the forests surrounding the city. It was an odor they could only talk about here, not experience, so it would be new to her. By the time he hovered over the rooftops, Pater Nos' curiosity had yielded in a shiver to the trepidation he wanted more than life itself to deny. "Putris Darken!"

"Gendau!" he fairly screeched this time, "shades of night!"

Pater Nos turned from his desk, his focus still not returned from his visit to the valley, when he was fairly knocked off his feet by Gendau, who entered like a whirlwind and sprawled full length to the floor. The tiny cylinder he was carrying rolled to a stop at the feet of Pater Nos.

"Gendau, will you ever learn to pace yourself?"

"I will skip supper tonight, your lordship, so sorry am I, and willing to do the rightful penance."

Pater Nos looked down at the little man. "You'll do nothing of the kind. Instead you'll eat double portions in the hopes you'll soon get taller and slower. Now hand me that vial." *The young one is clever.* Pater Nos smiled at the thought. *He has just nearly knocked me down and been rewarded for his trouble.*

Pater Nos turned to the note he was unrolling in tremulous fingers. "She knows!"

"My lord?" Gendau asked.

"Nothing. Fetch me a quill and piece, I will respond to this now. Then go and select two strong birds for the Giants. Do you know which ones they are?"

"Yes, my lord, the blue tickers with red feet, and I know which ones will make the journey for certain sure." Gendau looked up from the floor, proud of his knowledge.

"There's a lad, go now."

Gendau was on his feet in the flick of serpent's tongue.

Pater Nos chased him with the words "And slow down..."

But Gendau was already gone.

Pater Nos collapsed in his seat, laying his arms heavily upon the armrests. He gripped his staff that lay propped against the chair and began running his hands over it. He felt life within it, though it had been cut from its mother past one hundred and thirty years ago. It warmed to his touch. When Pater Nos died, the staff would be returned to its mother, planted in the ground near her, where it would take root again and provide for future wizards.

"Faithful friend and protector," he said, gazing at the staff. "Should I call her back?" The staff was mute, as always, but Pater Nos listened. His heart ached. At times like these he questioned the wisdom of what he had accomplished.

Until the school of the Senchai, wizards had no center, no place to share the knowledge that died with them. Pater Nos started the school and wizards arrived to teach and learn.

Emissaries from the five kingdoms and beyond began arriving with their questions. What of this blight on our crops? What of this law, or illness? What of this taste, that smell, what is it? Which breeding lines showed the most promise? The questions were as multitudinous as the answers scarce, but the Mosaic, which it came to be called, was their only resource and the good it did became legendary.

The wizards, with Pater Nos in the lead, adopted a curriculum of training with strict requirements for entry into the school.

As time went on, the five kingdoms agreed to a tax to support the school, a stipend they gladly paid, because the school had once and once again saved them all from war, or hunger, and in the case of the Catsyu, even from the evil of Putris Darken.

Now, his beloved Verdor was in danger. Pater Nos, not usually given to wasting time on what could have been, or might be, quietly wished he hadn't sent her. It was, after all, a drought, with some infertility among the women. It was a good first assignment for a wizard, Grand just three years. Now he feared he had sent her to her death. He knew what her response would be if he asked her to return—short and scathing, as well as it should be. She was trained well and Grand by all accounts.

Perhaps, thought Pater Nos, *her naiveté is cause for some hope.* He would give her all the help he could, but from his place here at the school. If he went there, even if they could together beat back these forces, the act would be a devastating lack of respect and confidence. The youngest student that entered here would prefer death to that humiliation. As for Verdor and the Giants, he realized, their fate was up to them.

Pater Nos arose from his chair with the heaviness of a parent about to lose a child to the world. *Deddimus be with her,* he prayed. It was now a question of how firm a foothold the Fouler had on the Valley and how resolute his Verifier would be.

Nine

WHAT IS IT IN YOU, VERDOR, that you think you can make everyone behave? Verdor made her way slowly along the path from Flen's home. *You take yourself too seriously; Pater Nos always told you so.*

She decided to find a place to sleep out under the stars, to collect her strength and digest her disappointment in general with her failure to gain Flen's change of heart as she had that of Hisash. Her shadow long to her right side, she watched it gliding over the ground as if it were a separate being or companion. "If I were a Giant, I would be about as tall as you," she said absently.

She recognized her mood. A night under the stars would help, a night to purify, to plan.

"Rest is a weapon," Pater Nos would often say during her apprenticeship with him. Verdor missed Pater Nos. He was like a father to her. She hadn't known her real father, Jordan, very long, though she remembered him with fondness. He had died just before she had entered the Mosaic School.

Jordan was of the Dardyea. It was his stories about the Mosaic that inspired a yearning for the vocation she now lived, especially the tale where Pater Nos confronted Putris Darkin and his hordes of Pokers. Belinda never tired of that story. "Tell me how the Pokers ran from the staff of Pater Nos. Did they come to hurt us? Those terrible Pokers. Could you chase a Poker, Jordan?"

Verdor looked up to the azure sky. *Can you see me now, Jordan?*

She remembered her last walk with him. She had held his hand one bright summer's eve similar to this one while they walked along the fields he worked but had little time to enjoy. The sun was just over his shoulder and dropping fast. The crickets were harping and a deer fly kept annoying her, buzzing around her head.

"I cannot abide the deer fly," she complained to him while swatting the air with her hand to keep the bug from alighting and biting her.

Her father was wearing his Dover, a broad-rimmed hat that protected him—from flies, the sun—and also marked his station in life as a field hand. The skin of his hand was rough, as rough as the cockleshells later given to her by Lord Pater Nos. But the face she looked up at was, though wind-burned and creased, gentle in a simplistic way. His hair was blond like hers, his nose was hers, and his eyes, kind, unassuming and intelligent. His was the face of a man familiar with hard work and resigned to the life he led, but who'd learned to find the joy in it.

"I can teach you how to kill it if you wish," he said to her.

"Kill it?"

"Yes, Bell, take its life. Have you never killed an insect, child?"

"I would have to catch it to kill it," she said with interest. "It's much too fast for me."

"You must fool it," he said. "Like this."

Jordan put his hat on her head and turned loose of her hand. He stood very still. The fly was immediately attracted to his blond hair and began to circle his head. Jordan placed his palm over the crown of his head and waited until the fly landed on the back of his left hand. Very slowly, Jordan brought the unsuspecting fly down low so Belinda could see it. The fly perched among the hairs on the back of Jordan's hand, working its way down to his skin. Belinda saw large yellow-green pupilless eyes looking at her or perhaps at the hand it was about to bite, she couldn't tell which.

"The fly takes time to ready its bite," he said. "If you are lucky, you will kill it before it bites the back of your hand. The fly must never suspect that any treachery is afoot!"

She never saw Jordan's right hand move. She heard the smack and the fly disappeared beneath his palm. When he lifted it, the fly rolled off onto the ground. Belinda squatted on her haunches. The deer fly didn't look as big now as it lay in the dust. The eyes hadn't changed, but she could tell there was no life in them.

"You took its life," she said.

"Yes, child." He took his hat from her and replaced it on his head. "You can't always reason with the one who will harm you."

Belinda reached up to take her father's hand again and the two continued their walk.

"Do you think the deerfly felt any pain?" she asked.

"I don't know, Belinda. I don't think about it."

***

Verdor climbed a rise above the path. From here, she had a good view of the surrounding countryside. Looking back, she could still see the roof of Flen's house while in front of her smoke rose continually from the soap works.

This would be a good place to spend the night, she thought.

It had been a difficult day. The Poker making itself visible to her at Hisash's house meant that there were likely more and they were becoming emboldened. *Putris Darken will not be far behind them. I have no plan when he comes.*

Flen was still foolishly bent on his Troca with Lorca.

Lorca and the rest of the Giants, with the exception of Hisash, were oblivious to the danger they were in.

Tomorrow, she would ask the Governor to summon the Giants for a meeting and tell them.

Verdor looked up to a sky that had darkened perceptibly. She spread her cloak on the ground and, using her staff, inscribed a coveret in the dirt around it, stepped inside, and sat down on her cloak. She placed her staff on the ground in front of her, crossed her legs, and focused on her breathing.

In her thirty-three years, she had never taken a life of any kind. She remembered the flash of her father's hand as it killed the fly and Jordan's words, "You can't always reason with the one who will harm you."

Ten

Darkness hovered over the ground like a dense fog, one black cloud after another. Hisash, her eyes accustomed to the dark, began to discern shapes and movements. She sat yet where she had fallen, off the side of the path.

The Poker that had addressed her left its perch and began to prowl back and forth in front of her like a lion guarding its kill. She could make out its skinny arms, pearl colored, like the moon sometimes looked behind the veiling curtain over her bedroom window. Its arms were quite as long as its legs, and dropped easily to the ground for balance as well as propelling itself along in sudden jerks and changes in direction.

Its smell revolted, reminding her of the sweet rancid odor of black ground ants whose nests she overturned at times when hunting swamp flowers for the soap works. The stink lingered at the back of her nose and throat, just above the base of her tongue. She softly snorted to remove it but it wouldn't leave her.

Several of the other Pokers, perhaps four in total, edged closer, nudging each other with bony shoulders, nipping and snarling right and left, all having settled on the same path to their quarry, her. The one guarding her grew increasingly agitated and fairly danced from one side of the path to the other in a clumsy minuet of hands and feet. Back and forth it whirled, all the while coughing threatening sounds, stopping only briefly to spray the ground from its rectum, further saturating the befouled air.

Seeing her guardian Poker preoccupied with the others, Hisash, who had been sitting with her feet stretched in front of her, slowly began to draw up her legs, so she could rock forward to a kneeling position. As she tried, slowly and carefully, to push herself up, her jerkin, caught beneath her on the stub of an old root, arrested any further movement, locking her to the ground. She could have easily torn the fabric, but not without drawing the attention of her captor from the others, who were now forming a half circle around it.

How like jackals they are.

She slowly moved her hand along her thigh, gripping the tight cloth to yank it free, when she discovered a lump in the lining. The leather pouch Verdor had given her. *What to do with it?* Her mind screamed for the answer.

Her captor actively confronted the intruders now. When one approached too closely, he chased it a short distance, tearing at it with the lone tooth in its snout.

The noise grew fearsome. The grunts became slashing screams. The sounds of predatory feet slapping the ground in attack and retreat were thunderous. The fray in full tilt now, several times one or two Pokers would get within one long pounce of being on her when her savior, with the quickness of a wolverine, would drive them back, its sides heaving with the effort. Clods of dirt and dust arose from the commotion, the battle creating its own wind, further darkening and choking the acrid air.

Then it happened.

Her guardian sank its tooth deep into the flank of a retreating Poker and caught it in bone. The unexpected twist of its neck and body as it attempted a quick withdrawal flipped it to its back. A nearby Poker dove in, black mouth gaping wide, wet slime streaming from its lone tooth. Ferret-like, feral eyes rolled back in its head, their phosphorescent color disappearing to become whitened orbs that shone above its snout.

A flash of white light jolted them upright, some almost falling over backward. The fireball from the hand of Hisash caught the most immediate attacker just below the groin, severing its leg before hitting a nearby tree stump. The injured Poker fell back onto the path, howling in stunned pain, staring at its severed leg, lifeless under the flickering light of the burning stump.

Hisash, unknowing what she'd done, was on her feet, racing in great strides down the path toward Lorca's house. She glanced over her shoulder repeatedly to see if she was pursued and what she glimpsed in the dying light of the burning stump were not four, but at least ten Pokers descending on their wounded comrade like fruit bats on a melon.

Each had driven its tooth into the writhing body missing a leg, and Hisash could hear moaning over the sucking sounds of the feeding frenzy. One of them, probably her guardian, she thought, sat apart from the group on its haunches, uninterested in the meal. Hisash swore she could feel its horrible eyes boring into her back as she swiftly left the scene behind.

Eleven

"WHAT IS IT, CHILD?"

Belinda knew she had been quiet too long.

Pater Nos looked up from the color he was mixing, or attempting to mix. The red he was looking for had eluded him now for two hours. He liked it when it was wet, but when it dried it "lost its excitement," he said. Pater Nos was teaching himself what he called "painting." Depicting scenes, any scene at all, from whatever he saw around him, be it a bowl of fruit or a larch tree out past the meadow. He had taken to carrying brushes, palette, and easel wherever he went. "What do you think?" he would ask Belinda, calling her attention to his latest endeavor.

Belinda would study the marks Pater Nos had made on the parchment, then study the tree he had attempted to paint, then again the parchment.

"I would look at the tree rather than the painting," she said, after deliberating down her freckled nose.

"Humph!" he said.

The fairies were teaching Pater Nos to paint. Now, it seemed, nothing could exist on its own but that he attempted to paint it.

"Why don't you just look at it?" she asked. "Even when you put it on the paper, it's still there, where it always was."

"Fairies say that if you paint something, you capture its soul."

"Did you capture the soul of that tree?" she asked

"Not yet, but I shall."

"When?"

"When I am good enough."

As far as Belinda could tell, Pater Nos had captured no souls yet, but by now, at the age of sixteen, she was used to his exploits of ceaseless learning. She did not understand why he wanted to paint on precious parchment what they both could look at easily enough. Her skepticism had no affect on him.

"Painting something helps me unite with it," he said.

"I don't understand."

"You will," he said.

How often had he told her that? "You will," he'd say with assuredness, as if it were as true as the night would fall on this day, as it did on all the past days of her life. She trusted his answer, never knowing him to be wrong, but suffered a youthful impatience for the day when "you will" would arrive, which, as Pater Nos had predicted so often, followed in due course.

"Understanding is like giving birth to new life," he once told her. "It is rarely accomplished without pain. For you, my love, the pain will be in the waiting." He chuckled as he said so.

Her need to understand was quite painful. It beat at her chest from the inside, as if it were a large bird trapped in her rib cage, flying panicked at the darkness. She was flushed one moment and short of breath the next, as if she had just run a race.

It wasn't all together painful. It was exciting too, like the time she finally understood the language of the Kunistae, once just guttural nonsense, impossible to decipher for years, then one day, clear to her. It was miraculous. The last piece of that puzzle just dropped into place and she understood. Exhausted but euphoric, she had raced around Pater Nos' study, picking up the most difficult tomes and reading them loudly. Slamming one shut, she would then choose another. "Ask me something in Kunistae," she challenged Pater Nos. She would burst apart if he didn't.

Today she felt like that too.

"Are you in your menses, love?"

"They are two weeks gone."

Her cycles had started over a year ago. The all knowing Pater Nos had helped her through the start, having prepared her long since, explaining things to her, as he could, in the way he had of making the world seem more wondrous than complicated. She was used to them now. This wasn't menses.

"So then, tell me, what brings this malady to my precious girl? When did it start? You look as if you want to jump out of yourself."

Belinda was silent for a time, tormenting herself for an answer.

"It started this afternoon, I think, just before Hails. No, just after."

"What were you doing?"

"Grand Singh had summoned us to help him with his irrigation waterways."

Pater Nos crossed the room to the desk where Belinda's head was now bent over an open book. She had not read a single line or turned one page. Pater Nos extended his palms over her and, satisfied that no spells were upon her, returned to his desk.

"Who is with you, Bell? Was it Thomar?"

A trace of a smile threatened his upper lip. He turned his head toward the wall, remembering. The two had taken to each other from their earliest days at the Mosaic School. Granted, it was a rocky start: Belinda had rendered up the only black eye ever in the history of the Mosaic, just one of many firsts his gifted student owned. Belinda, only a day new to the school, was about to be dismissed when Thomar, then in his fourth apprentice year and already known for his powers in elocution, explained to the satisfaction and amusement of Pater Nos how, indeed, it was his eye that struck her fist. The hobbledehoy did this, he said, only to gain knowledge of the wages of violence. He was happy to report that, in fact, violence is painful and not acceptable in a school where the quest for knowledge is tantamount, end of experiment, thank you.

"Did he touch you?"

"Yes, Grand Pater Nos."

"Tell me what you wish then."

"We were racing to the models, I was ahead of him by two good strides, I could hear his laughter at my back and it thrilled me and frightened me at the same time. I was never afraid of him before. I never ran so fast. Then I tripped on one of Grand Singh's gates. Thomar tripped over me and we were both in the water."

"Were you hurt? Was Thomar hurt?"

"No, Grand Pater Nos, we were both laughing. The water was freezing cold and we clung to each other laughing. Then we weren't laughing. He was looking at me. Well, not at me, but in me. I don't know how to say it."

"You're doing fine." Pater Nos had quietly crossed the room again and was again standing near her. "Continue, love."

"That's all. I didn't feel the cold any more. His eyes were warm, and big. I couldn't see anything else. I could swim in them. I was deaf to everything, but his breathing. His arms felt strong and safe, like my father's, only more. I was... "

"Stop, Child," Pater Nos looked down at her. He was smiling. "Say no more to me. I understand now."

"Stop? But why?"

"You must store the rest away in your heart. It is for you alone."

"What is happening to me?" There were tears in her eyes.

Pater Nos sat next to her on her study bench. He enfolded both of her hands within his. "Bellie, listen to me carefully. Do you remember your third year lessons when you were taught that everything, even the rocks, has a spirit?"

"Yes Grand Pater Nos."

" Your body, too, is no more than a home for your spirit, and the spirit within you, unlike the rocks, has many, many parts. You must never let your body try to control your spirit, because your spirit will have its way."

"I don't understand, Grand Pater Nos."

Pater Nos gently erased her tears with the pads of his thumbs, while holding her cheeks between her palms. He delighted in her. His gnarled hands smoothed the golden hair that parted her head evenly and fell to her shoulders. His sigh, mourned the change in her. Her blue eyes were more confident of late, forward-looking, more like a woman's. Belinda's childhood had slipped by, like the hours of a day, unstoppable. None of his powers could halt that. Already he missed the child, yet his joy thrived on the mysteries of her future, and that he, for a while yet, would be with her.

"Part of your spirit has flown from you and alighted within Thomar," he said. "And, I assure you, part of his spirit is now within you."

Pater Nos held her head, watching her eyes, waiting for the understanding that he knew would come to his student. Her pupils dilated almost imperceptibly, in recognition of what he didn't have to say, but said, so he too could hear it, hear its joy, share in its power.

"You're in love, Bellie. You're in love with Thomar."

Belinda gazed at her teacher, they both savored the long moment, the sound of his words, the understanding.

"I've painted him," she said, a smile teasing the corners of her lips.

"Yes you have, Bellie." Pater Nos leaned over to kiss her brow. "Yes you have."

Twelve

THE TIME TO KILL WAS NIGH.

The inevitability had loomed like a malevolent shadow from the moment Verdor had met the Poker at the home of Hisash. With the new day dawning, gifting the world with the reassurance that daylight brings, she allowed the hovering thought to descend to a place quite centrally within the loose fabric of a fledgling plan to defeat Putris Darken and his minions.

The Pokers are emboldened, she thought. They'd attacked Hisash in numbers. This she had seen during the night's meditation. How many waited now, hidden among the glens and woods of the Valley? Hundreds, certainly, perhaps thousands. They had their plan already, they had their orders.

"Beauty and harmony, the cycle of nature, is not deliberate or as orderly as it may appear," Pater Nos had told her in her thirtieth year at the school, the year called Traytson. A year of advanced sorcery, a year of learning to harness power from the very air, her Cept, given her during Dotson some ten years ago, now became both sword and shield. The two, teacher and student, were very close to being equals. Becoming Grand was almost guaranteed or she would not still be in the school. During Traytson, she learned to use her arms to focus energy and her mind to transport from one place to another.

"But make no mistake, the evil of the Dark One is as calculated as mathematics, and therein lies its weakness," Pater Nos had cautioned.

Traytson was a year of marvels for her. Pater Nos eagerly and thoroughly taught her, holding nothing back that would ensure her survival.

"Because there are no storm clouds doesn't mean that the forces that make lightning are not present in the air," he said.

Much of her learning occurred outside the school walls now. Lessons were given orally, on long walks in the countryside where herbs and medicinals were found. Where the natural state of the earth, its fire and ice, wind and heat, became her weapons of choice.

"From whence comes the permission to kill?" she had asked.

Pater Nos thought for a moment before answering.

"We give ourselves permission," he said finally. "This whole affair, this school, our mission, is about helping others. It is we, the wizards, who hold this world together. It is we who are a balance to the forces of evil. Someday that will change. But for now, it is our most sacred responsibility and stems from the permission we give ourselves through our training and study. It is why we train for so long. We winnow the less devoted in our own ranks."

"Will it change in my lifetime?"

"No, and not in the lifetimes of many wizards to come. But someday, through compassion and science, our jobs will be replaced."

"Then how do I kill, Grand Pater Nos?"

Pater Nos had casually reached out into the air with his right hand, as if plucking an imaginary apple from an overhead branch that only he could see, and seized upon a ball of fire, just bigger than his head. Then, seemingly without effort, he hurled the ball into the side of a nearby hill with such force that the ground shook beneath their feet. Instantly, the side of the hill was engulfed in flame, throwing great clods of dirt, stone, and sod hundreds of feet high. The air filled with the acrid odor of scorched dirt.

Pater Nos waved his left hand over his head and rent the sky above, as if torn with a spear. From the gash poured water, so much water that the fire was promptly doused and a large cresting wave threatened both teacher and student. Hissing, crackling steam darkened the sky from the snapping, popping red-hot stones caught in the deluge. Raising both hands, Grand Pater Nos made an arc with his fingertips and the landscape was suddenly restored to its original condition, as if nothing untoward had occurred. The green grasses flittered wistfully in the breeze, each blade in its original location.

Throughout the short demonstration, Pater Nos' facial expression had changed not one line or wink. He might as well have been reading one of his books in the comfort of his room.

"You kill without anger," he said, "without malice or passion."

"Can that be done?" she asked. "Can you take life without anger?"

"You must, or you become the evil. So rather than killing it, you give it new life, and you betray me and your training. Then you fall outside the Mosaic. You know what that means."

"Yes, Grand Pater Nos." There were some from the school who had gone to the other side, she knew. He would not hesitate to abandon her if she fell to evil.

"I have never killed so much as a fly. Will I be prepared if the time comes when I must kill?"

"You will," he answered. "Does the lioness hate the deer when she kills? Does she stalk the animal in anger?"

"No, Grand Pater Nos, she kills for her survival and that of her cubs."

"And the farmer who kills a hen to eat?"

"The farmer has no ill will against what he kills."

"Then you must learn from the lion and the farmer. When the time comes, as it will, you must give yourself permission. You will then kill swiftly and without anger. You will feel remorse. That's only natural. The farmer who kills the chicken to feed himself has remorse, but does not harbor or dwell on it. What he does is necessary. And so it will be for you. Do you accept this, Belinda?"

Her long years of training had prepared her for many things she had experienced after the lessons. She had come to trust Pater Nos' knowledge. It was then easy for her to answer, "I accept and understand."

Now, Verdor accepted what she must do—hunt and kill the Pokers or drive them out and find as well as confront the one who'd sent them. That he might kill frightened her. Verdor was aware that her circumstances were unusual. What startled her was how soon after graduation her untried skills would be tested. Surely, Pater Nos could not have known, not even imagined, what she would find when she crossed the Mohr Mountains into this Valley.

It was not the custom of the school to send new graduates into dangerous battles. Had he known, Pater Nos would have come here himself. Now it was too late. Pater Nos would never retrieve her in order to save her, nor would she ever retreat in the face of whatever plan Putris Darkin had already begun to execute.

"What does he look like?" she had asked Pater Nos when still in her fourth year.

"Who, Child?"

"Putris Darken." She had only breathed the name, too afraid to say it aloud.

"He may look like me or your mother. It is not possible to say. He changes form to suit his evil designs. He has a resting or normal appearance, a ghastly figure without a nose. He prefers the countenance of a young boy with raven black hair. But he could appear as anyone he wishes to."

"Could he look like me?"

"Yes, Bell, but he would have to capture you first and hold you alive. He can only mimic what lives. But he can invent his own creations, too."

His answer had worried her then and concerned her now as she stood, stretching last night's stiffness from her. She gathered her cloak and Cept. *Have I seen him already? Was he the Poker that fouled the home of Hisash just yesterday?*

She would apprise the Governor, Lorca, of her plan to fight as well as conscript the help of the Giants.

Verdor erased with her foot the circle she had scribed on the ground within which to sleep and meditate, then squatted on the ground to make water. The sun was peering over the Saget Mountains. In the distance, a column of smoke eerily defined itself against the morning fog, no doubt from the soap work fires.

She smelled him before she heard him. His was the smell of un-washed man; the smell of anger, the smell of fear. Ducking behind a nearby bush, she watched the giant stride the path that led to the city. A path she, too, was about to take. From her hiding place she watched Flen go by. There was a purpose in his gait and he was mumbling to himself in quiet, raging tones. His face was swollen and bruised from the bottle's chastisement last evening. The lumps on his chin and over his eyes, the forward set of his shoulders, all appeared to chase his scowl down the path well ahead of a lagging dignity. It was almost comical to watch him pass.

There was, however, no humor in what he was about this morn-ing.

Thirteen

FLEN STARTED OUT LATE for Burba. His head still throbbed from the beating he had received last night from the wine bottle. Some time had passed after his eyes opened before he was able to discern the blurry figurine that shared the space of oak decking directly in front of his swollen nose. The wine flask stood there resolute, appearing angry and ready for further orders from the wizard who, thankfully, had departed his home. Giving the bottle a wide berth, he lumbered to his open door where he stood in the archway and pissed on the footpath outside, closing his eyes against the smarting sunlight as he did so.

He looked neither to one side or the other as his feet stole great sections of ground from the path before him. Chickadees and starlings, startled by his thunderous footfalls, squawked and flapped to the safety of higher brush or trees to watch him pass. He took no notice of them.

His hand opened and closed on the handle of his hammer slung over his shoulder. He imagined the great sweeping blows he would inflict on Lorca's knees.

"What think you now?" he envisioned asking the broken governor pleading for mercy at his feet. "What? A boon from me? You would have me spare your life?" Flen snagged the leather pouch of orbs at his thigh and gave it a good shake. "You know that I would spare you, but one of these will taste your blood, and it will have its drink in full."

Over and over again he pictured Lorca's death. A sweeping blow to the legs would bring her down, then another to the base of her spine. She would be a mound of whimpering flesh eager to die, begging him to end her agony. "I will bend to you one last time," he mocked her in his mind, "and you will place your purple hat upon me, your governor. I will show mercy. I will allow you to choose the instrument of your death." Again, Flen shook the bag at his side, rattling the spheres within.

"Lorca may kill you instead, my good Flen."

Flen had taken two full strides before he realized someone had spoken to him.

"What then!" he bellowed, drawing to an abrupt stop. *Was I speaking aloud?* Flen quickly brought both hands to his hammer, tightening his grip on the long handle. "Who makes bold to address me unannounced?" he demanded, looking about quickly, yet seeing nothing. "Show yourself now as would make good manner, or hide like a coward's lap dog."

He looked around him, more slowly this time, examining the shaggy trees off to the side of his path, studying the rocks. Nothing, no one could be seen. *See how you upset yourself? Gain your bearing and be off, you have work to do.*

"I do not hide, good Giant. I am up here and would have a word with your lordship."

Flen jerked his head upward toward the sound of the voice, his hands choking the handle of his weapon. He stared into the leaves of the overhead tree branches and traced their lines back to the trunk only a step to the side of the path. He missed her the first time and, retracing where he had already looked, was startled to see her on the branch before him just past arm's reach. She sat on the branch, but it appeared that if someone were to cut the branch away she would still, somehow, be able to sit there without its support.

Flen was staring at a tender thing, not much taller, he judged, than the handle of his hammer. A young maiden, her skin the color of silk weed, she wore a diaphanous gown that clung to her, highlighting to great advantage the enticing curves of her body. The early sun filtered through the leaves at her back causing a halo effect about her head and shoulder-length auburn hair. Flen could not see her eyes clearly or make out the features of her face, but her silhouette was enough to pique his curiosity. *A fairy! I'll have her this very morning, by the oaths of Deddimus, and smash her under foot, damn me if I don't.*

Flen lowered his hammer, letting the business end fall to the ground. "Come down, my pet, and state your business, for you will find no harm in my company."

She was standing in front of him before he realized he had not seen her move. *It's their magic.* The hairs on the back of his neck were tickling him. He rubbed them quiet.

Flen had never seen a fairy before, although he had heard of them. The children believed in them. He had discussed them, ribald over cups of wine about their lecherous ways, running about the wood naked and fornicating amongst themselves, lusting insatiably after the cock.

He was wrong about her height; she was short by his standards, but taller than she appeared in the tree. Her body tried every seam of the gown, every line of the filmy material played on the available light to highlight rounded thighs, fulsome breasts, curving stomach. Flen gawked at her, so vulnerable she seemed, and his lower lip fell away from the pool of glistening spittle that threatened to spill down his chin.

She's as tall as the wizard Verdor, she is. The thought of the Senchai irked him. "What name have you?"

"You'll know that before you die, I promise you," she said calmly.

Before I die? What manner of nonsense is this? Flen pretended to ignore her answer.

"You're a fairy, now then, are you?"

"No."

He could see her eyes now, light blue, the pupils yet a lighter gray, and they frightened him. They looked dead, like the eyes of a spent mayfly. Her auburn hair was all the darker against the light skin of her neck. Flen backed away.

"Do you fear me, Flen?" the creature asked. "And you would have me this very morning by the oaths of Deddimus?"

She laughed, baring a row of fine teeth. Her beauty, despite her eyes, stood to heighten her mockery of him. He felt unmanned by her. Anger boiled.

"Mind your manners, witch," he snarled, "or I'll split you in twain."

Flen raised his hammer to threaten, but the hammer began to pull him up, first to his toes, then off the path. He tried to let go of the handle, but his hand was stuck fast.

The weapon began to climb the air, taking Flen upward with it. When he was twice his length above the ground, the hammer took an abrupt turn, dragging him through the woods, picking up speed as it went. Small trees were knocked aside; he caromed off larger ones with jarring, rib-pounding thuds. The hammer hurtled through the wood, moving as if in terror of being chased by him. Flen struck trees hard and often, showering the forest floor with their drying leaf buds, beating his breath out so that he had no cry within him. Suddenly the hammer deposited Flen at the feet of the woman in a pulsing heaving heap. He could only wince at the pain of his bruised and re-bruised body. Before he gained the strength to speak, the female addressed him again.

"My good Flen, I apologize for your jaunt in the woods, but I found it necessary that we start with good understanding. You see, Flen, I need your help, not your useless temper."

Flen stared at her, conserving his breath for living.

"We have common enemies, Flen. We can help each other. You go to kill Lorca, is this not true?"

Flen nodded.

"Good, but you could never kill her alone, Flen. She has friends or, should I say, a friend. Do you know of whom I speak?"

Another nod.

"Yes, the Senchai. She will not let you kill Lorca."

"Hmmpf."

"Her oath means nothing to her! She has sworn to not interfere, but she will abjure her oath, and help Lorca kill you instead. She will smash you and make your flight through the woods this morning seem like play."

Flen had gathered sufficient air to enable him to sit up. He looked for and saw his hammer lying on the ground next to him. In panic, he searched his waistband, relieved to discover his precious leather pouch still attached, the contents untouched within.

"Vicious…you …are," he said between gasps.

"Yes, I'm sure it was not pleasant, but I needed to get your attention." She stood beside him now and gently brushed a shank of hair from his forehead. "And, Flen," she said and smiled the woman's promise, looking upon him with kindness, "you will have me, but first you must help me."

Tenderness radiated from her, and it felt good.

"I will leave you now. And be back before you leave these woods. You'd best go and hide. The Senchai is just behind and will soon overtake you. You don't want her to find you in this condition, do you?"

Despite his pain, Flen reveled in her form, staring at her perfect bottom disappearing among the branches. *I will have her; she said it, by the oaths.* He managed a smile turned grimace in slowly gaining his feet, gathering his hammer and limping deeper into the woods to await the Senchai's passing.

He chose a spot just far enough back from the path to see anyone who might go by, resting against a large oak tree where he rubbed the soreness from his chest, ribs and thighs. He didn't wait long.

She moved like a ghost, making no sound on the path. He might have missed her had he not happened to look up in time to glimpse her hooded cloak floating along. No part of the Senchai's body was visible. Her cloak seemed uninhabited, preceded by a staff held in an unseen hand.

Verdor stopped parallel to him, the hood turning slightly in his direction, allowing Flen to see her face. She sniffed like a forest animal checking the air for signs of danger. Again, the wizard turned in the direction of the path and her face disappeared into her cloak. She did not look toward him again, but continued on after this briefest hesitation.

Flen held his breath all the while. It hurt when he breathed anyway, and he was loath to confront anyone else this morning, wishing to be left alone. Still, there was the fairy or whatever she was. *She will meet me again before I leave this forest, she spoke so.* He struggled with a tendril of fear that wound up his battered spine. He brought the full vision of her back in front of him as she had provocatively stood there before. *There's a promised share in the bounty of her, she spake thus, did she not? But how could I help her?* He shook this problem from his head, preferring to dwell on her enticements. *And those thighs.* The blood that should have been nourishing Flen's brain was being shunted to lower parts and even lower ideas. He licked his lips. *She will feel my manhood spearing her, then, by my leave, she will sup from my hand.*

Flen stood again, ignoring the pain, and his hammer in hand, set himself with expectation toward Burba. Despite his multiple discomforts, he was quite enthused. *What is that tune the children sing?* He attempted it, but his unpracticed voice regarded the notes as invaders and gave them no succor. Finally, he gave in to customary silence. Now however, as not before, he could mark the beauty of the wood, failing as it was to the drought. *Ah, the colors, so like autumn. Will we have no spring? And see the joyful birds there, how they look upon me from overhead.*

"And a sweet morning to you, feathered friends," he called out to them.

The birds watched him pass.

Fourteen

Putris Darkin stood imperiously over the Poker. "What think you of her, Jured?"

"She great power hav-ed, Lord Darkin, eh," Jured answered from his hands and knees. He dared not look up, but kept his wild eyes fixed on the floor of the cave. Small, damp, stones pressed into his bare palms and knees. He ignored the discomfort.

"Rise up from there, Jured, and act like a commander. Do I not seek your advice? Would my officers give counsel from their knees?"

Jured shuffled to an awkward upright stance, the position insisted upon by his lord, but unnatural to him and all Pokers, who preferred to walk ape-like, knuckles and feet to the ground. He forced himself to look upon his master, but his eyes refused to dwell there and flipped furtively sideways or down. Jured's serpent-like tongue, grooming obsessively, darted nervously from his maw and began to probe deeply within one nostril, then around his singular tooth. Six of his underlings were hanging on the cave walls, their mouths agape and Jured shuddered to think of their immediate future.

"I know she has power, fool," Putris Darkin said, "but is she as great as Pater Nos? Can she be defeated, and how?" He began to pace the length of the cave in quick strides. The flickering glow from a small fire cast his shadow on the rough walls, making the smallest of his movements appear ominous. He carried a hide whip coiled in one hand, long enough to reach almost any point within the cavernous room.

When he reached the far wall, his long cloak disappeared against the blackness leaving two pale hands floating above the cave floor.

Jured could pinpoint exactly when Darkin turned because his face, hidden within the cloak's hood when walking away, would reappear when approaching. Face and hands floated eerily, a bodiless apparition in a cloak that clung to the gaunt frame, as if the garment were soaking wet. Darkin was not as tall as the Giants, but a head taller than his enemy, the Senchai. His face was bloodless, accentuating his absent nose that appeared a dark void in the dim light of the cave. His milky face, now moving toward Jured, was mottled with healed wounds, blue veins protruding through delicate paper skin.

Jured never dared ask, but the rumors around the camps were that Darkin had lost his nose in the fight with Pater Nos. The story was that Pater Nos had also deprived Darkin of his staff, leaving his external powers impaired. Jured had no doubt that Darkin's inner powers were very much intact.

"I not presum-ed, your lordship," Jured said, "sure wise ist thou, eh eh. Sure ist wisdom you have-ed. Plan have-ed you to defeat Senchai."

Putris Darkin regarded his minion, fixing him with watery black eyes. "Naturally," he said, the sneer in his voice rising to a shrill pitch, echoing within the dome. "But even I must be mindful and how can I be with loathsome dogs like these." His whip lashed out with a loud crack, slicing the nearest hanging Poker across the midriff.

The Poker screamed, raising its snout to the ceiling as if imploring mercy from the jagged soot-blackened rock. The whip cut deeply into the Poker's torso, leaving an oily gash to leak a pearlescent, viscous ooze. The other cohorts screamed in terror, not sympathy, of what was ahead of them this night.

Putris Darkin returned to Jured.

"I hold you responsible for these spineless curs."

Jured's legs grew suddenly weak, nearly buckling under him. "With your leave. Willst I remove-ed all heads, so now."

"No, they will spend time with me." Darkin stroked the butt end of the whip. "I will instruct them in a soldier's discipline."

"As you wish-ed, your lordship, eh."

Putris Darkin laid the whip on a table and gestured Jured to sit, then sat down opposite. Producing a flame from the end of one finger, he lit a taper and pushed it to the center between them. The moans and mewling of the hanging Pokers filled the silent, dead air.

"Tell all!"

"Yes, lord." Jured anxiously rubbed his elbows. He did not like sitting at tables—why couldn't they squat on the floor, normal seating for Pokers? "I gait to home of Hisah, the giant, eh. Thee hath mark-ed well, your worship, I, no trouble hath to find, eh."

"Yes, yes get on."

"Entered did I, broughting down darkness did I. As thee teach-ed me. Wait for giant did I. Senchai but came-ed, eh."

"Does she have great beauty? Is this what that lecher Pater Nos sees in her?"

"I would suppose-ed she hath, eh, your worship, but none, eh, eh, beauty I see in any upright walkers. All horrible face I see, eh, eh." Jured flinched inwardly at what he'd just volunteered, but Putris Darkin took no notice of the slight.

"What did she say to you?" Darkin leaned forward, his cold breath chilling Jured's face. "Every word, now."

"She say no power I hath herein, leave now, she say."

"And?"

"I tell her, giant ist mine, death doth follow her, eh, eh."

"Did you work the spell? Was she impressed?"

"Fear did I see. But nay dread, eh. Caution were it, nay dread."

Putris Darkin sat back in his chair and stared upward into the black void as if he didn't like what he was hearing. "I will defeat her."

"Thee hast great power, thee willst kill her."

Jured's tongue flicked to his nostrils repeatedly and his eyes darted sideways. Although he tried, he was unable to stop these mannerisms. He didn't like being so close to his master. Jured wasn't sure who would kill whom. He knew only what he should say to avoid punishment. His eyes traced the circuitous lines of the coiled whip in the ghostly hand. Putris Darkin was, for a moment, seemingly preoccupied in thought.

"Then what?" he said finally.

"Leave, did I," Jured replied.

"And?"

Jured searched for the memory of what happened next. "Spy, did I," he blurted. "Senchai walk-ed about giant home, then leave-ed. Follow did I. She met giant called Hisah and frightened giant Hisah. Troca no more to giant. Sorrowful she did. Troca gone from her, eh."

"Spineless witch, that Hisash. She killed her father. I have every right to be here. She is mine."

"Thus said I, your lordship, eh."

Darkin's fingers were absently caressing the void where his nose once was, seeking and dislodging dried mucous from the open cavities. "Where did the Senchai go then?"

"To giant Flen house did she go, eh."

"Not so charming to my good Flen now, was she? He will be the key." Putris Darkin suddenly threw his head back and laughter erupted from him like a plosive bowel movement. Because of his absent nose, the outburst sounded more like the whine of a trapped animal, yet he sustained it, as if relishing the mirth of his thoughts. "The fool thinks me a fairy!" His whine siren filled the cave. "He would have me, Jured. He would have me! Neeee, neeeeeee. Can you comprehend the dolt?"

Jured joined in with as much of an attempted mimicry of the laugh as his snout would allow. His sounded more like snuffling. He was not now, nor was he ever, sure what this sort of reaction was about, but he deemed it wise to go along. He attributed his longevity to his ability to adapt to such bizarre behavior, while others, like those hanging above him, stupidly lumbered into mortal trouble.

Jured preferred to return to his report. "Nay, not charming. She not stay. Left in shortest time. Stay-ed night in fields. Follow Hisah, did I."

"And that's when these hyenas attacked her?"

"I make-ed talk with Hisah, tell her mine she ist. She very ist feared me. Them attack her, then, eh, eh." Jured gestured up the wall at the suffering Pokers. "She throw-ed fire, cut leg off-ed Daegar. Daegar eaten by them, eh." Again, Jured gestured upward. "Hisah away run-ed. I let go. She hath fire now, eh."

"Given to her no doubt by the Senchai. We will forget her for now. We still have the lout Flen. He will be enough. As for you, gather your charges in the woods nearest the city by tomorrow night. Hide well." Putris Darkin gathered his coiled whip and shook it at Jured. "I will have the skin of any that are seen by the Giants."

The meeting over, Jured rose from the table and quickly made his way toward the cave entrance. The last thing he saw in the flickering firelight was the ghostly, floating hand unwinding the hide whip. The hand moved in an abrupt downward and circular motion freeing the coils, which dropped below the firelight into the darkness. They lay motionless on the cold floor, momentarily at least, like a viper, hungry, ready for a night's feeding.

Fifteen

THERE WERE SUNDRY DETAILS to attend to before the killings started. Verdor pondered some of them as she walked the wooded path toward Burba. The blue sky, as brilliant as the azure pearls of Avoca, gave no hint to the seething evil of the world below, an evil that in Verdor's eyes seeped up from every crack and crevice of the parched ground over which her hurried pace shortened the time and distance to her fate.

She had only minutes ago smelled the giant Flen. He would be hiding off the path, she surmised, watching her pass, not unlike the way she'd surreptitiously watched him go by earlier. But the air held for her another announcement, her nose detected yet another odor, not unlike the sweetness of lilacs, but with a corrupted edge, as if someone had crushed a box elder beetle. This foul aroma rode the periphery of the lilac perfume and brought bile into her throat.

Putris Darkin has arrived! He is nearby. Mayhap he meets with Flen. For what purpose?

By now, Hisash would've apprised Lorca of the Pokers and Lorca would be consulting with her immediate cabinet. The council would be considering what to do. How and when to announce the bad news to the population? What scale invasion was this? Who would best be sent to the armory to clean and repair the long dormant steel of war?

Verdor knew they were waiting for her, but she needed time to bathe and prepare.

"Purify the body and mind first," Pater Nos had counseled. "Then from clarity, and not from anger, will you destroy."

Verdor abruptly changed direction and forced her way through brambles, low red-bush and choke weed, making her own path toward the Grune River. She moved with purpose as if she were a newly hatched turtle seeking water. She continued like this for some time with the sun at her back until, at last, cresting a drumlin, she found what she sought. Just below her where the field brush broke, giving way to a beach of fine sand, was a watering hole dug by the Giants into the bed of the Grune. They did this, it appeared, to create a pool within the dying River deep enough for their oxen to drink.

Verdor approached the oasis and immediately used her Cept to scratch a large half circle on the ground, starting and finishing at the water's edge. The arc was known as a Coveret. No evil could approach her if she stayed within its border. Inside the Coveret she could sleep, meditate, or, as now, prepare herself without fear of intrusion.

Removing her footwear, she stepped inside the crescent and lay her staff perpendicular to the pond so that just a few inches of the staff's tip was submerged. Verdor then removed her clothing, folding it as she had been taught, and placing these garments so that she was separated from them by the staff.

Kneeling, she bowed low to the water, cool and clear as a raindrop, so that her forehead touched the shimmering surface.

"Father, cleanse my thoughts for discernment and my mind from fear," Verdor submerged her hands up to her wrists and swirled the water thrice in a circular motion, "and my hands, that they touch not the corruption." Scooping with cupped hands, the wizard sat back on her heels and poured the water down her chest between her breasts. "And my body against the fouler." With wet fingers, she touched her soles. "And my feet, that they walk always in the light."

Next, Verdor mixed a quantity of a mud and sand slurry from the riverbank.

"Mother, cleanse me of my weaknesses. Fortify my will to my purpose." She vigorously scrubbed herself with the mixture, no part of her body left unwashed. In this fashion, she massaged the mud deep into her hair, down to her scalp, into her ears and between her toes. At no time did she lose contact with the water and therefore, through the water, contact with her Cept.

When the bathing ritual was complete, Verdor plunged into the river and let the feeble current assist her in removing the mud coating. Her blond hair undulating near the surface, her porcelain skin, slightly reddened from the scrubbing, shown ghostly through mud-clouded water on which she floated, luxuriating in the velvety coolness, noting again her Cept that lay inside the arc like a dutiful sentry. With it, she was vulnerable from neither land nor water. There was comfort in it. Its stalwart presence made her think of Thomar.

From the moment Master Singh had ceremoniously presented Thomar with it, Thomar's Cept was never further from him than his own hands. When he slept, it was near his bed. Verdor remembered how she'd found this amusing, not understanding how she would one day feel the same.

"Without your Cept, you are like a child without his blanket on wash day," she had teased him.

"You are smiling about my Cept being so near?" Thomar asked.

"Yes," she said.

"It must seem odd having it so close. I tried to keep it off to the side. Did it bother you? I can't be far from it; already it has become a part of me. Do you think that funny?"

"No."

He'd rolled to his back to stare at the ceiling of his room and she laid her head upon his bare chest. He was Grand now, with a new name, Lex Verd. To her, he would always be Thomar as she would always be Belinda to him.

Verdor would never see Thomar's Cept far from him again.

Reaching over him during that intimate evening they'd shared so long ago, she'd lazily traced his Cept's surface with a finger and grinned. "It seems so erotic now," she said. "I hold that old Singh never mentioned that possibility."

Thomar jabbed her side and Belinda screamed, bolting away, desperately trying to arrest the insistent index finger with both hands.

"Stop!" she screeched joyfully.

Once she'd pinned his hand to the bed, she paused, satisfied that she had the tickler trapped. "You men do worship your staffs!"

The words were trouble as she uttered them but she couldn't resist. Thomar's hand erupted free of her prison to catch her about the waist, and in one powerfully smooth motion, he'd trapped her beneath him, smothering her tittering laughter with a probing kiss.

Belinda's passion flared like a firestorm. She arched her back, pushing her breasts against his chest, moving her thighs to him expectantly. He separated his lips from hers and stared openly into her eyes.

A smile edged Thomar's mouth, his voice lust-laden, just above a whisper. "Then allow this wizard to put his staff in its place." He eased into her and her eyes closed, branding his kind, handome smile to her memory.

Thomar's smile stayed with her now, a smile that she missed beyond speaking, even as the Grune River cradled her in its cleansing water. She wanted to go back, to be held and caressed by her lover, to see the familiar walls of his chambers. But she knew she must put her wants aside.

Verdor left the water, and stood under the vast sky with the high sun as a mute witness. Water droplets rolled down her skin returning to their parent earth, leaving her as she would leave the life she knew, the one with which she had become comfortable.

I give myself permission to kill.

Not for Lord Pater Nos, not even for Thomar, would she fight. She would meet Putris Darkin, and live or die, as a Senchai wizard of the Mosaic.

"You are not a common sorcerer," Pater Nos had said, repeatedly.

Verdor closed her eyes and raised her face to the sky. With her back to the water, she spread her arms, palms up, ever so slightly from her sides. *"Facine Mudria, Facine Mudria an Verdor."* Come my mother, come to your Verdor. She repeated the mantra softly.

Slowly at first, energy surged into her naked body from the ground, entering through her heels, running up her legs and vibrating her spine, until it mushroomed in her brain and cascaded down both arms to her finger tips, arcing white lightning to her Cept. The staff began to hum as a plucked harp string, the sand beneath her feet dancing, puffing small clouds of grit around her within the Coveret she had drawn.

Verdor's arms rose, higher and higher still, the power increasing with them until the very air rumbled. The ground rolled, the river cresting to whitecaps as in a violent wind. When the backs of her hands touched above her head, her body locked to a tonic rigidity, each sinew pronounced, each vein and artery distended as if overloaded to the point of bursting. Her mind sought more and the earth obliged her, draining itself into her. In the flash of an instant, she realized what she must do.

Suddenly, there was release. Equanimity returned. The ground settled. The water once again became a limpid drinking pool of languid movement.

Verdor fell to her knees, covered her face with her hands, and wept at hearing the somber voice of Pater Nos: "Much will be asked of you, Verdor, my love."

She was alone now in the world.

"Loneliness is the most difficult," Pater Nos had instructed. "Hold Thomar how you may. Your time for love will be as scarce as your tasks will be multitudinous."

For the next hour, under the late morning sun, Verdor washed her garments and left them to dry atop the nearby bushes while she considered her decision. The price will be paid, the battle joined. Now she would send for what made her most vulnerable, but what gave her the best chance of success. She would request of the Mosaic to send her life's heart, Grand Wizard Lex Verd, her Thomar.

May Deddimus forgive me.

Noon had come and gone when she dressed herself and carefully erased the arc she had drawn at the water's edge. Then, for the second time that day, Verdor set out for the Governor's home.

Sixteen

"DOES SHE KNOW?"

Pater Nos looked at the floor. "No, Singh, I never told her."

"Nor would I have told her. Yet, the depth to his evil never stops surprising me. It would do him no good, even if he kills her, to regain it. You have seen to that."

"True, good friend, but it's not the Cept he's after."

"No?"

"He'll take it to spite me, but he wants more. He wants Verdor. He will not kill her. He will rape her, then put her in an arc somewhere and I'll not be able to find her. Then he will torment me the rest of my days."

"You saw this coming, Pater Nos."

"Yes, I knew this time might come. I could not know where or when, but I knew that he awaited her. He likely put the drought on the Giant's valley, knowing I would send a wizard."

"But Darkin couldn't know that you would send Verdor."

"No, but his was only to wait. In time, he knew, I would send her out somewhere. There was little to do about it, but go on with her training and prepare her as best I could. Which I have done."

"You have. Verdor will do you proud, and he won't find her so easy to undo. I wonder, however, why Putris Darkin didn't attack her before she arrived at Burba."

Pater Nos thought for a moment, stroking his beard.

"Darkin is no one's fool, good Singh. Verdor is unknown to him. He knows that I trained her, but he doesn't know her strengths. I believe he will let her deplete her energy protecting the Giants. When he thinks she is most vulnerable he will attack. But how he does that would be idle guessing."

"Then what about this epistle? What do you make of that? Did you see the bird?"

"Yes, I saw it. Gendau brought it to me when it arrived. Even he noticed its condition."

"Two primary feathers missing. Why would she select such a bird?"

Pater Nos allowed the question to linger unanswered. There was no sign a hawk had attacked the bird. Other than the missing feathers it was unharmed. *She must have sent it in this condition.*

He moved toward his window and clasping his hands behind his back, stared out into the darkness. His concern thickened the air like smoke from a smudge fire. "And that one got through. It's as if she wanted her message to be intercepted."

"You speak my thoughts, good Pater Nos"

"So, we should assume that it was."

"Yes, that would be wisest. And such a message! You know her better than I, but by my bunions, have you ever heard such drivel from her?"

"No, indeed not. She loves Thomar, that is sure, but it was always her private affair. This is not like her."

Pater Nos once again studied the troubling message in his hand.

Lex, my love,

I would you here with all my heart. My belly aches for your seed. My desires for you cloud my mind and befuddle my purpose. Please, render love's mercy. May I expect you in four days?

Verdor

"Have you looked into this further?" Singh asked.

"I have, but forgive me, I will keep my own council about that for now."

Pater Nos was not ready to believe what his amethyst sphere had shown him. To talk about it now would be impossible, unspeakable, as if he were watching a demon and not his beloved apprentice, the innocent Verdor.

He'd seen the high arched, rugged beams within the giant's house, the edges of a mattress and some of the bed coverings. Next to the bed, a large copper-clad trunk with a heavy iron hasp and hammered strap-hinges that girdled around the exterior to form clasps on the opposite side. Thomar looked directly at him through the convex gem that distorted his face slightly, but there was no mistaking the one who'd daily sat as his student, eager to glean the machinations of wizardry.

Then the sword descended as if materialized from thin air. Pater Nos nearly knocked the globe to the floor trying to thwart the deadly weapon's designated path. But even if he were able to reach within the rock, he would not, could not change what had not yet happened. Behind the blur of the flashing blade, he'd seen the open eyes of Thomar's severed head, the hand that held it aloft by the hair, then the arm, the creamy shoulder, the golden hair, the blood spattered face of his beloved Verdor. She gazed at Pater Nos through the misty purple orb, expressionless, as if in a trance.

Pater Nos had pushed the globe aside.

Singh interrupted the macabre reverie. "As you wish, my good Pater Nos. Shall we speak with Thomar? Shall we send him as Verdor requested?"

Pater Nos looked into the eyes of his old friend and said, "Yes, we will send Thomar. But as you trust me, I beg of you, do not look into this matter yourself."

***

Singh considered his old friend's request. Thomar was his Apprentice, his responsibility, and like a son to him. Would he be sending Thomar to be harmed?

Singh met his friend's gaze for a long minute.

Before him stood not only his friend and confidante of many years, but the one who built this school. Pater Nos had brought hope, peace and some measure of prosperity to a world that had known only greed, avarice and war. Singh studied the age-worn face, the white hair cascading about slightly bent shoulders, the tiredness in those eyes that seemed overtaken by burdens never expressed.

Pater Nos presented a frail form to whom Singh had, many years ago, pledged at first his allegiance and then, in time, his love. Pater Nos was his friend, the one who'd defeated Putris Darken on the plains of Bulgar, gaining at unimaginable risk the rational world they now enjoyed.

"Of course, my friend. As you wish." Singh turned toward the door of Pater Nos' chamber.

"You needn't trouble, I shall send Gendau." Pater Nos yelled up the attic steps, where both knew Gendau was preening the pigeons. The boy appeared. "Be a good lad and see if Master Lex Verd is in his chambers, will you? Tell him I would have a word with him directly, if it is convenient, then bring us two strong birds for the Giants. We must send—."

Gendau was already gone.

Singh couldn't help a brief smile at Pater Nos' brief look of irritation. "That boy," he remarked, a slight shake of his head.

Seventeen

HAVING COMPLETED HER BATHING ritual and prepared herself for war, the last item on Verdor's agenda before meeting with governor Lorca was to warn the fairies of the pending upheaval and possibly to enlist their help.

The fifth kingdom belonged to the Fairies. That was acknowledged by all, including the teachers at the Mosaic school. The Fairy kingdom, it could be said, had no boundaries. No rivers or mountains marked the perimeter of their domain because they, in fact, lived everywhere, within all kingdoms. They were never seen by most and rarely seen even by the wizards.

Fewer still knew their habits or kinship laws, although it was generally understood by all that fairies belonged to clans with names such as The Green Jacket Clan, The Red Cap Clan or The Black Shoe.

For the millennia before the mosaic school was founded, fairies were considered by many to be merely superstitions, the fodder of tall tales. The other kingdoms without exception included them in their stories. They were heroes or scapegoats for both good and bad fortune. If a child died in birth, then fairies had stolen the soul. If a piece of jewelry went unaccounted for, and the disappearance could not be attributed to a thief or a careless wearer, then fairies had stolen the item. Still, if the weather granted a favorable harvest and the storerooms were full against the coming winter, it was said with satisfaction, that fairies had favored their hosts.

No one who claimed the smallest amount of wisdom ever took them for granted. Few were surprised that one cool evening just after sundown, only a year after the founding of the mosaic school, forty fairies representing forty clans appeared to Lord Pater Nos, or so he said, and none doubted his word.

Each fairy stood no more than a thumb's length tall and sported a pair of wings that disappeared while in flight, like the wings of hummingbirds do, and fairies darted about in like fashion. The fairies' clothing was made from the down of duck feathers, puffing out their form, giving them the appearance of more substance of body than they truly possessed. Each wore the distinctive garment of its clan, the leathering shoes, or various colored jackets slitted for their gossamer, wasp like wings. Males wore hats that clung tightly to their tiny skulls, hiding ears pointed like the ears of a fruit bat, with draw strings tied under their chins. Females wore their hair long and free and many had hair longer than their bodies. With a delicate toss of their heads they could loop their hair over an arm. This was as practiced and as natural as an expert yeoman flips his bow over his shoulder. Pater Nos was reminded of the quick, involuntary motion with which a sparrow draws in its fanned tail after alighting upon a branch.

Delicately handsome, fairies' eyes were tiny aquamarines under long lashes, and their skin, wherever exposed, was almost translucent, giving only the hint of a skeleton beneath.

Fairies spoke in tones of tinkling crystal. Often, many spoke at the same time as if they could discern multiple conversations and points of view, as if every opinion or argument was heard simultaneously. When they spoke to Pater Nos, however, only one addressed him, although all spoke with perfect diction the language of all the kingdoms. Theirs, however, was the only tongue Pater Nos did not speak, because fairies never taught it to any, mainly for their own safety. And Pater Nos agreed.

They had observed Pater Nos for most of his life, deciding he was honorable and would not harm them. This belief in him led them to send their own emissaries to the school, finally making their presence officially known. Pater Nos, for his part, had long suspected their existence. During his youth even, he had seen their sign in the fields and woods. Clues being no more significant than a bent blade of grass to which not even the keen nose of a wolf paid heed. He had taken to the practice of leaving ground tobacco for them to find, and not just any tobacco either, but only the top leaves of the plant, the choicest and most valued cut.

So one evening, an evening of promise like the school itself, Pater Nos opened the door to his study to find his nose pleasantly assailed by the smell of ripened elderberries. Entering, he didn't notice them at first. The fairies all bowed low with their wings wrapped about them from one of the large books lying on his desk.

Thus began an evening of bargaining. At first, some fairies were frightened of Pater Nos, his voice boomed so that their wings quivered. He quickly learned to modulate his tone around them. Their leader wasted little time getting to his point.

"We applaud you," their leader said, "and we wish to be represented here to our mutual benefit."

"You are welcome, ah…"

"I am Raif Nek, king of Fairies, of all clans and all regions on land, and servant to my legions."

Raif Nek had risen to his feet, waving his arms about him, encouraging the others to follow suit or take their leisure, sitting where they had just been kneeling.

"Raif Nek." Pater Nos bowed low and gave them his name. "I am Lord of this School and Grand Wizard of the Senchai. As I said, welcome and as for mutual benefit, we at the school seek nothing but your friendship. In return we will do all in our power to aid you in whatever way we can."

A gentle tinkling response accompanied nodding heads and smiles from tiny, upturned faces. With that, one of their numbers lifted off the book and flew out the open window, a messenger to others of this initial response. Who could guess how many waited outside Pater Nos' room? Throughout the evening, tiny emissaries came and went at each juncture in the conversation. So many, in fact, that Pater Nos quit noticing. He couldn't say with any certainty that the one who left was the one who flew back in, or was yet another. They did this in a pattern known only to themselves, with no apparent protocol or pecking order.

Many items were discussed, some petty but mainly interesting.

"What race are you?" Pater Nos asked Raif Nek.

"We are the Tuatha, what you call fairies. Our numbers are as the grains of sand on the ocean's beach and under it. We have clans that live on land, as do we of the Tara branch, and clans that live in water, known as the Selkie. I am king of the Tara."

"And what do you seek of us?"

"We have concerns," Raif Nek responded. "The first, and to us the most important, is fire. In all your kingdoms, fires sweep over the land, burning our homes and scorching our wings so we cannot escape. Many perish in your fires. Why do you start such conflagrations?"

Through the long night many understandings were reached. As a result of the first and subsequent meetings, Pater Nos wrote a guide on the Tuatha for all kingdoms, a body of knowledge he passed on to all wizards. Nevertheless, the fairies remained a private race, still seen by very few.

***

Just before leaving the woods bordering Burba, Verdor once again left the path in search of a rock on which to sit. For a time she sat quite still, all her senses alert. Gently, with her toe, she pushed aside last fall's leaves that still blanketed the forest floor, exposing a small patch of the rich humus beneath. From her bag, she extracted a pinch of the tobacco as well as a pinch of the moo tea she was never without. Sprinkling them both on the bare earth, she murmured a blessing and covered the spot over again with the leaves.

Verdor then resumed her quiet, expectant posture while her eyes darted about in anticipation.

She always marveled that she never heard their approach. The sunlight was splintered by the overhead branches into singular rays of brightness that scattered about the ground like a patchwork quilt. Fairies appeared in like manner, as if from the air and wrought from the light rays themselves. They veritably covered the forest floor about the feet of the wizard. At once the quiet wood came alive with the laughter of tiny crystalline bells.

Some fairies alighted in Verdor's golden hair, others on her staff and others over her knees. Many flew around her head as if playing a game of "catch me." Their unbridled joy made Verdor smile, but too soon the tinkling merriment settled, and from behind a near tree a fairy emerged indistinct from the rest. For some reason, perhaps some markings or dress not apparent to Verdor, the others acquiesced to this fairy and a full quiet descended over the masses. The fairy alighted on Verdor's big toe and, folding her wings, bowed before announcing, "We love thee, savior." Fairies had labeled her "savior" since she first met them at the Mosaic School, yet Verdor didn't know why.

The fairy looked up to Verdor and the throng chorused the greeting in a thousand tiny voices.

Verdor thought that this must be what light would sound like if it made noise. "And I love all of you," she said in return.

The tinkling crescendoed like happy children on a market day, but soon there was quiet again.

"I am Mona," the fairy on Verdor's toe announced. "King Raif Nek sends you his fondest greetings and queen Luena sends you this adornment."

Mona unraveled a tiny satchel of cloth exposing a diamond-like stone glowing with the captured essence of a star. "Queen Luena begs you wear this, that you should never walk in darkness. Will you accept?"

"I will," Verdor responded without hesitation, "with deepest gratitude and fondest wishes in return for Queen Luena."

Mona raised the gem in her hands that two from the throng promptly seized and carried to Verdor's right ear. She suffered a light pinch that brought her finger to her earlobe, to the small stone now firmly attached. Verdor, who was normally not disposed to wearing trinkets of any kind, was grateful for this singular honor from the Queen. Removing her fingers from her ear prompted a fortissimo of approbation from the fairies, as well as exclamations praising Verdor's beauty. As if unable to resist, several began rearranging the wizard's golden hair about her forehead and behind her ear to highlight the gift to the boldest effect, again to great rejoicing.

Verdor smiled, heat flushing her face. "I am overwhelmed and humbled by the queen's love and generosity," she whispered. "Please thank her for me."

"What can we do for you, Savior? You have only to ask."

"There is danger for all of you in this valley."

"Fire?" Mona cried, clearly alarmed.

"Yes, such that has never been seen, I fear."

A long pause deepened the silence.

"We have seen him, Savior," Mona said finally. "The evil one."

"Do you know where he is?"

"Yes, he abides now in a deep cave. He knows fairies will not enter caves, but we watch the cave he occupies."

"Can you take me to him if I will to go?"

"Without hesitation, if that is your wish."

"Thank you, Mona. For now, all of you should leave this area. A great battle is upon us. Darken has come to destroy the Valley and he may well succeed."

"I will inform the King and await his instructions. Is there anything else?"

"Yes, I would ask a boon of thee."

"You have only to speak it, Savior."

"I will soon summon my lover, a Senchai wizard whose name is Lex Verd, but I call him Thomar."

"We know of him, Savior. We have seen you with him"

"In three or four nights time, he will be crossing the Mohrs on the same path by which I entered the Valley. Do you know the one?"

"Most certainly, Savior. With great joy we watched you arrive."

"I wish you to find him before he enters the Valley. He can't know that you are there. What I will ask you to do must be done in the dark of night."

Verdor moved off the rock and squatted closer to Mona. Her voice dropped to a quivering whisper, as if she was afraid of hearing herself tell Mona what she planned.

The woods quieted; not even a tree frog or cricket chortled in the shadows. The tittering of the fairies ended. Verdor's plea was met by a solemn silence and heard by a thousand tiny ears.

In a few moments, Verdor returned to her seat and said, "I stay in one of the Giants' Libraries. Do you know which one that is?"

"You stay at the home of Dair," Mona replied, "the keeper of a library. Yes, we know of it."

"Can you do what I ask?" Verdor said.

"He will protect his space at eventide. How can we get near him?"

"Before he sleeps he will mark a circle on the ground around him. You must be inside that circle before he draws it."

"It will be done, Savior."

"Leave this for him." Verdor removed a knife from her bag and cut a small lock of her hair, which she gave to Mona, who immediately passed the lock to a nearby attendant.

Verdor looked down at Mona. What she had just asked this fairy raised not an eyebrow on the tiny face. She was grateful for this trust.

"Thank you, Mona," Verdor swept her arm over the myriad heads to include each of them, "and thank you all."

The tinkling voices gathered in strength and the fairies took flight, many passing close to her face, touching her golden hair as if it were a talisman, steadily disappearing into the light from whence they'd came. Like a swarm of friendly bees, some toted the tobacco leaf bits Verdor had left while others carried the tea, all of which would be given to King Raif and Queen Luena.

Verdor sent a blessing after them on the air. When the last had vanished, the sun seemed to sense the gathering gloom in the valley and sank quickly along its path to the horizon, as if wishing to hide.

Verdor picked up her 'Cept, stood up from her rock seat, and for the third time that day set out for the Governor's Home.

The coming night promised to be a long one.

Eighteen

GRAND WIZARD LEX VERD shrugged his broad shoulders into his cloak, then tied the collar drawstring loosely about his neck. He was almost ready to leave. "What could she be up to?" he again wondered aloud.

She hadn't written in code. There were any number of those she could have chosen. The gist of the message almost appeared to be mockery.

Her belly aches for my seed? And she called me Lex. Was Singh right? Did she want the message to be intercepted? If so, why?

"Be cautious, Thomar, I like this not," Singh had warned during his goodbye embrace.

"Can you not look?"

"I cannot. Such is my promise to Pater Nos. I trust him, as you know."

"I will be cautious, Master."

There was no need for Thomar to call Singh master any more. They were equals now, but Thomar could no more stop that than he could call his own father by his first name.

He scooped his bag filled with necessities for his journey from his bed and lifted its strap over his head and one arm. He paused long enough for a short prayer, then took up his staff and turned toward his door, startled by a sharp knock.

"Would the Master Verd permit me the honor of accompanying him to the borders?" Gendau's head was no higher than the doorknob, but his energy towered over the school. He stood outside Thomar's door, shifting from foot to foot, beaming a dazzling smile.

"It would be my honor," Thomar replied. "In fact, I was about to find you to see if you would. I need a strong lad to help me with this satchel. Did you inform Lord Pater Nos of your plan?"

"I did, Master Verd, and he said I could if I could manage to walk as slow as you do."

"Then I'll have to lengthen my stride so as not to encumber you." Lex Verd tussled the boy's hair and relinquished his bag. Gendau ducked an arm and head through the strap and the bottom of the bag nearly trailed the ground.

The two set out together, silent for a while. Both were enjoying the freedom inherent to travel. They had a half-hour's walk to the boundaries where Gendau would have to turn back.

"May I speak, master Verd, about the good Lord Pater Nos?"

Verd looked down at the boy gamely carrying the heavy satchel and matching, even with less than half the leg, the gait with which Verd was covering ground.

"Of course you may, if it isn't confidences. It's not confidences, is it?"

"No, Master Verd. I would never betray a confidence!"

"Of course you wouldn't, I was only teasing you, Gendau. Speak freely."

"Lord Pater Nos looked into his globe to see the future, you know. I saw him."

"Yes, I know, young one. Does that upset you?"

"Only a great deal. I don't think he liked what he saw. In truth, he has been in a bad mood ever since."

"Have you seen him look before?"

"Yes I have, several times."

"And?"

"And what?"

The two passed under the last portal of the schoolyard wall and were now on a narrower cart path overgrown with wild grass. They waved to a group of apprentices tending Singh's irrigation models. Master Singh could be seen on a distant dam, pointing, instructing on the mechanics of controlling the precious liquid that was the life of the school.

"See how he loves his dams and aqueducts, Gendau. He is always making changes to them. When do you start with him?"

"Lord Pater Nos says I have to master my numbers first. Then I can go to Master Singh. I wish to be out of doors very badly too."

"Are you having trouble with your numbers?"

"Not in the sums, Master Verd, but the geometry vexes me."

'Well then, when I come back, bring your texts to me and I may have some ways to make it easier. We could work on it together."

At the rate they were walking, the school disappeared over the next rise, leaving ahead of them miles of open grassland, punctuated occasionally by low trees, to the foothills of the Mohrs.

"You were saying that you have seen Pater Nos look. What have you learned?"

"I? I have learned nothing, he does not let me look."

"But you have learned something, Gendau, what was it?"

Gendau thought for a moment. "I don't know, nothing ever changes."

"Exactly!"

The boy looked up at Thomar, knitted his eyebrows, and said, "I don't understand, Master."

"Do you see that robin over there? Look up in that tree. Count now, three branches from the bottom on the right. Do you see it?"

"Yes, I see it."

"Now, suppose you could look, and you knew which way it was going to fly when it leaves the tree. Would your knowing change that in any way?"

"No, I suppose it wouldn't."

"Well then, suppose you looked and saw that it will fly toward the sun, right into the path of that hawk up there. What would you do then?"

The two squinted into the brilliant blue expanse. Gendau took a moment to find the raptor, shielding his eyes with cupped hands. A red-tailed hawk circled well above the level of the sun.

"I would run and tell the robin to fly the other way, so the hawk wouldn't see it and take its life."

"Is it not possible the robin can fly toward the sun, in the path of death, yet the hawk, being blinded by the sun as we are, would not even see her?"

"It is truly possible."

"Then what do you learn from that? What did your looking teach you?"

"I would need to think on that a while, Master. Unless you care to give me the answer."

"It might be better if you think on it for a while, Gendau. Some things you would better teach yourself. If I try to teach you, you may learn only what I know, and not what the truth is."

Gendau scratched his thick, floppy hair and walked in silence for a short while.

"Do you not worry about what Pater Nos saw, Master Verd?" he asked.

"No."

"What if you fly into the path of the hawk?"

Lex Verd stopped, knelt to the ground and took the boy in his arms. There were tears in the lad's eyes. Lex Verd wiped them away, smiling. "Then I would hope that the hawk doesn't see me."

"Will you come back to m… the Mosaic?"

"I plan to. And don't forget, Gendau, I'm no one's easy prey. Even if the hawk sees me, he will have the devil's own time trying to catch me. I've good legs for running."

"You could outrun a Hawk?"

"If I needed to. I heard you are quite fast too. Care to race?"

"You're old, master Verd!"

"Old, is it?" Verd's eyebrows arched skyward. "Do you see that post out there?"

The boundary post some distance away marked the border of the Mosaic campus where Gendau would turn back. Just the square top peeked above the high grass.

The two grinned at each other. "Give me my satchel and I'll give you a head start."

Gendau yielded the bag. "No head start will be taken."

The two bolted like frightened deer. The very wind would have been jealous of their swiftness. At the end, Lex Verd won by two convincing strides and Gendau mentioned how reassured he was—if Master Verd could beat him, what chance would the Evil One have?

They both stood together catching their breath and a few minutes passed before Gendau said, "If I could see the future, it would take all my strength to not try to change it. I know that I would try to save that robin from the hawk."

Lex placed a hand on the boy's shoulder. "I am proud of you, Gendau. You already know Lord Pater Nos' dilemma."

"Has he ever tried to change the future?"

"No, not in the way you are thinking, and you're right, it takes great discipline. That's what makes Lord Pater Nos such a great wizard. But you and I change our future every day. We just don't think about it much."

"How, Master Verd?"

"Just by studying your lessons diligently, you save yourself from a life of drudgery, from a life with little joy. Is that not changing your future? Suppose you decided to be lazy? Could you not guess what your future would be like then?"

Thomar made the good-byes quick and jovial before setting off toward the Mohr's jagged peaks rising in the distance. The sun was just starting its decline, slowly coloring the mountains green to ochre and then to a blush of purple. Tall pines swarmed up their sides to a height where they seemed to grow tired as if by common agreement, surrendering the high peaks to snow as white as a swan's wings glowing against the azure sky. All of his life Thomar had studied these color changes, through all seasons, and had never seen one display the same as yesterday's or last week's, or last year's. *A daily gift,* he thought, marvelous to behold, energizing his legs that gobbled the ground before them. Each foot loath to touch the earth for more than an instant; each competing for distance with the staff that thumped the ground alongside of them.

Thomar expected to reach the base of the foothills by evening, when darkness would force him to camp. *In three nights, I will hold her in my arms.* He was surprised at how much he missed Belinda. If he could, he would think of her always, but his work kept him occupied and exhausted. He arose early and fell into bed late, with barely the energy for night prayers. So, there was precious little time for daydreaming about her. But now there was such time. He smiled to himself. He would make good use of it.

What has she gotten into?

Something serious judging by all the clues: the warning of Master Singh at their goodbye, the tears of worry from Gendau. Even the idea that Lord Pater Nos had looked into the future was disconcerting. Pater Nos rarely looked, the skill was not to be encouraged. Of course, Pater Nos would look; with his precious Belinda's concern, he wouldn't be able to stop himself. Still, knowing all would change nothing of what might be. Verd refused to let speculation dampen his high spirits as his strides shortened the distance to his lover.

"Hey, Ho!" So lost in thought was he, and in his singleness of purpose, he was startled at the red flash of fur that crossed the path nearly tripping him.

"On your way to your den, are you?" he said to the Vixen. He noticed the rows of tits on the animal's belly. "Home to feed the wee wanes, then? What, with no luck in the hunt?" The fox stopped trotting to face Thomar and sat back on its haunches. Thomar came to an abrupt stop. "Come here, then Mrs. Fox and I may have something to fortify that rich milk you'll soon be parting with."

The wizard hunkered down, laying his staff to the path's side and began rummaging through his satchel. The fox sauntered closer and sitting again, waited expectantly. Thomar withdrew a large chunk of cheese and split it down the middle, using his thumbs to divide the dinner. "It's too much for me, don't you know," he said. He split that half again, dropping one part to the ground and offering the other to the animal.

"This is for you," he said, "and mind that you eat it. It won't do those kits any good if their mom dies of hunger, will it?"

The fox gulped the cheese and Thomar scratched it behind its ears. He admired its intelligent eyes, the deep red fur, the long white-tipped tail. When the fox had finished, she turned her head and licked Thomar's hand. Then, without hesitation, she picked up the other half of the cheese from the path and bounded into the high grass.

"Stay away from the hen coops," he scolded after.

In like manner, and with as little delay, Thomar had his staff in hand and was again thumping toward the distant hills and his beloved's arms. He owed the fox his gratitude for startling him from his reverie. He must stay more alert.

"You have two minds," Singh always told him. "Someday it will be your undoing."

Thomar pictured the frown on his master's face over his lack of discipline. The path to the Giants' valley was indeed a pastoral scene, worthy of his appreciation, but he mustn't forget that this road could be as dangerous as the landscape was beautiful. Were this not so, his love would not be sending for him.

He bent to his task with a more watchful eye.

Nineteen

FLEN WAS APPROACHING the edge of the forest where the trees stopped and the firebreak—open fields that surrounded the city—began. From there it was a short walk by his giant's steps to Burba's outer gates. His desperate anger at the world, and especially Lorca, had diminished but only a whit, eclipsed to a small degree by his concern about the return of the Fairy, so he called her. She had made a promise. She needed his help. *And help her I will. The poor darling needs you, good Flen. And your hammer, too.* Flen felt the weighty heft of it on one shoulder.

He slowed his pace to give the fairy time to catch up. *She will see me again before I leave this wood.* Flen was reluctant to move on, but short of stopping altogether to wait, he was beginning to despair of her pledge. Only a few long paces remained 'til he was out from under the canopy of the treetops and his anger flared.

"To Nye with them, and all the lying fairies. Never have there been ten women to equal a good man. Lying, treacherous, deceiving…"

He bashed his hammer against the broad trunk of a nearby tree to impress upon the splintering bark the truth of his words.

"Lying." BOOM. "Treacherous." BOOM. "Deceiving…," until a quantity of drought-saddened leaves showered his feet.

Flen was bent on continuing his lesson to the whole forest if he must, except for the pain that quickly equaled, then overtook his tantrum; a nasty reminder to his ribs and back of the flying tour through the trees, inflicted by the very one he awaited. He stopped hammering and walked back to the path groaning. He fell to his knees, allowing the iron head to fall to ground before him.

Gasping from his efforts, his rope-like muscles glistened under a sheen of sweat. Despite his pain, Flen took the moment to admire his swollen power. He flexed his arm, making the muscles jump. They reminded him of the voluptuous curves of the fairy's thighs and his breathing quickened. He flexed again, this time under the palm of his other hand, feeling his muscles' fluid movement. *This is what she would feel like under me.* He slid one hand to his groin.

"I will not wait, I will have her writhing beneath me, by all the power of Deddimus, I will." He tore at his codpiece, freeing his engorged penis into his grasp.

"Very impressive," she said, "but you will have to wait if you wish to see me writhing beneath you." The Fairy had appeared as if from the air and was walking toward him. She gave her head a quick lift, tossing her hair to one shoulder. Her full lips curved to hint at humor. "You must first fulfill your end of the bargain."

"Damn your foul manners, witch. Cannot a man make piss in the woods without prying eyes on his every movement?" *Was I speaking aloud?* Flen quickly covered himself but did not stand.

"Then I beg your pardon, abjectly, good Flen."

The same shimmering gown caressed each limb and curve with every silky movement. The Fairy stopped directly and fearlessly in front of him, her full breasts jutting impudently; their nipples poking the fabric just below the level of Flen's widened eyes.

"Are you done...making piss," she asked, "or do you require more time?"

If Flen could lift his arms, he would have only to reach out and take this lovely creature. But, he was fastened to the ground as if his knees had sent down roots. His hands lay helplessly at his sides, also stuck, until she reached down for one of them and placed it over an ample breast. Her nipple was hard beneath the veil-like covering. Never had a woman presented herself so willingly to him. She placed one of her hands over the top of his, pushing it firmly over the mound.

"You want me, good Flen."

Flen could say nothing. His bottom lip drooped from his lower teeth, releasing a stream of saliva to dribble in a thin, viscous flow to his engorged lap. He didn't see her other hand move, but the slap to his face reverberated through the trees and sent him cartwheeling off the path. He rolled to a sitting position, several feet from the mauled tree.

The blow had separated him uncomfortably from his weapon, for all the good that his hammer would do him. Confused and helpless, he waited for the ringing in his right ear to stop. The Fairy was again standing nearby, though he couldn't recall seeing her move. Her fingers were training the tendrils of his hair, gently, even tenderly, pushing his locks back from his forehead. One of her thighs brushed against his shoulder and the touch radiated through him. Flen sat in stunned silence, craning his neck, seeking the tenderness of her fingers playing atop his head. There was no fight within him now.

"I regret the discipline, Flen, but I was losing your attention."

"Mmmn." Flen nodded once.

"We have much to discuss, good Giant," she crooned. She moved around in front of him then straddled his extended legs, smiling up to his face.

"Mmmn."

"Tell me about the Troca. Flen, are you listening? We don't want any more unpleasantness do we, Flen?"

An answer formed on his lips, but his voice echoed within his skull, sounding distant, as if someone else were talking. "It's the law," he mumbled.

"Yes, tell me all about it." Her fingers had moved to his chest, preoccupied with the hair behind his open collar. "Does Lorca have to fight you?"

"No, she can give over her office to me instead."

"Will she fight you?"

"I will kill Lorca."

"Of course, you will. But I asked if she will fight you under the law?"

Flen stared dully back at her. The thought that Lorca would not fight hadn't occurred to him. "I know not." The indignity that this incongruity presented aroused him. His umbrage reawakened. "I will kill her anyway."

"Verdor will help her. Verdor will help her kill you instead." The Fairy stood and walked a few steps away from the sitting giant, hips swaying suggestively as she moved, leaving Flen to stare salaciously while digesting this notion.

"Nonsense!" he said.

"Oh? Is it?"

"Hisash spake that the Senchai are sworn to not interfere with Kingdom law. She cannot help Lorca. It would be impossible. I will kill Lorca when she fights me." His voice trailed off at the condescension on the Fairy's face. He searched her countenance for some answer, a comfort, noticing again, as during her first visit with him, that her eyes appeared odd. The pupils were cat-like and seemed to change with the angle of her head. How strange that such eyes should besmirch such a magnificent face.

"Hisash lied," the Fairy said with no more interest than stating a mundane fact about the weather. "She lied and Verdor lies."

'Then I will kill the Senchai also."

The Fairy laughed. "Come now, Flen. I didn't put all those bruises on your handsome face, did I? Where did they come from? Perhaps an unfortunate duel with a wine bottle?"

Flen felt cornered. How had the Fairy learned about the affair with the flask? *There is much magic afoot and hereabouts.*

"Don't worry, Flen, you have me to help you." She once again straddled his legs. Flen had no trouble avoiding her discomforting eyes for the swell of her breasts. Her voice was comforting, soothing him, giving him confidence. "We shall kill them both and you shall become Governor. Would you like that, good Flen?"

"How, lovely Fairy?"

She laid a gentle hand to Flen's cheek and pushed his face to one side, forcing his gaze to the tree he had battered, a large hickory of sufficient girth that his long arms could not reach around. Energy flowed from her hand through his cheek and out through his eyes.

The tree began to tremble, rocking, vibrating so violently that its roots shook loose the soil that had buried them for nearly a century. Thick bark separated from the trunk and fell in large chunks to the percolating earth. High branches bent as if pummeled by hurricane winds from all sides at once. The power pouring out his eyes intensified until the tree was moaning, howling, screeching like a tortured animal. The cacophony built to a siren noise that hurt the giant's ears, and then suddenly, with a piercing, tearing, sound, the tree exploded. Large chunks of wood and massive burls of torn branches whirred past the cowering Flen. The force of the wind lifted his hair and folded back his ears, matting his cheeks against the bone of his face.

He had seen trees that were hit by lightning, but he'd not seen one suffer such utter destruction as this. Not a piece of root remained in the ground. Through the haze of dust blanketing the forest floor he saw tree parts torn against the grain, not split, but twisted apart, lying about like flotsam on beach sand. The Fairy allowed the giant time to absorb the scene. The power made Flen giddy with satisfaction.

The Fairy turned Flen's face back to her, staring into his eyes. "You did that, Flen," she said. "Not even Verdor has such power." She sat back, her bottom provocatively resting over Flen's thighs, just above his knees.

"What do you want of me?" he asked.

Her eyes entranced Flen. Her face achieved a certain grimace, a suggestion of passion or an amount of ardor, but those pupils were still dormant, un-alive. There was more comfort in the eyes of a dead possum he had once found in his rain barrel.

Take your leave of this, he told himself in a last effort to corral his minimal good sense. Once she shifted in his lap, he was again captured by a lust that crowded out any chance of salvation.

"Soon, I will tell you," she said. "Where will this battle, this Troca, take place?"

"In a field by the soap works. It is where all public meetings are."

"Excellent, it is sufficient," she said, more to herself than Flen. "Will all the Giants attend?"

"All."

"If Lorca gives over her power without a fight, will the gathering take place?"

Flen hesitated. He wasn't sure. His face still burning from her previous chastisement, he feared provoking the Fairy and stabbed at an answer:

" All will come," he said emphatically, hoping he was correct. *Hisash, that cowardly hag, would know this answer.*

His vulnerability before the fairy attached itself to his self-confidence like lichen to a rock, which in time breaks down to sand. He dared a question: "Why do you wish to know where the Troca will take place?"

If the Fairy was annoyed, to his relief, she showed none.

"I need to know where to help you." Her voice sounded sweet and she spoke to him now as if he were a pet kitten. He liked this. "While you kill Lorca," she said, "I will attend Verdor to make sure she gives the governor no advantage. I won't have that witch hurting my Flen. It just won't do."

She stroked his face with her delicate fingers and Flen's arousal soaked him like a warm soapy bath. *She said 'my Flen'.*

"Why won't you tell me your name?" he complained mildly, hoping she would continue in this almost playful tone.

"Dear Flen, would you like a name for me? Why don't you call me your little Bobolink? Will that do?" She smiled at him. That is, her lips smiled; her eyes had not changed. Flen tried not to look at them.

"Yes…Bobolink…" Flen boldly placed a hand on her thigh, yet she seemed unaware. The sheer cloth covering her leg heightened the mystery, stoking his lust. He tried to speak but began to stammer. " Wh-when, my Bobolink, will-will I have thee?"

Bobolink rocked to her knees, and pushed herself to her feet, a hand barely brushing his bloated loincloth. Flen was eye level with her breasts, a challenge he dare not take. She bent forward to kiss the top of his head and one of these magnificent orbs brushed his nose. His breath stopped.

"When you kill Lorca, my sweet Flen, then you will have your Bobolink."

She turned from him, sashayed across the clearing, and disappeared amidst the trees.

A thought staggered Flen's brain. *Her breath was cold!* Flen's conscious mind quickly gained control, slamming the fledgling misgiving as if with a great hammer, reminding him the Fairy had called him "my sweet."

Shortly, Flen gained his feet, sought out his hammer, checked the precious contents of his leather pouch, which he'd nearly forgotten, and with a last look at the sundered tree, set off with long strides toward Burba. His face assumed the accustomed snarl, but his chin jutted in high optimism. Every past second of his misguided life paled against the moment of fame ahead of him. He strode toward his destiny like a brazen rooster struts a hen coop. Like the cock, Flen knew there was really nothing of importance to life outside himself. Yes, of course, the Valley was in trouble, any fool could see that. All the more reason that his mission could not wait. His time had come. Bobolink would fawn over his victory. They would rule the land together, yet she would be subservient to him, he would insist on that.

***

Verdor, having been waylaid by her meeting with the fairies, was again behind Flen on her path toward Burba. She came upon the hickory's destruction as early evening shadows lent their own sense of foreboding to the dismal scene. Her sorrow for the tree was a sorrow for the entire valley. This kind of destruction might soon be common, so prevalent, in fact, that those Giants who survived the coming maelstrom would take no more notice of it than the grass beneath their feet. She stopped, remembering Pater Nos and a time in her past when she was still Belinda.

126

"Life is a balance, Bell," Pater Nos said, "and a precarious one."

The two, master and apprentice, stood over the dead animal lying in blood-stained grass only a few feet from its burrow. A woodchuck, caught by...what? A fox? The furry throat had been slashed, the neck broken, yet the animal was uneaten. What filled fourteen-year-old Belinda with such sorrow were the six babies suckling their mother's body. Their chattering and mewling signaled that they were unsuccessful in drawing nourishment from the corpse.

Belinda knelt on the ground and picked up one of the pups, gently turning the baby over. The tiny body barely filled her small palm. A pink tongue lapped her finger. Half-open eyes suggested a hopefulness that made the girl sadder yet as the pup gnawed her fingernail.

Tears wetted Belinda's cheeks. "I don't see the balance in this, Lord Pater Nos, only meanness."

"It appears that way, and you may be right, but the balance for this is here."

"Where? Will a wolf eat that mean fox?"

"Mayhap the fox will live to an old age and die in its den. That is not what balance means."

"We can help these babies, Lord Pater Nos. We can take them home and raise them. I will use my free time, none from study. Can we please?" Belinda nuzzled the baby woodchuck with her nose, the fur slick and soft, smelling of earth.

"Child, only their mother knows how to raise them and I'm afraid..."

"She's dead, Lord Pater Nos. Please, we must do something."

"Give me your hand, Bell." The grand wizard knelt beside her. "We must leave this place."

Belinda jerked her shoulder away from him. "You can fix this!" Tears streamed down her face. "You can give her back her life. You are the Pater Nos!"

"No, Bell. I cannot. The death of the mother grieves me, but death in nature is part of life. We cannot interfere."

Bell jumped to her feet, still clutching the baby animal, and ran several yards away where she fell to her knees once more in the high grass.

Pater Nos followed and again knelt beside her. "What happened here is not evil, Bell. This is natural."

"I hate you! I will not go with you. You are mean. You are cruel."

"I will leave you to your grief," Pater Nos said. "Come when you are ready." He placed a coveret on her, stood and started off toward the Mosaic School.

"I will not come. I will never go with you."

The baby woodchucks died during the night. Under a somber moon, Belinda tenderly corralled them with their mother into a grave that she gouged from the soft earth with a stick. Shortly after mid-morning she found her way back to the Mosaic, throwing herself into the open arms of her waiting teacher.

She shook herself free of the memory and focused on the hickory. What had happened to this tree was not natural nor was any balance to be discovered here. Besides, if the Evil One was leaving her a message with this destruction, she would leave him one as well. Verdor knelt on the disturbed ground.

Both of her hands made alternating circles in the dirt. Each pass she scooped a handful that she allowed to pour back through her fingers. Over and over she repeated this with her eyes closed so that she did not see, but imagined a swirl of activity about her. Pieces and parts, splinters and bark, sand and roots, surely, steadily, joined to their original places in earth and tree to make both whole again.

The work tired her, but she could not stop now.

She heard the voice of Grand Lord Pater Nos in her head: *You are the balance.*

Twenty

"WHERE IS SHE?"

Lorca addressed the question to the walls. She paced the black slate floor of the hall adjoining her house where the cabinet meetings took place. Her house was situated on the very perimeter of Burba so that on the easterly side she could see the sunrise over the fields and hills beyond the firebreak. Out a westerly window, she viewed the very heart of the city.

The meeting hall was an addition to the south side. A large room even by Giant standards, the interior walls were white stucco, interspersed by tree-trunk like support columns holding up a high vaulted ceiling made from split timbers under a slate roof. Most of the other Giant homes were roofed in traditional thatch.

The room measured one hundred feet square with the most modern glass windows that towered even over a Giant's head. Lorca paused at each to study the landscape to the east. Dried, crumbling and dust covered grasses stretched to the firebreak. The scene reflected what she felt. Her strength seemed to recede from her and her courage dried like the grasses before her. The news Hisash had brought was most unwelcome. Verdor, hopefully, would arrive soon. How good it would be to share her burdens, though she knew she alone must face decisions she feared to make, and she would need to decide on them soon.

"There were ten of these, these Pokers, you say?" Lorca asked Hisash.

"Yes, Governor, ten at least. It was dark to where I couldn't see much beyond the path."

Lorca stopped pacing and, with hands clasped behind her, she faced Hisash.

"Do you wonder that they have trapped Verdor? Wasn't she behind you?"

"I don't know, Governor."

Hisash sat in one of the large chairs that ringed the conference table, wringing her hands as if to cleanse them. Lorca advanced on Hisash, regarding her warily, then called down the hallway for Nakus.

"Climb the tower and give the bell three and two," Lorca ordered. "And chop them fine."

If Nakus was alarmed in any way, she didn't show it, but quietly receded from the hall. Shortly, the bell began summoning the council.

Lorca and Hisash listened for a moment, and then Lorca asked, "What are your plans, Hisash? Are you done with Flen and the Troca?"

"With my heart in my mouth, and my life at your service I beg your forgiveness, Governor." Hisash stood up. "I am done with the Troca. It was my foolish pride and jealousy. But…"

"Go on, Hisash, but what?"

"I fear that Flen is of no such mind, unless the Senchai can change him. It was I who filled his empty head with this ambition."

The bell in the tower continued to toll the alarm. Hisash and Lorca again gazed upward at the summons, a depressing noise, not uplifting like a normal bells' call.

When the walls swallowed the last ominous notes, Lorca turned to Hisash. "Can I count on you?"

"Yes, Governor."

Lorca studied her former lover's eyes. "We will talk, but not now. I will give you a letter to take to Dropeye at the soap works. He is next in charge to Noish, is he not?"

"Yes, Governor."

"Fine. Noish will already be on his way to the council. You might pass him as you go. This letter will instruct Dropeye to shut down the soap works. Be sure the fires are out, all of them. It will be a holiday of sorts. All but the Fiercers will return to their homes. They, all of them, with saw and ax, will come here and wait outside for me. As for you, you will then return to this council. There will be shock and disbelief at your news. Brook no argument from anyone, is that clear?"

"Yes, Governor."

"I remain hopeful that the Senchai returns by then. I don't know if I, without her, can convince the council of the danger we are in. And when they hear that I have closed the soap works, they will be angry. As for Flen and the Troca, I will deal with him as I must. Perhaps he may yet see to reason." Lorca wrote furiously from her place at the head of the long table. She folded the parchment, sealed it and handed the missive to Hisash.

Hisash made quick strides toward the door, leaving Lorca to ponder the import of the news she carried. The soap works had never been shut down in her lifetime. Parts of it for repairs, yes, but never the entire affair. This would idle most of the Giants in the valley as all jobs had one end purpose—to manufacture soap.

Lorca again called out for Nakus. The scribe appeared wearing a worried, furrowed look, but said nothing.

"Nakus, who would know most about the armory?" Lorca asked.

"That would be Skin Doo, your worship."

"Nakus, you needn't call me that. We can't forget ourselves in these times, eh, old friend?"

"Yes, your wor…governor. Forgive me. Skin Doo is the eldest son of Lensor the Fiercer. He can be found at the armory on his days off. What he does there I don't know."

"Good, send for Skin Doo and have him at this meeting. Tell him I will need a report on the state of the weaponry."

"Would that he can do that, Governor, he's just a lad."

"Would that we can fight what is coming with weapons, Nakus, though I doubt they will do us any good, whatever shape they are in."

There was a loud banging at the door of the house, so forceful and persistent that the long poles of the embroidered tapestries high on the walls swayed, audibly clicking in their brackets.

"Deddimus, give me patience, but that would likely be Flen," Lorca said. "Be kind and go let him in before he breaks something, will you, Nakus?"

"I would as soon run him off, Governor."

"No, Nakus, we know what he wants, and what he wants breaks no law. Let him in. He would attend this meeting as a council member anyway."

Nakus left the hall and soon Lorca heard Flen's booming voice resonating through the corridors. He grew louder upon his approach. "Troca!" he bellowed, "Troca! I won't be denied! Trocaaaaaaa!"

Flen stood at the doorway to the great hall, red of face, hammer over one shoulder.

"You will not enter this room with a weapon, good Flen. You know the penalty for that, don't you?" Lorca calmly challenged the blustering giant.

Flen's offensive collapsed. He looked confused, undone, and Lorca pressed her advantage.

"Set your hammer there on the wall and Nakus will find us a bully wine to share and we will hear your grievance like old friends with a difference of opinion, neh?"

"Fetch the wine then," Flen replied, "but I'll countenance none of your smooth tongue to dissuade me, Lorca. You will fight me as the law allows."

Flen swaggered into the hall without his hammer, his pouch jouncing at his waist, the contents ticking. Lorca said nothing about this. Flen withdrew from the table his customary chair and sat ceremoniously as if the very room honored his arrival.

"Of course, Flen, but did you not hear the summons?" Lorca said.

"I heard it, and a timely one it is. Now the whole council will know my intent."

Lorca paused a moment to allow the giant to settle himself.

"Then you will hear with everyone else," she said, "that we have more pressing matters than your Troca."

Flen bristled visibly. "A dainty trick, no doubt. But I'll not be put off with a ruse."

Nakus entered the hall with several flasks and numerous goblets on a large pewter tray that she set gingerly on the table. "Some of the others have arrived, Governor." Nakus placed one goblet at the head of the table, Lorca's customary seat. The Governor had approached her chair, but did not sit. Nakus then placed another cup, to the left side of Flen, avoiding the reproachful eyes of Lorca as she did so. Flen failed to notice the slight, he was more intent on the drink. She then distributed the rest of the cups around the table, one in front of each chair.

When Nakus returned to distribute the flasks, Lorca said to her quietly, "Show the rest in, Nakus, then ready your quill and book. Be sharp to your task this evening. This may well be a most important meeting and I wish the books to show that I followed the laws of our forebears."

Flen brooded over his goblet, which he had filled. Upon first meeting, a stranger would be certain that the giant was making a great effort to contain a righteous anger. But to those who knew Flen, it was just the familiar thumb-thumping and head shaking of one whose precious time was being wasted by the ineptitude surrounding him. At any moment, his face might puff up like an adder's, intent on a violent outburst, and then the next, he would settle as if rethinking a finer point to his strategy.

Lorca tried to set him aside from her thoughts when the other council members arrived.

All presented concerned faces and went straight away to their chairs with only terse greetings and blessings. Nakus noted their presence in her log. Councilors at large: Osah, Osish, Piash, Duron the water keeper, Noish of the soap works, who radiated indignation—he had heard the order to close his soap works. Entwas the herder was there, Pusah the grainer and finally, Telf the woods keeper.

"We are all present, except Hisash," Nakus announced.

"We begin." Lorca said. "Nakus?"

Nakus began the prayer that bowed all heads. The council had mumbled the words a thousand times, yet for Lorca tonight the words had more meaning. The council members, unaware of the reason for the abrupt summons, seemed quietly fearful. The bell had made the difference. The 'three and two count chopped fine'—meaning three rings followed by two in rapid succession—was a code known by all. Trouble was at hand. So they prayed now with unusual fervency:

"Dedimus in Chaka…" The words droned on in quiet desperation to their hopeful conclusion, reminding the supplicants of their vulnerability in this world, "…silvic in slok Chaka. Dedimus, Exichay e Dedimus in silvic ichitay. Amen."

Lorca placed her palms on the table and waited for the quiet moment that would follow the prayer. Bowed heads righted themselves immediately, except for Flen's who deigned to dwell yet a few more moments with his god. Silence weighted the air. Lorca struggled with the horrifying image that she hoped to make real to these unsuspecting ears.

All eyes regarded her. Each Giant seemed struck with a prescience of disaster, thinking likely of their homes or partners still tending hearths, of children or tasks uncompleted.

"We are occupied." Lorca said gently. "By forces we are nearly powerless against. Our survival as a race is threatened."

Twenty-One

DARKNESS ASSERTED ITSELF, and those subservient to it retreated to their lairs or beds. The day was over, gone like the days in Thomar's past, stolen by insatiable time. For him the closing of each day always brought a smidgeon of regret, gone before he was ready. Today was, after all, not just a day to the world, but a day in the wizard's life.

Thomar's strong legs had carried him further up the mountain than even he expected. He was pleased with his progress. Night prayers, soon to be said, were not only spoken by habit or custom, but through fear of not. Who could be so confident in The Giver's benevolence to close his eyes without praises? Lex always thought that night prayers sounded direful, like those said at the death of a friend, at least the ones he had learned in school. He usually made up his own, with hope to the promised tomorrow.

He had chosen his camp well, on high ground and dry, just at the line of truce where the trees stopped and the snow would begin. Dead wood for his fire was plentiful here. Lex had only to scoop up the fallen and in little time and effort had sufficient tinder to give him heat against the chill of the coming night.

When the fire was raging he happily began to whistle a tune he was composing for Belinda. Still whistling, he took his staff and with his back to the fire, scribed a broad coveret in the dirt. While he did so, he saw, or perhaps he only sensed, a movement out of the corner of his eye, which caused him to stop and focus his attention on the ground. Just then an aspen leaf turned over, sucked by the draft created by his fire. In the inconsistent firelight, the leaf blinked a shadow several times larger than itself. The shadow danced, there, then gone, then back again until at last it lay still. The leaf was one from the pile of leaves he had gathered, not too close to the fire, on which he would sleep with his cloak tightly about him.

Something felt odd. For a moment he sensed a presence within his circle of protection. *Night fears*, he thought, dismissing them. Thomar continued his ritual work.

That done, he sat with the fire warming his back. With his staff beside him on the ground, he looked up at the clear night sky. The stars were close, stunning in their brightness.

"I would that I could give one of you to my love," he said aloud.

He reached into his satchel and withdrew the lute he had been carrying in secret for a while. Vanity would not allow him to practice within earshot of anyone. He had little talent for the instrument and even fewer melodic chords was he able to coax from the strings. And why should he insinuate his music on another's quiet? That is, until he became accomplished enough, which he was determined to do.

Shifting his weight on the leafy seat, he angled his body toward the fire and tuned the lute. He began by softly whistling the song he wished to play. Clumsy fingers groped several bars to familiarity, then strummed them, whistling for accompaniment. He now attempted new notes, singing instead of whistling. His voice, contrary to that of the instrument, was rich and flowed easily, like a melodic river from his insides. If only the lute would cooperate, playing seemed so simple, yet he was constantly surprised at how stubborn these four strings could be. They would not meet his fingers and seemed to rebel against them instead.

Lex struggled through the first measures again and then applied the words he had invented thus far to go with them:

I would rather touch your fine gold hair,
Than stroke the ermine's tail
I would rather hold your gentle hand

Than hear the nightjar's wail.
Your eyes of blue, your skin so fair
Your lips of rosy hue,
Quench me like a summer morn's
Purest leafy dew.

He could get this far only with fits and starts and many miss-fingerings on the lute's neck. Nor did the words flow the way he'd imagined they would by now.

Finally, good sense, not frustration, overtook the lovesick minstrel and he replaced the lute in his satchel, satisfied with how Belinda's song was progressing. He was very excited at the prospect of playing for her soon. On nights like this, going to sleep was truly a discipline for him. He would have liked to spend the night practicing or spend the star-light hours divining new verses for her. He was sure he could create the longest love-song ever composed. But, he also knew he needed sleep.

Night prayers were whispered on breath that lay upon the cold air like smoke. The myriad stars overhead listened dispassionately. The brilliant crescent moon seemed to turn toward him. With considerable difficulty, the Senchai was able to concentrate on the holy words. He then banked the fire, wrapped himself in his cloak, reached out and touched his staff, which lay beside him on his leafy bed. With hope that his prayers were heard, Lex Verd closed his eyes on one more of his allotted days.

That night, Thomar was tormented by dreams. In them, Belinda had come to him eagerly, he thought, but when he tried to embrace her, she would move, floating just above his grasp, or she would rapidly diminish as if he were looking through the wrong end of Pater Nos' spy glass. Worse, he seemed tied to the ground on which he lay and, when she drifted about, he could not reach her. Time after time he attempted holding her, but she would elude him. He searched for her eyes, which also tried to escape him, and when he was finally able to see them, they were overflowing with tears.

"Belinda, my love, why do you weep so?" he begged over and over again.

He fought the invisible restraints, his body jerking back and forth, but he could not loosen the earth's grasp. In one final desperate and violent shake, he found himself awake, staring at the pale gray, pre-dawn sky.

A bright morning star just over the horizon fought valiantly against the dawn, refusing to yield its claim on heaven. The new day's mountain air was crisp, biting his nostrils. He was panting for breath, his shirt soaked through with sweat, and one of his hands was closed tightly.

Thomar recognized his fear immediately, a hollowed-out, dull throb in his bowels. He felt desperately alone and sat up on his leaf bed. In the awakening light, he turned his fisted hand palm side toward him, bringing it close to his face before slowly, painfully, opening it. A lock of blond hair was matted against his wet palm. Belinda's! He knew as much before his mind could process the bizarre event. Now he feared for her. He reached for his staff.

Gone.

Twenty-Two

EVEN THOUGH THE NIGHT was warm, one of the Fiercers started a small fire. They were men of fire, who spent the stock of their days and the store of their bodies ensuring the fires at the soap works would never extinguish. The fires mustn't go out, to be sure, but they were also required to burn with optimal heat. The coaling qualities of the wood that fed these fires were bred into the trees, felled, split and seasoned by the skilled hands under the watchful eyes of these men.

How natural, then, for them to have fire on which to focus and pass their time waiting.

The woods, the trees, were the Fiercers' world. Any of the ninety or so giants assembled could spot a diseased limb or harmful mold in a glance. So accustomed to each other's company, and so familiar with their work, were they that there was little need for conversation. They had lived their days in each other's shadows from the time they were small.

Trees, large ones, dropped around them, axes cleaved air and wood with controlled abandon. The sound of their work, the death screech of toppling oaks, the earth "thumping" when trees crashed to the forest floor, was a constant din in the forests where they labored. The noise alone would be trying to anyone not raised to it. Yet, even above this racket, if an axe entered a dense knot or a tree splintered or might fall in an unforeseen way, the Giants would hear the difference, and would move, in unison, away from the danger. They lived on that difference, and those who never heard had long since been winnowed from their ranks by a crushed arm, or worse.

There was always too much for a Fiercer to do—pruning, clearing undergrowth, chopping and splitting, carrying, stacking cords and stoking fires—and these never-ending tasks kept them in constant motion from early to late, when they would return to their homes and wives, secretly eager to start the next day's labor. The ordinariness of their lives, the satisfaction of great chunks of work accomplished, even their tiredness at day's end kept them content.

They were not temperate men, but gnarled like the hickories they tended. Callused, thick fingers were impatient to work. This evening, having been summoned by Lorca, they milled around the fire carving splinters from their palms or just listening to their own night sounds, the spitting, the jostling and broken laughter from a lewd joke, or the shearing sound of axe on whetstone. Idleness confused, making them nervous. They had names like Torsten or Beargus as if their mothers knew their destinies before they left the cradle.

They knew of the valley's problems, of course—the drought, the barrenness of the oxen and even their wives—yet they were content to let their leaders handle them. The Fiercers had even heard that a wizard visited the Kingdom. Other than the crude joke from one of the younger among them that only a Fiercer could satisfy a Senchai in the bed chamber, there was little interest in what the governs said or did as long as the work was there. But now the work had stopped.

The whole day crew had been summoned to the governor's house at the close of their shift and now the night shift was arriving. Some had been milling about Lorca's courtyard for over an hour. More and more small fires were lit. More giants gathered. They began to occupy themselves with taunts and challenges. Feats of strength were attempted, wagers made, anything to keep in motion.

"What do you make of this, Menshun?" one asked the senior Fiercer.

"I don't like it," Menshun replied without taking his eyes from the flames. "I like none of it."

"And she broke the clodding line!"

"Nay, that!"

"'Tis true enough, they cool as we speak, all fires out, I came from there direct."

"Deddimus, the woman's mind has foundered. It will take days to start them again"

Silence followed these words into the black sky and, like the sparks from their fires, hovered over the giants like smoke on a rainy day. Could their work really stop for days?

"I avow that Flen should show her those children of his and we be done with her," one of the voices broke the quiet.

"Stow that!" Menshun rebuked the man. "Lorca will have a reason for this, we'll see rightly, by the by."

The lower door leading out to the courtyard at the back of the house where the Fiercers had gathered opened, and Lorca stepped through. She was followed by Nakus, her scribe, and yet another. This would be the Senchai wizard, the Fiercers surmised.

Giants stepped aside, yielding a path to their governor. Almost all the men stood a head taller. They studied her face when she passed, looking for any cues, perhaps of weakness, indecision, or fear. They garnered only that she moved through them easily.

"Open the Maps," she commanded Nakus when they had reached one of the fires. Only the sounds of shifting feet and rubbing shoulders could be heard. Those nearest tried to see what Lorca was doing. She knelt and, with the help of Nakus, found small stones to hold the corners of the map to the ground, close to the firelight. Lorca and Nakus then stood. Verdor the wizard was close by, quietly watching. Just over half the average Fiercer's height, she appeared a child among hulking adults.

"Who is chief among you?" Lorca demanded.

Menshun stepped forward from the throng.

"Ah, Menshun Ram, it has been a goodly time since last we met."

Even for a giant, Menshun was big. Not only taller than most of the others, his shoulders were broader, straining against the leather shirt that covered them. He was confident in his bearing. A day's growth of beard shadowed his jaw in the faint firelight. His mouth was set, his arms and legs fluid, a man ready and able to handle whatever was ahead. He carried a sheathed broad axe deftly on one shoulder as if it were naturally a part of him like his muscled arms.

"I am senior of the day-lot," he said, bowing to the governor. "It is not good news that sponsors this meet, I'll wager." Menshun made a cursory bow to the Senchai also. Giants closed the void left when Menshun stepped forward, leaving the five surrounded.

"You know Nakus, Menshun. This is Verdor, Grand Wizard of the Senchai. She will have instructions for you this night. Listen to her and do what she says." Lorca addressed not only Menshun, but also all the assembled. She then spoke to Menshun directly in a quieter voice. "See to this map, good Menshun."

The two knelt shoulder to shoulder and hovered over the map.

"I will speak to you of calamity unheard, and it will call for you to do things unnatural to you, but you must do them now and without question." Lorca's finger traced an area of the map to the Northwest of the city. "First, clear this line. Clear it to the ground. Cut the stumps low. Remove, but do not burn any brush or branches. Leave no root or branch large enough to hide a cat. I would like you to double the firebreak around the city. But there will be no time for that."

Menshun said nothing. What she was asking was a horror to a Fiercer. The clearing of generations-old forest nurtured to its prime would have disastrous effects on their whole economy. The age-tested cycle of work would be destroyed, the repercussions felt for many years to come.

Lorca said quietly, "Menshun, we may not have many more days or even hours. What you and your men do this night might be our only hope for survival. What is left of the wood may support those who survive the coming battle, but if we do not act now, then little else will matter."

Her warning passed through the ranks of Fiercers and the quiet gave way to fearful murmuring.

"Who attacks us?" Menshun tried to listen, but his mind kept tripping over the order to clear the virgin growth. He shook his head and blinked, trying to dismiss what he'd just heard. *Surely*, he thought, *I am dreaming.*

"Putris Darkin is in our valley," Lorca said.

Normally, Menshun would deride this statement. Putris Darkin was fantasy. His own mother had threatened to leave him on a hillside where the Dark One would find him if he did not behave. Menshun had never given the creature a single serious thought his entire adult life. Now, fully grown, valuing only what he could taste and see—the sublime beauty of a keen edge on his ax, the speed of his men at reducing a two hundred year old tree to cordwood in minutes, the sacredness of his work where nothing was wasted—all seemed to vaporize. One nightmare of incongruity seemed to follow the next.

Now he knelt with a governor and a Senchai wizard nearby. He thought that neither could ever understand his world. These were things that appeared in dreams, mysticism and magic, things he did not believe nor talk about.

"What do we do with the trees?" he heard himself asking.

"Wall the city, corral the oxen. The herders will assist you. The Senchai could put a magic ring around the city, but it would exhaust her. She said it would be easier to have a physical barrier to enchant than to use energy only for a ring of this size. Then only Giants would be able to pass this ring. I don't understand it myself, but we have no time to argue. Her ring, which she calls a coveret, on your wall may protect us within. The rest, the homes outside, the forests, the soap works, will be at the mercy of dark powers. The Grainers are already at work emptying the storehouses."

"The Council agrees to this?"

"Yes, but only by my vote. They were split. You should know, Menshun, that what seems to you to be madness is quite real, I assure you. But, I may not survive tomorrow morning. What I tell you now may well be countermanded by then."

"Flen?"

"Yes, he presses the Troca. I will fight him at dawn."

"Give over, Lorca, you have no chance."

"If I give over, you'll have no time to do what I ask."

"Have you seen this Dark One?"

"No, but the Senchai tells me it is here and I believe her. And, Hisash has seen numbers of his minions, the Pokers."

Still kneeling, Menshun scratched his chin. He was at a moment of decision, yet he stalled, grasping for anything.

"Hisash is a child," he said.

"Young, but no child. The Senchai has seen one also."

Menshun turned, looking toward the wizard. She appeared pretty, but frail with little more weight to her than the small branch of a tree. Could she have such power as was said about her? The wizard met his gaze steadily. The truth was in her. He saw it with eyes trained to see what was not apparent. Like he could foresee where the trilliums would bloom in his woods even before their shoots followed the spring thaw.

He had grown up with Lorca, he knew her, yet the wizard he had only just met engendered the same level of lifetime trust within him.

"How do I get the men to agree with this?" he said to Lorca. "You must know how they will be."

The murmuring of the men intruded on the night air, quiet expressions of disbelief. Menshun heard "Virgin forest..." "planted by our founders..." "impossible..." "ruination..." rumble through the crowd.

The familiar scent of the wood smoke helped assure him, settling his misgivings. The night was warm and friendly, starkly at odds with this impending disaster.

"If you believe me, then you must make them believe you," Lorca said. "Much depends on it. If they do not act tonight, then it may be too late. Remember, Menshun, it is only a plan, it is the best I can think of, and the wizard agrees. Yet, even this may not work against the powers we face."

Menshun stood and considered the throng of men before him, uncharacteristically motionless, waiting for his words. He looked to his left and addressed one of them, "Gather my first axe men here and now." Then he turned back toward Lorca. "My hopes are with you in your battle this morning. Flen is a fool."

"Think on your own task," she replied. "Not on me."

They looked at each other; their eyes speaking that which their lips saw no need. He would do what she asked of him. Lorca turned and, with Nakus, walked back into her house, leaving Verdor with the Fiercers.

Twenty-Three

THE SUN GLEAMED RED on the skyline, its appearance like a comforting hand on Thomar's shoulder, blessing him and fulfilling its unfailing promise of rebirth. Still seated, Thomar swiveled toward it and began trying to calm his spirit. He closed his eyes and took in a series of deep breaths, releasing them slowly, evenly. When he opened his eyes again, the sun was half exposed, the brilliance sufficient to see that his circle had not been broken. Whatever had robbed him of his Cept had been within the area of the coveret before he'd drawn the circle.

He studied the lock of hair in his hand once again. He didn't need the increasing light to affirm the strand, indeed, belonged to Belinda. Each individual hair seemed to emanate light, yellow gold, like ripened wheat shafts under a low sun at eventide. His staff missing, a lock of Belinda's hair left for what? A sign, certainly.

Belinda behind this burglary?

Who else could be? She had communion with fairies, he knew. She met with them often, something only she and Lord Pater Nos were able to do. The fairies would be invisible to him and might have been within his coveret before he made it. But why? Why would she leave him so vulnerable? He carefully placed Belinda's hair within a fold of cloth, then tucked the parcel deep within his bag.

Summon him only to betray him? Impossible. She would never have gone to the dark side—unthinkable. He loved her. Belinda knew there were forces that could kill him if they discovered him so compromised. So why?

Within his Coveret, he was still safe. He used the time to think. *Of course!* Belinda was in desperate trouble. Maybe even captured. Some foulness or other put her up to this. There was no other reason. Thomar was ashamed of himself. *How brittle is your trust in her.*

Soon, just when the rising sun cast its first shadows, he decided his course. Leaving only his lute within the circle so the instrument might stay safe, he stepped away, onto the path toward the snow capped peaks. In continuing toward the valley, he was placing his hope and life in Belinda's plan. Without his Cept, he worried how he could help her. *I must do something.*

Thomar finished eating what was left of the cheese and bread he had carried while he walked up, toward the snow. Without his staff he felt lopsided, even exposed. His feet fooled him like a landed sailor's after being away at sea. Empty hands swung at his sides uncomfortably, as if they belonged to someone else. His strides, though still strong, lacked the cheerfulness and anticipation that marked the start of this journey.

His heart felt like a stone in his chest. Part of him was willing to accept whatever Belinda's scheme was, though she devised it without consulting him, and another part complained that he had been left defenseless, a sheep among wolves. His beloved had done this to him. For the first time in their relationship, one defined by their life's work that included separation for days and even weeks, Thomar imagined his anticipated meeting with her. It would not be a lover's reunion, desperate to embrace, when no voice was necessary other than the pleasured mewling of their kisses. First, their speech would define and qualify, question and challenge. Their words would bump, jostle and confuse. And sadly, Thomar thought, they might disguise true feelings. Their touching would wait.

"What has happened?" he wondered aloud.

The snow, now up to his knees, ignored his question. Thomar quickened his pace. The sun gave him some comfort, warming his back. His efforts through the snow, lifting each leg high and putting it down again, began to turn his concentration from his troubles to just making headway up the deep path to the mountain's peak. At the summit, he stopped and looked at the Giant's valley below. He saw what he knew Belinda had seen: the tree line and beneath that, the brown and tans of a valley in drought. A smell she must have noticed was there also. In fact the stench was quite powerful, even noxious.

"'Tis an evil odor," he said and his eyes narrowed. He searched the landscape below him.

The snow less than ankle deep on the down side, he made short work of gaining the tree line. When he entered the scrub pines and then the taller trees below them, the path had dried, the walking easier still. Suddenly the hairs on the nape of his neck warned him he was being watched. They told him something else, too. Whatever was watching him had been awaiting his arrival and had brought the stink with it.

Out of nowhere, a blow slammed the back of his head and he fell forward. *Odd,* he thought, for he'd felt no pain. He was sure darkness had descended the instant before he'd been struck. His mind worried this puzzle only briefly on his plummet to the gritty path, for a sibilant voice said, "Bind him tightest, eh eh."

Before Thomar surrendered to the comfort of unconsciousness he heard the same voice again, fainter this time: "Master most please-ed to steal Senchai, eh eh. Ist bountiful easy."

Twenty-Four

THE FIERCERS WORKED through the night. By morning Governor Lorca saw the evidence of their labors in looking out the west windows of her home. The firebreak was widening. The fallen timber had been dragged toward the edge of the city and a crude, but stout wall of logs erected around at least one third of Burba's perimeter. If work continued at this pace, they would be half way around by noon.

Flen would countermand her order the minute she was dead. The wall's construction would cease. The changes painful to look upon must be beyond painful to the Fiercers, she thought, who, with the dawn's light, would take in the full scope of their night's toil. Trees planted by their grandfathers summarily felled left the land badly used, ugly even, as if plundered by a marauding army of massive locusts.

Lorca gazed silently through her window, but instead of the destruction, saw old Governor Maysi instead. *Do you still believe in me, Maysi? Do you regret pushing my name so hard before the council, dear friend?*

Lorca had served as Maysi's assistant governor from the time she was a young woman. Those were good years, prosperous, the Valley had thrived. Many children were born. And water, how wantonly they had used it. But who could have foreseen a time when the now precious liquid would be rationed so stringently?

Lorca was very content serving the old man. Maysi was like a father to her and she loved him. He taught her not only the workings of government, but also how to weigh and juggle the diverse opinions and personalities of their race. Their feelings about each other were mutually tender.

Then his headaches started. Lord Pater Nos was sent for and with him came all the hope and knowledge of the reputed Mosaic School. That was the first time Lorca had seen a wizard. Though she had been sending emissaries to the school on a regular basis, none had ever come to their valley. Once Lord Pater Nos arrived, however, there was little he could do, or would do, save giving old Maysi some respite from the pain. Lorca often thought that Maysi had accepted his death and required no further help from Pater Nos.

Pater Nos had brought with him a child, his apprentice, he said, and that child was Verdor. How shy she had been then, and how well she had grown into her office. *Have I grown into mine, Maysi?*

A cough behind turned Lorca from the window to Hisash standing near the door.

"Did you sleep, Governor?" she asked timidly.

"A trifle, good Hisash, is it time?"

"It is time for you to give over, Governor."

"That will do, Hisash. I will hear no more of it."

Lorca noted the tears on Hisash's face, approached her, and touched her gently on the cheek.

"You know, my love, that Menshun needs all the time I can gain for him," Lorca said. "When I am dead the work will stop and we will be that much more defenseless."

"We have the Senchai, Lorca. She can protect us."

Lorca wiped the tears from Hisash's cheeks and said, "She needs the circle, Love. She needs our city enclosed. You heard her say that. It has to be done this way. Now, Hisash, I need you to be strong. You will still be assistant governor and, may Deddimus help you, you must keep Flen from destroying us all. I cannot continue unless I am sure of your strength. Are you resolved, dearest? Please, say so."

Hisash stepped back. "I am resolved, Dear One, and may Deddimus give you godly strength."

"Then we go. Is my sword ready?"

"Skin Doo has brought several from the armory. Verdor has asked for one too, though I know not for what. They are in the courtyard awaiting your selection."

The two walked from the great hall toward the courtyard on the south side of the governor's house. The battle would be in the same yard where only a few hours ago Lorca had met with the Fiercers.

Flen had protested, saying he wanted the fight at the traditional grounds above the soap works, but he had been voted down by the Council. The soap works were now outside the protective wall currently under construction. And Lorca, with the help of Senchai Verdor, had successfully convinced the Council that a large assembly might be dangerously exposed, though half of the voting body still did not yet believe that the Valley was under attack.

"Folly!" they murmured among themselves, intimating that the order to destroy the forests was criminal. Yet none would publicly call a Senchai a liar. Verdor had said she'd seen a Poker and her word swayed the final vote on the location of the duel, if nothing else. To effect a compromise, Lorca suggested the Troca be fought at dawn rather than waiting the lawful three days in exchange for Flen relinquishing his insistence on the fight's location. Some of the Council reasoned within Lorca's hearing that since she had minimal time to make her fortifications, the damage would not be insurmountable by the time Lorca was dead and Flen was firmly in office.

When Hisash and Lorca entered the courtyard, only the Council had assembled to witness the affair. Verdor was not present. Their council chairs had been taken away from the main hall and placed around the wall of the yard. No one sat, but milled about two distinct camps, one for Flen and one for Lorca.

Hisash walked with Lorca to the center of the yard and, without looking at her again, retraced her steps to the perimeter to join Lorca's supporters. The sun now up, its rays lit the top of the western wall, turning it from the customary dark brown to brilliant clay red. Lorca stood alone, her sword in hand. It all seemed so foolish, so wasteful, as if she were caught in a bad dream, her only hope a quick end to her life.

A loud thump from the far side of the yard shook the ground, and Lorca saw her adversary wielding his heavy hammer that seemed light in his hands. He smashed it down on a large stump that Lorca had not seen before and which, she assumed, Flen had brought with him early this morning.

Stripped to the waist, Flen jousted imaginary foes, his undulating muscles glistening in the early light while he feinted and thrust, slamming his hammer to the stump.

He has oiled himself? What a foolish man, Lorca thought.

Flen cast his gaze to the ground at his back, to five spheres arranged on a length of board covered in dead grass in descending order of size, the largest the size of a melon to the smallest, no larger than an oxen's bullocks.

"He has brought his own gallery," Lorca said and laughed aloud, quieting the others. Flen looked at her with steady eyes. In that instant, she understood how close to hysteria she had come and stayed the mirth. If she didn't maintain some control over herself, the battle was already lost.

Several concerned voices arose from the gallery of twelve. "'Tis cruel," one shouted, "bring the nog!"

Entwas the herder left Flen's supporters and carried a flask across the yard.

"Will you quaff the nog, Lorca?" he asked, his expression grave. His eyes showed genuine concern.

"Nah, the quaff," Lorca retorted. "And how is Lisa, good Entwas, has the croup left her yet?"

"Never mind my wife. I didn't think you would carry this. Give over Lorca, it's not worth your life."

"Tell me, Entwas, what's a life worth? Me thinks you would die for your oxen, neh?"

"It wouldn't be for the animals, it would be for the Vall..." his voice trailed off.

"Then go, good man, let me choose my destiny. Besides, I am not unarmed." Lorca cut the air with exaggerated movement. "This sword fits my hand, I swear." She winked at him.

Blushing crimson, Entwas left Lorca alone in the middle of the courtyard.

Flen was still darting and shifting about, waving the heavy hammer, stopping only to quickly scan the yard, the wall, even the branches of overhanging trees. *Is he expecting someone?*

With each moment that passed, apprehension eroded Lorca's resolve. She had no idea how to wage a battle against Flen or anyone. She'd realized this fact only last night, in the few moments she'd had alone after the preparations to protect the city had been made and all the necessary papers signed.

Nakus approached her with a sheaf, making no eye contact upon presenting her with the file of papers to sign that would close Lorca's responsibilities concerning the Troca. Flen joined the two, smelling of ammonia mixed with rotting flesh. His eyes shone with the anticipation of a young child opening a gift. He would soon be governor, and better, he would soon kill—a killing denied him all these years.

"This is the law of the Troca as set down by the ancients," Nakus said. "Ye two are clear that no quarter will be asked nor given, that this is a fight to death?"

Her lower lip trembled but she had no trouble meeting Flen's eyes. Lorca worried briefly that Nakus might attack Flen.

"I understand," Lorca said.

"And I," Flen said.

"Your hat, Governor," Nakus said.

Lorca removed the purple hat and handed it to Nakus.

"When this business is done," Nakus said, turning a hateful stare upon Flen, "the winner will retrieve this hat from the ground where I drop it. Nog having been refused by Lorca, the same is now offered you, Flen."

Flen sneered at the insult. "You drink it, Nakus, and say goodbye to your job. You won't have it before the sun is too much higher, I'll warrant."

"I'd sooner cut my own throat than work for you, you mange ridden—."

"That will do, good Nakus," Lorca said. "When you serve the law, good friend, you serve me well."

Nakus looked at her friend and employer for the first time that morning, tears clinging to her eyelashes like tiny diamonds.

"Will you need the time for prayer?" she asked.

"I will take the prescribed time, Nakus," Lorca said stoutly, "but I have already prayed."

"She stalls!" Flen cried, looking disgusted.

"She has her right, Flen," Nakus replied.

Flen swaggered back to his hammer and his spherical supporters.

"You have but three minutes for prayer, Governor. Then you must…" Nakus pressed her lips together.

"How goes Menshun's wall?" Lorca asked.

"They are half around. The Senchai told them to place the logs end to end to speed the way. It will not be as stout, but it will complete the circle sooner. They should be finished soon."

"Will that be enough?"

"It will buy time. So says Verdor, my governor"

"Good, I will stall this if I can."

"Governor," Nakus'voice quavered.

"Now, Nakus, we have said our good-byes. You wouldn't make it harder on an old friend, would you?"

Nakus hesitated before replying. "No," she said finally. Her chin fell to her chest.

"Nakus, I want you to work closely with Hisash. Can you do that? Can you work with her?"

"Aye, I can do that for you. You have my word. Between the two of us, we should be able to keep the valley running for a while longer, Deddimus willing."

"Good, then I am ready, Go drop the hat."

Nakus turned toward the perimeter walls and dropped the purple hat to the ground in the midst of Lorca's friends.

His hammer over his head, Flen charged Lorca, bellowing a cry, his tongue dangling from one side of his open mouth. Lorca parried the blow with her sword, the pain shot up to her armpits. She almost dropped her weapon.

Flen's momentum carried him past her, but within a few steps, he pivoted, hesitating long enough to glance about the courtyard wall.

What does he seek?

"Well done, Lorca," Flen said, his upper lip curling back to expose brown teeth. "Will you make a match of it then?"

Lorca held her tongue and Flen came at her again, the hammer brought low this time to her knees, forcing her to jump outside the arc of the swing.

Flen returned a flurry of swings and some very near misses. Lorca heard gasp after gasp from the gallery, and gamely thwarted blows coming faster and faster. Her arms began to tire, her knees on the verge of buckling. Flen seemed to gain strength while she neared exhaustion, and he was astonishingly fast, his movements fluid, his hammer ringing against the sword, yet none a deathblow.

He began circling her and she fought for breath.

He is toying with me. He wishes to show his skill to the others.

At his next attack, Lorca's trembling legs gave out and she fell to her knees on the paving stones, her arms shaking uncontrollably. Flen darted at her, aiming for her head, and she deflected the hammer, the clanging sword vibrating painfully

She knew she was done, too busy defending herself to mount any sort of counterattack. She let the tip of the heavy sword fall to the ground, Flen circling about her, and Lorca with barely enough strength to follow him with her eyes.

Shouts rose from both sides of the courtyard.

"Give over, Lorca."

"Spare her, Flen."

Flen feinted to the left and struck Lorca a blow to her head with the handle. She fell forward, stunned, courting the edge of darkness, the roars of the crowd muted now, like echoes under a bridge. Rough fingers yanked the collar of her shirt and, choking, she was dragged over stone pavers that pummeled her hips.

Let me breathe, Deddimus, just let me breathe.

A brilliant pain of white light and Lorca realized a moment's peace, her head lying on Flen's stump. She filled her lungs slowly, the air burning, giving no comfort. She tried, but couldn't move her feet, the hilt of the sword smooth yet in her hand.

Flen stepped over her to kick the weapon away, the blade clanking against the stones.

The sun now up over the wall, Lorca noticed a tear in the knee of her leggings. *I must repair that soon,* she thought, *clothing costs a goodly sum.* The stump scratched her chin. Her vision blurred. She worked to focus on a singular black rock within the surrounding wall. *Today is the day of my death. How strange that I have no fear of it. Dying is quite easy, really.* She slipped to unconsciousness, welcoming the darkness.

The odor of ammonia mingling with rotting flesh woke Lorca to Flen straddling her body, adjusting her head on his stump, a move she had neither the strength nor the inclination to deny. He suddenly left her for his spheres, his audience lined up on the board at the base of the wall.

He will kill me with one of those. He has planned an execution.

Flen plucked one of his audience and hurried back to Lorca. The orb was a cold weight at the nape of her neck. .

"*Breathe, Lorca,*" Old Maysi unexpectedly whispered in her ears. "*You cannot let him kill you in this way.*"

Lorca's head throbbed, the pain returning some clarity of mind. Marshalling what little strength she had left, she curled her hands under her torso and pushed herself up off the block. The ball rolled down her back and clicked against the hard surface of the stones.

A sharp blow to the ribs, she curled into a fetal position, her head striking the ground, and she again flirted with blacking out. Breathing was even more difficult, Flen towering over her, vexing unintelligibly over something. He abruptly grabbed her ankles and violently jerked her body out straight again.

"You'll not move again, you witch, or I'll kick your lungs out of your chest," he snarled. He replaced her head on the stump and again the ball weighted the nape of her neck. He crossed into her line of sight and retrieved his hammer. She heard him singsong a word—Bortal, it seemed—then he disappeared from view. She sensed his feet near her right shoulder.

"No!" she said breathlessly and shook her head, dislodging the ball. Old Maysi appeared to her suddenly, a ghostly figure from a foggy realm.

"He wants to take your life, he wants to end you," Maysi cried. *"This fool will end you!"*

Rage abruptly enveloped her, and, with unknown will, she pushed herself to her hands and knees. Flen returned another kick to her ribs, a resounding crack, taking the last of her air. She refused to collapse, Flen straddling her a second time, fighting her, pushing her down. A glimpse of the orb in his hand brought with it the realization that he would need both hands to seize her by the ankles again.

Help me, Deddimus, Lorca prayed and blindly kicked behind her, her face meeting the stone floor of the courtyard the next instant, but not before a heel of her boot met a soft, squishy mass.

At first there was no sound and then Flen collapsed beside her like a felled oak. He drew his arms and knees to his chest, bleating like a goat, spittle dribbling from his gaping mouth.

Old Maysi whispered to Lorca, *"Get to your sword."*

She managed to rise to her feet and bent at the waist on unsteady legs, she looked about, her gaze lighting on the sword lying near the wall. She staggered across the courtyard and dragged the gleaming blade back to where Flen curled, holding his damaged testicles.

Lorca dropped to her knees near his head and, grasping the hilt with both hands, buttressed the handle against her midriff before guiding the point of the blade to the soft underside of Flen's chin. Ruby drops of fresh blood spilled from the puncture, rivering along the blade's keen edge to stain Flen's collar.

Flen jerked back in vain.

The other council members drew close, forming a tight ring around the combatants. No one dared make a sound.

"Give...over...or die," Lorca said between gasps, the pain of her broken ribs robbing her of a decent breath. "Decide!"

"Give," Flen muttered, his voice strained as if fearful of dropping his jaw even minutely.

"Surrender...your hammer...and tools of office. You are...done here, accept...these...terms.

"Acshept," he said, barely above a whisper.

Lorca hesitated. Her intuition told her not to trust him. She had the legal right to kill him and he had been more than intent on killing her. She hoped to see old Maysi one more time, perhaps he had the answer, but he was gone. She fell back into the arms of Hisash while Nakus hovered over the former executioner, daring him to an aggressive move of any sort.

Lorca looked up into the smiling eyes of Hisash. "Help me up," she told her.

Gently Hisash and Nakus pulled her to her feet. Lorca stumbled forward, pulling the two with the weight of her body in moving toward the west wall of the courtyard. The three slowly but steadily made their way to the purple hat. Lorca extended one arm gingerly and plucked the hat from the ground to her head. Hisash and Nakus held the symbol of her office there.

"Take me...to see the wall," Lorca said to them, "Then take me to my bed."

Twenty-Five

THOMAR REGAINED CONSCIOUSNESS lying on a cold, damp, surface. *'Tis the womb of darkness,* he thought. A terrible odor like decomposing carrion assaulted his nose. Had he been dropped in a cesspool, or a dry well with dead animals? He tentatively breathed in short staccato bursts through his mouth. If the air were poisonous, he reasoned, he would not have awakened.

He relaxed as well as his throbbing head would allow. The sack over his head felt oily against the skin of his face. His hands tied behind him, the cords dug deeply and painfully into his wrists. Worried about circulation, he tried to move his fingers, only to have them tingle painfully. He opened and closed his fists against each other.

How long have I been lying here, he wondered.

The rustling of nearby movement told him that he was not alone. He now remembered the scent, the same stink from the mountain path. *I am a captive. Is Belinda a captive also?*

"Verdor?" he called out.

" Ist awak-ed," a phlegm-coated voice said.

"And lucky for your hide that he is, you might have killed him." The second speaker sounded clear, youthful even.

Thomar raised his head. "Who's there?"

"Remove the blindfold," the second speaker commanded.

Stinking hands jostled Thomar's head, tearing a rope from his neck that had secured the head cover and viciously abrading his neck in the process. The stench was near unbearable. *Are they rotting alive?* he wondered of his captors.

Thomar discovered that he was in a large cave. Solid walls arched upward from their base. Stalactites, like an inverted mountain range, pointed down menacingly from high overhead, glistening wetly. A single torch on a nearby wall offered feeble encouragement to the dismal scene. A small table supported only the waxy lump of a spent candle.

"Our war room, do you approve, Senchai?" the second speaker asked.

"Who are you?" Thomar blinked the grit from his eyes and a strikingly handsome, boyish face hovered into view. Though young looking, and quite beautiful, there was no innocence, only a sinister malevolence born perhaps of an ancient and darker time. The boy's countenance, his brooding stare, as well as the manner of movement seemed practiced and sure of a future very much in its control—a signature normally ascribed to leaders of long standing, good or bad.

The boy studied Thomar as an artist might squint at a still-life subject about to be copied to canvas. A high forehead ended at a dark hairline, the hair drawn back tightly, shining purple-black like the sheen of a raven's wing. The nose was well sculpted, thin bridge, perfectly straight, gently feminine bulbs at the nostrils. The complexion flawless, not so much as a pimple scar, yet pale, as if cave dwelling were the normal domain. The cheekbones were high and slightly pronounced, causing a thin shadow to fall over sullen cheeks. The lips were sensual and full, reminding Thomar of a pouting, spoiled-child.

At about five feet and ten inches tall, this "boy" stared down at Thomar with eyes darker than anything he had ever seen. They seemed to radiate blackness and everything evil. He wore a dark full-length cloak that hid every part of his body, but the tips of black leather boots and two pale, almost delicately graceful hands, one of which held a coiled bull snake whip.

'Tis the very eye of evil.

"Surely you know us." The boy struck a stunned look of embarrassed disappointment. "Why, we are the reason you exist. We are the nexus to your virtue. It's very amusing, don't you think, that you don't know us? We are offended." He swirled his cloak in turning away, striding toward the table. Then Thomar noticed the Pokers, prostrate on the ground, barely visible. They looked at first like dark lumps just below the candle's direct light.

His captor, standing at the table now and facing the wall of gray stone behind, said, "We know you, Lex Verd. We have been watching your remarkably average career for some time now." Suddenly his voice changed to a higher-pitch of contempt. "Leave us, you jackals, and go join the others." The Pokers, six in number, arose quickly and shuffled deeper into the cave, each with an eye furtively darting toward the whip in their leader's hand.

"Putris Darkin," Thomar said. "Why have you taken me?"

"Taken? Aha, no. That was too easy. I think you were given to me. A gambit by Verdor, no doubt. A clever one, she is. And the why? Well then, that's for me to figure out. It's all so very . . ." Darkin shrugged his cloaked shoulders, "intriguing."

Darkin turned and faced the Senchai, saying nothing for a while, just watching.

"What have you done with your Cept, Wizard?" Darkin asked finally.

"My Cept was taken from me during the night," Thomar replied.

"Taken?"

"Yes, taken, and I know naught of its whereabouts." Thomar squirmed onto his back, trying to give his hands some position of comfort, but this maneuver only made his pain worse and he rolled back.

Darkin seemed amused. His black eyes gleamed.

"So, you have been duped. Is that it? A Grand Wizard of the Mosaic School has been duped. A delicious mystery, isn't it?"

"What have you done to Verdor?"

"Done? My, my, but you give us too much credit. It's very endearing, really. It's a shame what we will do to you." Putris Darkin studied his captive, tapping his chin with the handle of his whip. "But there is time for that later. Tell me, Thomar, that is what she calls you, isn't it? Thomar?"

Thomar remained quiet.

"How noble of you. He doesn't wish to speak of his love. I know you are lovers, Thomar. I saw the message she sent you. How her loins hunger for you." Putris Darkin said this in a falsetto voice, a mocking imitation of a lovelorn woman.

"I love her."

"Why would she betray you, Thomar?"

"She didn't. She wouldn't."

"Oh, come now, Thomar. You may be blinded by love, but we can see. She knew we would intercept the pigeons. Only an idiot would choose such birds for that journey to the Mosaic. But you being here tells me at least one got through." After a moment of consideration, he added, "Verdor is many things, Thomar, but she is not an idiot."

The pain in Thomar's wrists was growing more acute, his fingers swollen and numb.

"Then you tell me, Putris Darkin, why would she want me captured by the likes of you?"

The whip lashed out through the semidarkness, the tasseled burl on the end catching Thomar's left cheek just under his eye, opening a deep cut to the gum line of his upper jaw.

Thomar's head snapped back and he tasted the sweet-sour warmth of blood filling his mouth. He tried to spit but because of the hole in his cheek he merely gurgled saliva and blood through the laceration. Thomar closed his eyes trying to detach his mind from the searing pain. He concentrated on his breathing until the onslaught passed to a dull aching throb. The tip of his tongue then tried, in vain, to assess the damage.

"We don't believe we like your impudence, Lex Verd, Grand Wizard," Darkin said and shook the now recoiled whip. "You might keep in mind that we would enjoy taking you apart inch by inch with this, so it would behoove you not to vex us."

Putris Darkin leaned back against the table, folding his arms in front of him, the whip plainly visible. "Shall we begin again?" he said.

A trickle of blood coursed warm and wet along Thomar's neck.

"I'll tell you what I think, Thomar." Putris Darkin was once again pleasantly conversational. "I think I am being set-up. I think I am the pigeon here. What do you think of that?"

"I know naught of that."

"Of course you know naught. You have too little imagination. You are content to fix the broken sparrow wing or feed the furry animals. What a perfect waste of your power. And to let your staff slip away in the darkness. My, just what would Master Singh think of his student now?"

Thomar shifted his body again to relieve the ache creeping into his hip and back. The bleeding had slowed and was coagulating to sticky grease. The wound throbbed. The awkward position of being trundled and unable to move enough to stretch, even slightly, was becoming difficult to bear. Now there was the whip. He felt somewhat relieved, however, that Belinda was likely still free.

"What do you want of Verdor?" Thomar asked, the wound making speech difficult at best. "She has done nothing to you."

"She has my staff."

Thomar blinked.

"You didn't know. You really didn't know, did you? Of course! The exquisite irony has been lost on you all these years. Pater Nos stole it from me and gave it to her."

Thomar knew this to be a lie. Pater Nos had defeated Putris Darkin and deprived him of his staff, but Thomar had never heard that the staff was given to Verdor, or any other. If this were remotely true and Verdor now carried Darkin's staff, she surely didn't know either. What came from that legendary battle was the knowledge that Putris Darkin couldn't be killed so Pater Nos did the next best thing by depriving him of much of his power to cause mischief.

"Then we are both cooking in the same kettle, Putris Darkin. If Verdor now has both of them."

"True, very true. But we shall get ours back. As for you," Putris Darkin smiled like a well-fed cobra, "you will soon see how fondly we regard your ilk."

"Why do you want it back? It will do you no good."

"Of course, it won't. That cursed Pater Nos has seen to that. But we will take it, anyway. It is ours, just like we will take your precious Belinda."

"Leave her be, Darkin, she has not wronged you."

Darkin laughed at this. His hideous laughter, sharp and piercing, climbed the walls of the cave to echo deeply within hidden recesses. "Don't you see, you fool? We care not a Poker's tooth about Verdor. It is Pater Nos we will punish. He will spend the rest of his days in misery. He will die knowing that his precious protégé will suffer every day of her life. We will hide her in the blackest hole. She will be one of the living dead for a century."

Darkin's face clouded. He seemed focused on a distant place or memory. His next words were measured. "Pater Nos will know this. By the gates of Nye, he will hear her screams every time he lays his head on a pillow. And," Putris Darkin brightened to joy, "and he will be unable to help her. Oh, the rapture of it. And they say we can't be happy." Again his laughter echoed from deep in the cave.

Thomar shuddered in the fight to control his anger. His hands struggled against their binds. *"Be calm, my child. Often your anger is the only thing you can control."* Master Singh's lesson came to him as if it had been taught this morning.

"Verdor will not let you just walk into her coveret and take her away," Thomar said.

"No, of course she won't let us in, but she will let you in. She will let the love of her life in. Oh, yes, she will."

"Do you think I will betray her? You delude yourself."

"Oh, we think you will. Yes, we know you will." Putris Darkin stroked his chin with his free hand and the same malevolent smile returned to his face. "That is why your head is still on your shoulders. But we grow weary of this prattle. You are dismissed." He knocked the butt of his whip on the table and several Pokers appeared. "Take him deep. We cannot have Pater Nos detecting him. Mind that you check his bonds. If he escapes, you will beg me to die. Oh yes, give him water, we want him alive." Darkin turned toward the entrance of the cave, his cloak billowing majestically behind him. "For now," he added, more to himself than to the Pokers.

The Pokers lifted Thomar from under his bound arms and legs. Wherever they touched him their hands left a gooey residue like the slime from a beached pike fish and their stench left Thomar reluctant to draw breath. He struggled against the panic of a drowning man.

Deeper down into the bowels of the cave, the room narrowed. Fiery torches along the corridor lit their way. Ahead he heard the din of activity, the commotion of hordes, akin to the mixed sounds of an army making ready for battle. The noise grew louder with each step his handlers took.

Thomar didn't recognize any of the few utterances rising above the grunts, groans and snarls. They were in a language not studied at the school. He feared being taken to the nether world, one he didn't expect to ever see. *Could this be Nye?*

"What happens to us when we die?" Thomar remembered asking Master Singh when still a young boy. Singh looked up from his models and plans for irrigating the school gardens, the question unrelated to what Thomar was studying at the time.

"That, my boy, is a question of hope," Singh said. "We at the Mosaic hope that if we live charitably, then our spirits will join the great life force, making it stronger. It will be very pleasant for us."

"If we are not charitable, then do we go to Nye?"

"Where did you hear that word, young one?"

"Longdale said that Thistle would go to Nye if she didn't share the jump-the-rope. "

"Hmm." Singh hesitated, then said, "Yes. Some believe that Nye awaits those of us who are not good to others."

"Do you believe there is a Nye? Where the evil ones go when they die?"

"What I believe, Thomar, is that those of us who are evil are already living in Nye. You don't have to die to go there. It's an unhappy place."

"Will Thistle go to Nye, Master Singh?"

"No, Thomar. Thistle will learn to share and, when she does, she will be happy. Happy children do not go to Nye, they are not allowed there."

"Then I'll be happy always," Thomar announced with satisfaction.

"Then you'll never need to worry about Nye."

Now, while Thomar was being dragged through the dank cavernous room, he wondered if Singh had made a mistake.

The way opened upon a vast arena, the smell so oppressive that bile burned his throat. Hundreds of small fires cast twitching shadows across the high dome of an inner cave. Two Pokers jostled him through the cavern, while many thousand pairs of eyes regarded him with a mixture of hunger and dull contempt, but no fear, and not a trace of pity.

Twenty-Six

"ENTER."

Verdor heard the response to her knock and knew before seeing the Governor that she was having difficulty breathing. She approached the foot of the bed quietly.

Lorca lay on her back under a down quilt, only her head exposed. She breathed in shallow gasps. Hisash and Nakus had helped her limp into her bed. "Try and sleep," they'd told her, but Verdor knew that there would be none of that. Not only was breathing difficult, but by her grimacing she appeared to be suffering pain no matter her position on the bed. She nonetheless managed a smile when Verdor entered.

"Do not speak," Verdor said. "With your permission I will tend you."

Lorca nodded.

Verdor pulled the covers back exposing Lorca's upper body, which was clothed in a thin undergarment. The light fabric covered a body wrap through which arose the scent of a gule weed poultice. She turned and drew a chair to the side of Lorca's bed, then sat.

Verdor placed her hands over the bandage. "Have you coughed any blood?"

Lorca shook her head.

"That is well." She began to move her hands over the area starting at Lorca's side, working toward the mid-line of her chest and then back again. "You will feel some heat and some discomfort. Then you will sleep."

Gentle warmth radiated from Verdor's palms. She began to feel Lorca's tension drain from her and with it, in delicate pulses, the pain would leave also.

"You can help me with this," Verdor said.

Lorca looked at her.

"Close your eyes, Governor. Imagine that I am opening a small door or a spigot in your side. Let your pain flow through that door and into my hands. Think of a soft summer's rain cleansing you, washing over you, healing you.

Verdor continued to speak to her in low tones, all the while her hands caressing Lorca's wounded body. "Flen humiliated you. He demeaned you and your office with his little spheres of execution. I sense a great rage in you. The same rage that kept you alive is now a hindrance to your healing. You cannot allow this anger to live within you."

Already Lorca's breathing became more even.

"Anger hardens the heart and confounds love. It blocks all kinds of good things and especially it delays healing. This too you must let go, let it flow out the spigot. Let it be gone. Can you do this, Governor?"

Lorca did not answer. She appeared to be sleeping.

***

Fear and rage bled from her damaged body. Her mind opened and Lorca watched the effluent of hatred flow in reds and violets, a river in spate, undulating toward, then through the exit Verdor's hands created. Healing energy from those same hands, which appeared as white light behind her closed eyelids, flowed in to fill the void. The whiteness infused itself within each minute part of her body, particularly surrounding her broken ribs, cauterizing internal bleeding, reducing swollen tissues. Her ribs began to knit themselves. They pushed outward to reform their natural curve. Lorca's breathing became deeper and satisfying.

Sleep came easily, smothering her cares about the wall, the valley and the mortal danger threatening her race.

***

Hisash had quietly entered the room and stood watching from inside the door. When it appeared that Verdor had finished her ministrations, Hisash approached. "What think you, Senchai?" she whispered.

"She will be fine, her lungs are sound."

"Did you cure her?"

"I merely unblocked her. Her body cured itself."

"A bad day for her. I thought she had no chance."

"She has remarkable strengths, not unlike you, Hisash."

"I wish that were true, but I am always frightened."

"Fear may keep you alive."

"We have not been attacked, Senchai. Do you still think we will be?"

Verdor stood and returned the chair to the wall from where she had taken it. She then accompanied Hisash toward the bedroom door.

"The ring around the city has bought us precious time. It may have slowed Putris Darkin or at least altered his plans, but he will attack."

"Can we defeat him?"

"We may contain him. He cannot be killed."

"Will the Pokers come?"

"In great numbers, I suspect. Darkin will use them to panic us, but we should do well enough with them. They cannot cross the ring. Have all the Giants been summoned? Are they all within it?"

The two exited Lorca's bedroom and walked together through the Governor's house. They passed the scullery where Nakus was cooking what smelled like hen soup. Verdor stepped into the kitchen. "She sleeps now, good Nakus, but a bowl of that broth will suit her when she awakens."

"So it will, good Senchai. It will do no less for you. Can you break fast with us?"

"Now that my nose has discovered your cooking, my stomach will settle for nothing else. I'll return in an hour. Will it be done by then?"

"It will, and there will be a loaf to fortify it and a wine so dry it will pucker a lizard's lips. There's no denying that we have much to be thankful for this day."

"Aye, good Nakus."

She left Nakus to her stove and rejoined Hisash, who continued their conversation.

"Most, or likely all, have arrived. There are few of us who live outside the city anyway. Flen and a few others."

"Where is Flen? Have you seen him since the Troca?"

"He was seen shuffling home with a decided limp, him with his pants about his ankles and holding what's most dear to him. It's a right tender cargo 'tis sure. I'm told he was as bent over as our Lorca."

"Send someone to fetch him. The coveret will stay open to Giants who wish to pass. Flen is in grave danger if he does not remain within the city."

The two were now standing at the entry door of Lorca's.

"Forgive me, Senchai, for I have much to learn about forgiveness, but I care little enough for the man."

"It is not only his personal danger, but he is dangerous, perhaps more so in his humiliation. I fear he has communion with the evil one."

"Is it so?"

"It's a suspicion. He should be watched. Will you see to it?"

"I will send some stout Fiercers," Hisash said. "He will not listen to me. Besides, if those horrible Pokers should appear, I'd prefer to be nearer you. I have no courage for their ilk."

***

In talking with Hisash, Verdor had omitted any mention of the devastated tree that she had repaired on her way toward Burba. She was certain that Flen, strong as he was, couldn't accomplish that destruction without help, help not of this world. A fool like Flen would be easy prey for the Fouler.

Verdor made her way to the city's perimeter and the Fiercer's wall, which was progressing at the expense of the ancient forests around. The streets of Burba all but disappeared beneath the feet of busy giants, intent on the wall's construction. They had worked through the night. The oxen had been corralled within the new boundary and all hands carried and stacked the trees the Fiercers were chopping down at an astounding rate. Men piled the logs and women and children filled the joints between them with lesser limbs and cutoff branches so that the end result was a wall that appeared impenetrable and rose to the level of the rooftops. A gangway had been attached to the upper inside. From this the Giants could observe any activity from directly below to the receding firebreak.

Some paused in their work watching Verdor pass by. Many considered her with open contempt. Verdor understood their anger. She, after all, was the one responsible for the devastation to their children's livelihood. They of course would wonder why. A wall? For what? Against an enemy that no one among them had seen other than young Hisash, a Bracker's daughter. In her walking about, Verdor had heard the rumors concerning Hisash's mother having been insane.

"Was there not proof in that, good Heamy? Did she not step off the brackering ring as if it were a bath she was takin'?"

Verdor ignored these fears.

At the leading edge of the new construction, she found the one she sought. "A word with you, good Menshun."

Menshun broke away from his men after a few terse orders and followed Verdor to an open, if not quiet, place.

"Your work goes well," she said.

"Well enough."

"How do your men feel?"

"The way I would expect, Senchai. They do this for love and loyalty to me. But their hearts are not in it. In truth, I wonder myself why we have to destroy so much."

"In a short time there will be destruction beyond your belief. The powers of a dark world are aligned against us. I know this to be so."

"Yet even you have not seen this Putris Darkin. A single Poker, what is that? Surely you can kill it."

"No, I have not seen him, but he is here. I do not feel him either, so he must be deep in the ground. But he will come."

"If he will come, then what good will this wall do?"

"The wall, with my spell, will help keep the Pokers from crossing the circle you create. Darkin is after me. He has likely planned this for a long time, perhaps even from the time I started at the Mosaic school as a child. Even so, it's not me he vets his evil on."

"Who then? What does he want?"

"He wants revenge against Pater Nos. He will seek it through me."

"Can you stop him?"

"That is my prayer and hope. If he captures me, then the Mosaic will fall. Pater Nos' love for me makes him vulnerable to failure. Lord Pater Nos may have seen this day coming, I suspect that he has, or at least the possibility of it. I see now that more is at stake here than your Valley."

***

Menshun passed an arm across his forehead, smearing beads of sweat that wet his eyelids. He looked around at the upheaval of work, listened to the chorus of axes and the groaning of straining backs. *Is all this hopeless?* he wondered to himself. "What more can we do?" he asked.

"Tell your Fiercers to work in teams of two. No one is to be isolated from now on. Each shall have a strong hickory club. When the Pokers attack they will do so in droves. They are slashers. They have a single tooth in their snouts that looks ugly and useless. Make no mistake that they use it well. Tell your men that if they are attacked they should fight back to back. They should not let their heels be exposed. If they fall, it will be the end of them."

"Will clubs work?"

"Yes."

"'Why not axes?"

"Axes may get stuck in their bones, which are very dense. Clubs are best."

Menshun considered Verdor. She was just under half his height, frail as a milkweed pod. A handsome one, for her size, she was a prize, he guessed, for the small men of other kingdoms. Never in his wildest imaginings would he have chosen her to plan such a battle, which she and no one else could see coming. Yet, in her eyes was an undeniable truth. He could see no other way but to obey this wispy creature from beyond his Valley.

"Are they disciplined warriors, these Pokers?" he asked.

"No. That's the only good thing about them. They seek out weakness to attack in overwhelming numbers. However, if the resistance is stiff, they will likely move on to easier quarry."

"What's in it for them? Why do they fight so?"

"That is just what they are. It is all they know. Besides…"

Menshun leaned closer to her. Yesterday he was pruning trees. Today he was preparing a war for the life of the Giants. If anyone but Verdor was before him, he felt sure, he would find a jar of nog and finish out the day watching the stars come out one by one. She held him to believe what every one of his senses had already denied. "Besides what?" he said.

"The Pokers fight from fear."

"Fear."

"Yes. They fear their master and would sooner run toward their deaths than provoke his wrath. What we fight is evil that is beyond mortal comprehension. It feeds itself on loathsome deeds, growing stronger. Horror is its dinner. Think of a snake feeding on itself. It seizes its own tail and begins to nourish by causing its own demise. Putris Darkin is like that snake, but he will not die. He could not stop nor would he ever want to. He enjoys what he does."

"Why do you tell me this, Senchai?"

"Because you must persuade your men that soon and likely suddenly they will be fighting for their lives and the lives of their neighbors."

"What warning is there?"

"There is only their smell and sometimes darkness will descend as if a storm cloud covered the sun when they are near. That is, if it is not already dark when they attack."

"Anything else?"

"Do not rely entirely on the wall. They will not be able to cross it, but Putris Darkin will have assumed that I would use it. He may have a way to penetrate it, I don't know. Just be ready."

"How fares the governor?"

"She will be up and around by evensong, I'm sure." Verdor turned toward the governor's house. "I will eat with Nakus," she said, "And see to Lorca. I'll return soon."

"Senchai," Menshun stopped her with a hand on her arm. "Why does he do this?"

"Because he has the power."

"Is there any hope for us?"

"Our hope lies in his greed. He lusts to be the most powerful, so he must humble Lord Pater Nos. He would do this through me"

"If you were to leave this valley, would the Dark One depart from us?"

"He will. I would have been gone already except for one plain truth, good Menshun."

"Which is?"

"Before he leaves, Putris Darkin will destroy this Valley anyway. He will leave no blade of grass unburned. Not a weed will grow here for a thousand years. He will do this for the perverse joy that he finds in it, and then pursue me to the next kingdom, where he will do the same. On my oath, Menshun, I would give myself to him if he would stop. But he will not."

"How do you know him so, Senchai?"

"'Tis a fair question, Menshun. And an easy answer, though you may not understand it. I know him because I know myself."

Menshun studied Verdor's eyes. He didn't understand what she had just said, but he said nothing. After a moment, he turned from her and walked back to his wall.

Twenty-Seven

FLEN STUMBLED ACROSS his threshold. He'd had trouble with the door because to do so required him to straighten up enough to work the stubborn latch. He grumbled to himself that he had not yet repaired the cursed thing.

He had walked, rather limped, the whole way home with his head never above the level of his waist. The searing cramps in his lower abdomen were more bearable in that position and he was able to avoid the eyes he knew would be all the merrier because of his plight. News of his torment sped through the valley on wagging tongues. Within the same hour that it took Flen to roll to a sitting position, after having been kicked by Lorca, his defeat had added the Governor's name to some ballad that was likely already being composed.

"The witch! To do such a thing! Kick a good man so. A strumpet she is, and a coward. No man's work, that. Only a woman would do such a thing." He complained all the way home, grumbling between wincing stops and breath- taking painful spasms. "No honor there in that one." He berated himself for ever trusting a woman to fight fair. "The governor she is, too. Bah!"

Flen had left the tools of his trade on the courtyard floor where they had fallen from his hands. With their loss, his humiliation was complete. He could not dwell on that now, the throbbing in his groin was worse for his journey, but he would be damned if he'd lay in that yard another minute. His only thought now was the redemption in a stout bottle, and then laying down in his bed. Somewhere along his way home, he had shed his pants. He cared nothing for his nakedness to the world but cradled his tender manhood in the cup of one hand. His testicles were like scalded nerve endings when touched, but letting them hang on their own was worse. They were already thrice their normal size and his scrotum was a raging purple-black color. Seeing this gave him a fright. *Will they survive?*

"That foul witch. May she rot in Nye with Pokers ramming her."

The steps to his wine cellar were agony, but there was no other way. Every descending foot fall to the next tread caused screaming pain up his back and into his armpits. Twice he became nauseous and dizzy and had to stop until it passed.

Still bent at the waist, he found the shelf where his nog and wine were stored. Fumbling blindly, he seized a tall bottle and with one hand yet cupping his crotch, he smashed the neck from the bottle on the edge of the shelf. Glass and wine exploded, soaking his hand and sleeve. Tilting his head, he examined his handiwork in the dim light available from a small web covered window tucked up under the floor joists.

The bottle had broken cleanly. He drew the flask near to his lips sideways and poured its contents into the side of his mouth, slurping and gulping while probing the liquid with his tongue for dangerous shards. More wine fell to the floor than to the pit of his stomach, but the effect on his pain was magic.

He straightened himself slowly and determined that the cramps in his bowels had diminished. He freed his genitals, then clamped both large hands on another bottle. He twisted the stopper off and tossed it to the dirt floor. He then drank as if he had just crawled over a desert.

The ascent was easier, though slow. By bowing his legs he was able to isolate the offending appendages and thereby, if careful, avoided the daggers there. His arms now carried four bottles. They would comfort him soon. He would lay abed now and finish his healing. Flen turned into his bedroom doorway. The throbbing began again fresh and hopeless. Beads of perspiration bloomed over his eyebrows. What he saw in his bed startled him.

She lay there, though it would be better to say that she had insinuated herself on his bed. Languorous, her thighs melded into the quilts. Her bare bottom peeked out from a filmy gown. Her lovely face pouted all the innocence of a praying mantis. Flen nearly dropped the wine.

"Bbbbobolink!"

"Dear Flen, you are hurt. Did that guttersnipe injure my love?"

"Lorca has…"

"Shhh," the Bobolink had placed her finger in front of her lips. "Shh," she repeated. "Lorca had naught to do with this, good Flen."

"You're not angry?"

"Angry?" The Bobolink laughed. "Good Flen, I am proud of my giant."

She rolled to her side. Her breasts, now facing him, swelled over her low neckline. Flen momentarily forgot his pain for his confusion. He stood by the side of his bed, clutching his medicine the way a toddler enfolds a doll, unsure of what he should do now. *The Bobolink is proud of me?*

"Come, lie with me," she said, making the decision for him. Her left hand patted the open space next to her.

"I am, I am, unable to service you." He shrugged, then became aware of his nakedness. He turned sideways to her.

She rose to her knees quickly and walked on them to the edge of the bed, holding out her arms, inviting him. Taking his bottles, she carefully set three of them at the foot of the bed. The fourth she opened and this time watching him, surrounded the tip of the bottle with her lips. Finally, she tilted the bottle back and drank deeply, then standing on the edge of the mattress, she placed the opening against Flen's lips. He let her pour the wine. The bottle was cold against his mouth.

"If you lie with me," she breathed, " I will tell you a secret."

"You mock me thus. I have no desire." He pointed to his swollen parts. "Curse Lorca. A pit viper, that one."

"Come," she urged him, "lie here and I will heal you. Would you like that, Flen? Would you like me to heal you?"

She pushed the empty wine bottle off the bed where it clacked on the floorboards. Flen slowly lifted one knee upon the bed and then the other. The Bobolink gently pulled him by his arm. She proved to be strong and had little difficulty supporting his massive shoulders while she helped him recline.

"There, there," she said. She maneuvered him easily.

Flen found her voice comforting, but her breath, so close at fleeting moments, had a deep chill, as if she carried ice within her mouth. He dismissed this, concentrating instead on her delicate hands and fingers which were now massaging his inner thighs. "You must relax," she said. "You must separate yourself from your pain. I will show you how."

Flen watched her while she worked. She was beautiful. No woman in the Valley could compare. Everything about her captivated him: her breasts, her rounded thighs, and the way the swale of her back dipped toward her bottom. She changed her position to his other side then back again. All the while her fingers never stopped massaging his legs, first one then the other. Starting low at his calves, she steadily probed and kneaded upward.

She loves me, Flen thought. Surely, no woman had ever touched him with such tenderness. He doubted his own forgotten mother had ever been so kind to him. Flen was suspicious to his core of every insect or bird that crossed his lonesome yard's boundary, even of his fellow giants who approached him on the streets for even small conversation about the weather or crops. He recoiled from all of them. They wished to steal from him, if not his treasure, then perhaps to borrow of his time, or even pump him for some tidbit of information. They were all up to something. He trusted no one.

But now there was the Bobolink. Yes, her breath was ice cold, but that wasn't her fault. He could overlook this minor flaw. He had only to consider the prize that was now in his bed with him. In his bed with him! He dare not think on that too long lest he be dreaming and too soon awaken. The barricades he had built over the decades from his imaginings, never from any experience, not counting the disdainful glances of the town's women or the taunting of their nasty juveniles, were crumbling under Bobolink's tender ministrations. This is love, he was sure of it. Well worth the pain now diminishing with every pass of her hands over his thighs. *I have found a mate. And why shouldn't I? Am I a troll to look upon?* Only when he was deep into his wine had he ever felt anything close to love. And here he was more sober than not, yet feeling as drunk as he had ever been.

Still her hands worked on him. "You did not lose to Lorca, my darling."

"The witch cheated me, 'tis sure."

"No, my love, Lorca didn't cheat you. The Senchai did."

Flen lifted his head from his pillow. "The wizard?"

"Of course. Think on it, Flen. Could Lorca really defeat you without Verdor's help? You could break Lorca's back with one hand."

Flen let her words mold their meanings between his ears. He pushed himself up to his elbows.

"Flen, lie back, let me heal you."

Flen reclined.

"Now you know my secret, but there is time for revenge."

"How do you know this?" Flen asked.

"I saw her, Flen. While you were in the courtyard I watched her."

"What did she do?"

"Put a spell on you, my love. The Senchai cheated you of your victory."

"She is sworn not to interfere. It is their way. All know that."

"But she broke her vow, Flen. She is in love with Lorca; she wouldn't let you kill her lover."

"A Senchai foresworn?" Flen pushed to his elbows again to stare at the woman massaging his legs, her knuckles close, nudging his manhood. His testicles had stopped hurting and returned to their normal size and color.

"There you have it, Flen. You did not lose. You should be governor at this very moment."

Flen collapsed back to his pillow

"Good Flen, lie still now. Let me help you relax." Her hands had become more insistent on the flesh of his loin, awakening more familiar and welcomed stirrings. Thinking became difficult.

"How can you help me?" he asked.

The Bobolink suddenly grasped one of Flen's testicles and her squeeze startled him but there was no pain. He liked her hand there.

"Do you feel pain?" she asked.

"None." Flen was back up on his elbows, his lower lip drooping below his gums.

"Then, you see, it is not only the Senchai who has power. I can help you, Flen, if you help me." She added this last with another gentle squeeze. "I can make you governor in a fortnight, but I need your help." She began to roll the organ in her hand. "She cheated you, Flen. She humiliated you. You were laughed at. The mighty Flen has become her fool."

Flen heard her words, but his attention was on her hands. His loins had responded, his breaths shallow. Tiny beads of moisture gathered over his upper lip. He was ready to grasp her hands and place them where he desperately wanted them, but she seemed to sense his need and shifted both her hands to his erect penis. Flen gasped.

"Oh, Flen, my big strong Flen, you are ready for me."

"Ready." Flen pulled the back of one hand across his mouth.

"Can I count on you, good Giant? Will you help me make you governor?"

"Yes, Yes." His hands tore into the quilt next to his hips.

"You are very, very, very wise." She stroked him with each word. Flen's head slammed back against the pillow, his mouth gaped. Abruptly she let go of him, then slid her body up over his chest so that her breasts taunted just beneath his chin. With her right hand she reached past his ear and probed under his pillow. Again he felt the chill of her breath on his neck. "See this," she said. From under his head she extracted a glass sphere no bigger than a plum. "Take it," she urged.

Flen was annoyed by the distraction but there was now an edge to her voice that he dare not ignore. He took the sphere from her hand. The ball was smooth and cool to his fingers. A soft buzz emanated from the object that Flen felt rather than heard. He was sure if he carried it into his dark closet, the orb would glow.

"It's a fine globe," he said laying it on the bed next to him. "Now tell me how very wise I am, child, can you not see I am a boiling pot?"

The Bobolink withdrew from him and sat on the edge of his bed facing away. Flen struggled to find meaning in her sudden change.

"Have I offended thee, beautiful Bobolink?"

Bobolink turned toward him, twisting at the waist. Her breasts strained maddeningly against her chemise. "You do not take me seriously," she pouted. "I only wish to help you gain your rightful place. Have you thought about what lies ahead of you if you are not governor? I will not abide a common field hand."

Flen had not thought about his next days, preoccupied as he'd been with his pain. His office of executioner stripped from him, how would he support himself? The soap works? He was qualified for nothing. He had no skills. To him would fall the most menial of tasks. What would that be? Likely he would be spreading the scum garnered by the brackers into the open fields. Desperation seeped into the void previously occupied by his libido.

He picked up the sphere he had set on the bed and swinging his legs around, sat next to his love. She had turned back again, facing the wall. The object hummed in his hand, reminding him of his precious globes, his tools of execution. *You ungrateful scoundrel. She is trying to help you and you toy with her.*

"Bobolink, my love, tell me how to help you and it will be done." His sorrow was genuine and he placed it before her. He was a puppy whose tail had just been stepped on, and like puppies do when they are hurt by their masters, seemed to think, by dog logic that it must have been its fault.

The Bobolink brightened. She turned toward him and was again smiling. Flen smiled back at her. When she parted her lips to speak Flen thought he saw a wisp of steam escape from her, similar to that of breath on frigid air. He blinked the incongruity away, concentrating instead on her lovely smile.

"I have friends," she said

"Friends? What friends?" He imagined more fairies like her.

"Those whom I count on to defeat Lorca and that wicked thief and liar, Senchai Verdor. Those who will make you governor."

"Then bring them here. They will find me hospitable. Are they in hiding? There is no need of that"

"We are grateful for your kind offer, good Flen, but for them to travel out here would do no one any good. They must enter the city, which they cannot yet do."

"I will see to it that they can." Flen waved a magnanimous hand in dismissal of the problem.

Bobolink persisted. "Verdor has a ring around the city, a coveret, which neither they nor I can cross. We must do so in secret. That vicious Lorca and her lover, Verdor, must not know. Verdor is a powerful wizard and if we are discovered, all will be lost. She will kill me. I need your help, my love. If we cannot enter the city, then I cannot help you. And Flen, my dear, dear Giant," she was stoking his cheek with her hand, "I live to see you governor, where you should be, with me at your side. You want that, don't you? You want me, don't you, Flen?" She allowed Flen to gather her to a seat on his lap, a child at story time gazing up into his face.

Flen was undone by the tears he saw brimming at her eyelids. "How can I get you past the ring, my love? You have only to ask."

"With that," she said, indicating with a nod toward the orb in Flen's hand. Flen had forgotten about it.

"What is it, what does it do?"

"We will tunnel under the ring and enter the city from underground. It's the only way. But my power is not strong in the earth. The orb will guide us when we dig. Without it we may get lost."

Flen rolled the glass in his hand, sensing the soft vibrations. "What do I do with it?"

"You must bring it into the city and hide it."

"Where?"

"The basement of any home or building. Can you do that unseen?"

"I can hide it in the basement of the Library of Tomes. I always go there, so no one will suspect me."

"Good, then we will come to it there."

The soft conspiracy, the whispering of her voice, his tremulous answers, reminded Flen of school chums eyeing a cooling pie on someone's back porch from their vantage point in nearby high grass. But it occurred to Flen that it was no pie-stealing in the offing.

"It's just Lorca and the wizard you're after?"

"Good Flen, I have need only of the wizard. It is for you that I will kill Lorca, unless you wish me not to. But then how will you become governor?"

Flen scratched the stubble on his chin. He thought of long future days working in hayfields under a relentless sun. "No," he said, "Kill the governor. Kill the governor."

Later, toward dark, when their plans were set, the Bobolink spread her legs for the Giant. He, nearly blind with lust, began spurting his seed before he entered her. That would prove to be the climax of his pleasure, however, because when he'd finished within her, he couldn't withdraw fast enough. Her belly was as ice cold as her breath and during the few shocking moments he pumped her, she laughed. Not the laughter of pleasure, but that of the victor. In truth, it sounded to Flen, as he lay spent next to her, that her's was the pealing mirth of the deranged.

She left him soon afterwards with an unmistakable warning in her eyes from which any semblance of her earlier warmth had fled. He lay alone on his back and stared up at the ceiling. He allowed his vacant mind to wonder about with whom he had just made a pact. He was reluctant to admit, even to himself in the privacy of his own chambers, that she frightened him. But, it would not matter. He would be governor soon. He would set things to right then. The glass sphere weighed heavily in his hand then fell to his side. Flen surrendered to a fitful night's sleep.

Twenty-Eight

"Mona."

Verdor called softly into the night air. She had managed to steal away from Lorca and the activity at the wall. The Governor had arisen from her bed late that afternoon and returned to work. Even those aligned with Flen were forthright in their congratulations on her victory. Witnessing Flen's cruelty had changed their minds.

Many were still reluctant to believe they were under attack, with no visible evidence of it, but Lorca's triumph over the powerful executioner had earned her some leeway. There was different news about which to gossip, no shortage of talk. Verdor overheard one young woman's version: "She played the opossum, so. Had our boyo thinking there was no fight in her, then up she rises and kicks him a gagger in his joint, she did."

Verdor waited patiently for the fairies to appear. She had made a seat of a low tree stump just beyond the newly felled timbers that Menshun and the others were assembling. The ring had been completed. Now the trees went to buttressing the wall. The night was warm and dry, and windless, a grudging gift of the drought. A bright sliver of waning moon hung above her amid a million winking companions.

Mona arrived on the light of those stars. She was not alone. An army of fairies jostled and tittered their way forward seeing who could get closest to Verdor. "Savior, savior" was heard in their glass voices. Some flew boldly to her and sat on the toes of her shoes, others flew around her head like moths, reaching out and touching the Senchai's golden hair for the good luck in doing so.

"The King and Queen's love is with you, Savior."

"I thank them for that, Mona." Verdor reached up and touched the star ear ornament the queen had given her. "It has become a part of me," she said, "I go nowhere without it now. Do you like it, Mona?"

"It is rare beauty, but fades next to your own, Savior."

"Thank you, Mona, and how are you?"

"I am in sorrow because of your troubles. How may we help you?"

"Be at peace, Mona. Together we will overcome this evil. We must all be strong."

The fairies had opened a clearing in their numbers, then produced a pillow on which Mona might sit. They placed it at the feet of Verdor.

"Have you seen him?" she asked.

"With these eyes, I have seen your Thomar. The Pokers have taken him into a cave a half day's walk on your legs."

"Did he look well?"

"He was unconscious. They trussed and blindfolded him. I could not tell how he was, but if he were dead, they would have left him on the mountain."

"How many Pokers have you seen?"

"Less than ten, Savior, but we think there are many more in the cave. How they got in there we don't know."

"Yes, there are likely many by now. They will attack soon, but I don't know how. Perhaps they will tunnel under my ring or try to burn it. They will attempt to panic the Giants."

"We await your will, Savior."

Verdor looked about her, addressing the multitudes. "Thank you, Mona, and thank all of you." The quiet gave way to joyous nattering. "I will give you a powder," Verdor said. "Put a small amount on each of you and you will be able to cross my ring at will."

Verdor reached into her bag and produced a small packet of red colored powder. She laid it on the ground in front of Mona. Mona raised a hand and the packet disappeared back into the throngs. "Soon," Verdor continued, "if all goes well, I will need a goodly number of you to carry a heavy trunk that will be in my room. Can you do that, Mona?"

"Where would you like the trunk carried to, my Savior?"

"To the very heart of your kingdom, if King Raif Nek gives his permission. It is only there where no mortal has ever been, that I can trust it will never be opened."

Mona didn't ask what would be the contents of this trunk. That would be the king's business.

"When the trunk is ready, may I summon you again?"

"I am as close as your right hand, Savior. You need only to call out."

"Good, then take care. If Putris Darkin comes with fire, you should save yourselves. Leave the Valley."

"You are kind in our regard, Savior, and we love you for it."

"I count on your love and am strengthened by it, Mona. Please watch the cave and report to me."

"My prayer is that you are reunited soon with your Thomar, my Savior."

"Thomar will be safe as long as Putris Darkin is not successful. If I am captured then his life is over, and mine. But we cannot think such thoughts, can we, Mona?"

"No, Savior. You will be victorious."

"Goodnight then, Mona, and to all of you." She blew kisses off the palm of her hand.

The fairies flew by her in happy parade. Verdor wondered about victory. If it became theirs, what would be the cost? Would she ever see Thomar again? She would weep for him. But Thomar's life, as her own, was of little consequence if the Mosaic school did not survive.

The last of the fairies disappeared into the moon shadows. Verdor looked up at the slender crescent light, then slowly over the starry heaven.

While a child, she and Lord Pater Nos had spent many happier nights than this one, gazing at the heavens. She loved those intimate hours with him, calling them "mystery nights," because of all the questions without answers which he unfolded before her. The two would sit near each other on the roof of the school with only the starlight to guide their hands. They sipped the hot Drogha tea. His voice then was like an instrument that played on the darkness, resonating against the black wall that enclosed them.

During those times he shared with her ideas that, she knew, he'd brooded over before he ever gave voice to them. Belinda discovered then that it wasn't the stars that captured her imagination but the interminable space behind them.

Often those were vexing nights. Nights that took her mind to uncomfortable places, but always places of learning.

"Why do we bother?" she once asked Pater Nos.

"Ask that question honestly," he replied.

Belinda thought a moment. "Why do I bother?" she said, now embarrassed.

"That's better, and it is a good question. Unfortunately I cannot answer for you, only for myself."

"Then why do you bother?"

"Because I value myself. I love the virtue in me. I love the wisdom that discipline has earned. I will not hide it. I will show it on the highest mountain if I must. If it were not so I could love no one."

From the stars she learned humility and, of course, from Pater Nos, the greatest wizard of all, about whom it was said he could stop the sun in its path, he who would share his time and mind with a girl child. On the roof, she learned that even he found life to be about questions more than answers.

On one of those nights he told her, "If you live a thousand years, Belinda, your physical life is but a moment in time compared to the age of the moon and stars,"

The very young Belinda felt diminished by his comment.

"But our spirits live on," she protested. "Are we not, then, as old as the moon?"

"Perhaps," he answered

"But you told me that all things have a spirit and that our spirit cannot pass."

"My dearest love, I only told you what I believe. I have thought on it my whole life. I have seen too much to think any other way. But in the end, no one knows. You must decide what you believe, but you don't have to decide tonight."

Belinda was silent for a long while, her face burning. Pater Nos had ruined the mystery night. She wanted to leave and return to her bed. Once again, as he had often done, he had turned things around.

"We live in hope, my heart. That is the only promise I can give you. There is no answer for that question."

Belinda wanted to cover her ears. His voice was stinging her. Yet, he continued, "Not I, nor anyone knows. So have a care with your moment here. Mind that you don't squander it."

Now, Verdor stood from her seat and gathered her cloak about her shoulders. There was a chill to the night air. She turned toward Menshun's wall. Her moment was close at hand. Loneliness gnawed at her. She worried about Thomar. He whom she loved most, she had betrayed. Where would her courage come without him?

She could transport herself over the Mohrs and be home by dawn. But that was just a thought.

"Night fears," Pater Nos had called them. "Very common, not to be taken seriously—nothing a good night's sleep won't chase away."

Verdor was tired. She walked in the direction of her bed. All that could be had been done. The time had come to leave this night to its course in the universe.

Twenty-Nine

SLEEP HAD FORSAKEN HISASH. Her thrashing about proved a poor means of making the hours pass, but she was grateful for the bed and stayed there longer than she normally might. The bed, to her, was an indication that she had truly been forgiven. Trust would come in time. She was determined to prove herself.

"Lorca requests that you take the room next to mine," Nakus had told her, "and she bids you good night." That was all, enough for now.

Dawn was close. Hisash could sense it. The city was quiet. All the Giants, except for those patrolling the wall, were in their homes sleeping or trying to. The window showed her only blackness, too dark, as if the night fed itself desperately before its imminent defeat.

Hisash rose from her bed and dressed. She fumbled her way to the scullery to find Nakus boiling water and cracking eggs.

Nakus looked up from her cooking. "Cool outside."

"Is it so?"

"Aye, Lorca went out and returned for her cloak. A bite to the air, she said."

"Is she still out there?"

"She is. Walking the wall with one or the other Fiercer."

"Will the attack come today, do you think?"

"Who can say? It will or won't. Will you break the fast with us?"

"I will with thanks, but I will walk first, my mind being unsettled."

Hisash departed the scullery, took a cloak from a rack in the great hall, and left the house. She stepped out onto the cobbles and discovered that Nakus was right. She gathered the cloak about her tightly and walked toward the wall. She had walked these streets from childhood so the darkness was no hindrance to her, but it bantered with her mind, creating fears. Night was never a friend to her, but since her experience with the Pokers, it frightened her more than ever. She steeled herself. Lorca was out there somewhere, and she would have words with her.

In the few minutes it took Hisash to round the corner at the end of the street, the black night sky had given over to a charcoal gray. The few stars were fading. Buildings took on definition: cornices poked out from rooflines and shutters on second stories outlined themselves against the flat stucco walls on which they hung. The distant Mohrs appeared darkly against the lightening sky. She would see the sun rising over them soon.

Hisash was, at first, relieved to see another giant up ahead. She thought of calling out so that the other would stop and wait on her to share the walk. She opened her mouth, but in the time it took to draw a breath, she changed her mind.

There was something strange about the other night traveler. He or she walked too close to the houses, stepping in and out of dark doorways and stopping often, as if to listen, before starting again furtively along the way. Sneaking about was unusual for a Giant. Hisash decided to watch and follow.

The hulking shape became a moving silhouette against the gray and charcoal buildings, the gait familiar.

Could that be Flen? Hisash wondered. The small hairs above her collar warned her to move on. This is not your business, they told her. There is foul work afoot here. Just yesterday Flen couldn't walk. Could that really be him? Why does he sneak about so?

The giant continued to duck and dodge, taking advantage of each shadow, doorway and post for several blocks, unaware that he had already been seen.

Finally, the sneaking giant arrived at what he apparently sought. Just then, the sun cast a lance from the far mountaintops, slaying the night. Flen turned his face about, looked up and down the street, then ducked under the lintel of the Library of Tomes.

Hisash waited just outside the door for him, but he was inside over-long and her curiosity needled when she heard the unmistakable sound of flint on steel. A common sound in this city, where a block of the fire starting material was placed behind every door in the event that the house should be entered after dark.

The sun, though still new, certainly cast enough light through the windows so that a taper should not be necessary. That is, unless Flen were going to the basement.

Not all homes had cellars. Most of them were built over simple cisterns where the water was captured from the roofs for bathing and cooking. But the Library of Tomes had a full basement for additional space. The storage of books and documents down there proved unwise because of the molds and spiders that could damage them, so the basement remained a dark empty place, only rarely entered. Now, it seemed to Hisash, that the basement was indeed Flen's destination. She entered the Library.

Flen was a querulous cuss and fearsome to look upon. But, what was there to fear? He had, after all, shared the governing table with her for several years now, and she thought him more stupid than dangerous.

She traced Flen's steps across the gray floorboards, past the tall shelves that lined the walls and divided the room like a maze. The hairs on the nape of her neck tickled in warning. He was acting strangely, with his sneaking and ducking into doorways. And she had seen first hand his cruelty toward Lorca. He was up to something.

Hisash snorted her fears away. Flen was just another man. A necessary inconvenience. Another of those males who bumped the periphery of her life and, like her father, left nothing but unpleasantness in their wake. She didn't hate all men, but she was amply ready to do without them. She had not yet told the scoundrel how she felt about his treatment of Lorca.

"Flen, I know you're here, and I would a word with you." Her voice echoed against the web-covered stones of the foundation and died in the musty air. She had reached the dirt floor and saw candle-light behind a column, but she did not see Flen. He was somewhere in the cavernous room. There was no other way out. Her widened eyes struggled to adjust.

"Will you speak, Flen? There's no need to hide."

Silence.

Then she noticed the sphere lying in the far corner on the dirt floor, emitting a soft, phosphorescent glow, humming a low sound, a beckoning evil—not a curiosity, but something to be turned away from and left alone.

Hisash's mouth was dry. Whatever Flen was about was best left for daylight and the company of others. Without another word she turned back toward the stairs.

A fist slammed her temple and dropped Hisash to the floor; darkness closed in on her, a humming sound, the sphere, she realized. The noise seemed close, as if the object vibrated the ground against which her ear rested. Then Hisash blacked out.

Thirty

THOMAR LAY DEEP in Darkin's cave, his hands still tightly bound behind his back. The cave grew quiet. The Pokers had heard the humming also. A thousand ears concentrated. For a brief time no one moved, standing or sitting where they were, stewing in their own smell. Then, as if of one body, they flooded one side of the cave like a sea wave and began digging.

Thomar propped one shoulder against the cave wall to watch the excitement. What seemed at first to be haphazard digging evolved into a methodical and productive tunneling. Pokers formed long lines. The leaders, digging with claw-like hands, were passing the excavated dirt to the next who continued the chucking behind and behind again. A hill of dirt and stone began to form, inching closer and closer to where he lay. Thomar began to worry that he might be buried alive. His two guards had joined in the excavating, paying him only intermittent attention.

More dirt piles created more shadows. By lying flat Thomar could put himself in complete darkness. He began to work on his bindings, rubbing them against a rock. The hide thongs were tough and after an hour he had made little progress. By the look of the hills of dirt that grew within the cavern, the tunnel was making rapid headway.

The attack has begun.

Thomar guessed the tunnel was part of the plan. *They will dig under Belinda's coveret, which she will surely have made. It is the only way they*

can attack her. Would she have thought of this? Would she have a plan?
He must warn her. Whatever her plan for him was, he wouldn't stay
here while the valley lay in danger. The Pokers would have difficulty
with Belinda, he knew, but they could murder the Giants with ease.

Look at them, he thought, seeing the workers bent to their labor.
There is no joy in this work. For them it is a hunger for evil.

The Pokers worked with the efficiency of ants removing and moving dirt. Dirt stuck to their sticky skin, causing them to blend and
disappear against the cave walls with only their eyes glinting into the
semi darkness. The Pokers' eyes appeared like a million fireflies dancing their mating ritual against a night-darkened field.

More and more torches that had lit the cave now found their way
into the tunnel. The cave grew darker.

Lex concentrated on his bindings. His powers were limited without
his staff. Without his hands he was near helpless. He must free them.

The vixen's tongue startled him when it licked his face. He drew
back his head, barely recognizing in the poor light the flash of white
fur on the fox's chest.

"So it's you, Mrs. Fox. A welcome sight you are. But you didn't
leave your wee wanes for the likes of me, now?"

The fox jumped over his prone body and nudged her way into the
gap between the cave wall and his bound hands.

"There's shame in that, you know!" he scolded her in a hushed
voice. "And for a piece of cheese, would you make them all orphans
and myself responsible? It's a hard position you put me in, there."

In no time the fox had gnawed through the bindings.

"Still, I'm glad for your company." Thomar drew his hands in front
of him, rubbing his wrists. His hands had gone numb. He banged
them against the floor cave. The vixen had already started gnawing
the binds of his ankles and soon they lay in pieces on the ground.
Without a backward look, the fox disappeared behind a near mound
and was gone.

"And mind that you get right on home and there'll be no more such
steppin' out," he called softly after her. His smile cracked open his lip

wound again, which began to bleed. He lay still in the position they had left him and gently caressed the wound with his fingertips. The cut began to knit itself and in minutes the pain had left him. Much better, he smiled again. *I can't be looking like cut bait.*

He sat upright, keeping his hands behind his back. Two Pokers appeared from the din. Without a word one of them shoved Lex, turning him to his stomach. They could see that his hands were no longer tied. They watched transfixed on the wizard's palms; his fingers splayed apart and then closed together repeatedly. Their dirt-covered faces showed puzzlement. Hooded eyebrows raised in alarm, their confusion had nothing to do with Lex's bindings, which lay strewn about the cave floor. They had not the least interest in his bindings or how he became loose from them. The last quandary of their dying brains was over the deep chest pain for which they could make no scream. They couldn't see within themselves, so they had no way to know that the pain they were feeling was caused by their hearts drying to powder and crumbling like ash to fall within the void left by the absent organ.

Lex stood and quietly stepped over their bodies, heading to the cave entrance. If he had his staff, he could transport himself. But now he could only run to Belinda. She would give him entrance and he would help her defeat the multitude of Pokers that were tunneling toward her. He passed through the diggers unhindered. Those that stopped in their work long enough to notice the departing form shared the same fate of the two he had just left. They dropped over dead and were cleared by the others along with the dirt and stones. In this manner he left the main cave like a pathfinder clearing his way through a dense, vine-entangled forest, swinging his arms like a pair of deadly knives.

The entrance was only a short distance ahead now. Thomar could smell slips of fresh air and his nose searched them with a desperate hunger. He doubled his pace through the first cave and past the desk with the spent taper where Putris Darkin had torn Lex's cheek. Running now, he crashed into an invisible barrier and fell backward.

Sure, he thought, *I should have expected this.*

He approached the wall. His hands traced it as high as he could reach and to both sides where the barrier was well rooted against the cave walls. There was no sense in wasting himself. Even if he had his staff, penetrating this would be difficult. Without the staff he might as well start digging with his hands like the Pokers below were doing.

The Pokers! They're digging toward Burba! What a fool I am!

Thomar was in such a hurry to breathe fresh air he had overlooked the obvious. He could battle the Pokers at this end of the cave. He could kill them all now—trap them in their own tunnel. *You idiot!* Verd was truly angry with himself. He kicked the wall of the cave, hurting his toes.

"So, you don't care for our hospitality?" Darkin's youthful voice was slick with mockery. "How very rude of a wizard of the Mosaic, though not altogether unexpected."

Thomar looked about him but saw nothing. "Will you show yourself, then?"

"Oh, no. Do battle with you now? No, we like it better this way. Besides, we are not ready to kill you." The voice had come from the other side of the barrier. Darkin was just outside the cave entrance in the open air where his power would be greatest.

Lex turned and raced back toward the inner cave. The second barrier nearly knocked him unconscious. He aroused himself to the impudent laughter of an indulged adolescent.

"We can't have you going back down there, my friend. Think of the mischief you could cause."

Lex threw his hands up. A cannonade of fire originating from them slammed against the barrier, shaking the ground, then exploding into a harmless shower of sparks.

"Oh my, a temper tantrum. Now what have you been taught about that, Thomar?"

"It's myself I'm angry with," Thomar said. "But you, you'll have no easier time getting near her. You may as well come in here and join me."

The bodiless voice seemed to be moving back and forth across the cave entrance, maddeningly close to the wizard, until the voice seemed to be hovering over his head.

"We've had this conversation, Lex. Do you recall what I told you?"

"I will not play with you, Darkin,"

"You're such a disappointment. I simply don't know what the beautiful Verdor, ah, Belinda sees in you."

Thomar remained silent. Suddenly his clothing was stripped from him; torn away by invisible hands. He stood naked.

"What manner of folly is this?"

For long moments, there was no response from his tormentor. Lex had the feeling of being watched, no, of being studied, much how he felt when Darkin stood near his bound body with the bullwhip.

The air at the cave entrance began to shimmer like heat waves rising. Soon a shape began to form from the unsettled air.

"We'll have those," the still unformed shape said in a voice that was Thomar's own.

His clothing was swept on a breeze through the barrier to the entrance of the cave. Before Thomar's startled eyes stood himself, as if he had crossed the barrier and turned back to look within the cave.

"Why, you look surprised," his double's eyebrows arched above his own grinning eyes. "This is what she had planned, don't you think? Isn't this why she gave you to me?"

Lex stared. A panicked anger ballooned in his chest but he said nothing.

"How would you say it? I won't keep her waiting for the love she's a-wanting. And see," Thomar's mirror image breathed on his hand, "our breath is warm. How do we do it?"

The evil one turned away, laughing Lex's own boisterous laugh, and disappeared beyond the cave entrance.

Thirty-One

"No one should be without a club."

Verdor knelt down beside the mound of stout clubs. The Fiercers had cut them during the night and they formed a hill of several thousand freshly de-barked and gleaming white under the new sun. She hefted one and found it adequate—an ash pole, dense at its thickened top and narrowing to a good grip, longer than she was tall.

"Remember,' she told the Giants, "fight back to back or in a circle facing outward. When they come they will be frightening and attempt to panic you. If you run they will catch you from behind and you will be killed."

"How big are they?" someone asked.

"The size of a large dog. They can walk upright but they prefer to run like a dog."

"Will there be any warning or will they just come from the air?"

Verdor ignored the sarcasm. "There may be warning," she replied. "It will likely be a sudden change to darkness, but not always. You will smell them."

"What of the children?" another asked.

"Those unable to fight will be vulnerable. The Pokers will attack the weakest. Guard the children well. Keep them close by."

The Giants began selecting clubs from the pile. Some of the adolescents began to playfully attack each other, poking and jabbing. Adults looked on quietly.

"They don't believe."

Verdor turned to Menshun's voice behind her shoulder.

"I know. Soon they will."

"We have never been attacked by any army, now you tell us that there is an army sprung from fantasy and wives' tales."

"I know it's hard, good Menshun, but their survival depends on their readiness. You must convince them."

"I can only do so much. We are not warriors. What you ask of us is inconceivable. See how they already regard our defense."

Some of the Giants, tired of their stick play had set their clubs aside and had moved too far from them. Children began playing with each other too far from a parent.

"You must convince them, Menshun."

"Can you show us what we will be fighting? Can you give us some sign to believe in? Show us one Poker and I'll have the whole city in arms."

"No, my friend, I can't do that. You have only the word of a Senchai wizard and, of course, the word of Hisash."

"For me that is enough. But for them," Menshun tipped his head toward the others, "there is no difference between today and two days ago except for the wall, and many think that was a foolish waste of our industry."

"The wise will live, Menshun. The foolish will perish. I have done all that I could to persuade them."

Menshun looked about him. The sun was brilliant in a cloudless sky. The Wall had been constructed surrounding the city and separating the Giants from their world of forests and of work. They were idle now. *Soon they would weary of their incarceration and leave the protection of the wall,* he thought.

He had secured the wellhead, placing a guard at it. The water from the well was bitter, but the River was low and inaccessible to them. He had ordered his Fiercers to bring the grain to the armory. If the siege was long, he felt, they would not starve.

Pusah had objected to moving the grain and had appealed to the governor. Lorca had agreed with Menshun, but his Fiercers had grumbled at the order. They were not Grainers. They were forest men. The work with dusty grain sacks was demeaning. But they also knew Menshun and no one would deny him. Not from fear did they obey, but from a respect between men who risk themselves daily under his governance. Their trust was capital he had earned over the years. He was now spending that capital at a fast pace. He wondered for how long they would go on listening to him. *If only there was some sign.*

"They will come, Menshun," Verdor said as if she'd read his mind. "And they will come soon, Perhaps tonight or tomorrow."

"Is there anything else that you can tell me, anything I can pass along to my men?"

"I met with the fairies last night," she said. "They told me that the Pokers abide in great numbers within a cave not too distant from here. Perhaps thousands, though they didn't know for sure."

Menshun's eyebrows arched briefly. *Now it's fairies,* he thought. *She said it as though she were relating the price of eggs.* He would keep this information to himself. He had lived his life by what he could touch and move or cut down and build. All the Fiercers had. What he had just heard was absurd. He knew his men and if he told them that the Senchai spoke to fairies, his remaining capital would vanish.

He searched the wizard's face. Again, there was truth in her eyes, carved there as in granite by a stoneworker's chisel.

"Why don't we go to the cave and burn them out?" Menshun asked.

"Your lives would be worthless if you walk past my ring. Putris Darkin is out there. He awaits such a mistake."

Enough. Menshun couldn't listen to more. Their plight grew more and more amazing. This woman had asked him to clear thousand-year-old trees and he had done so. She spoke of fairies and Pokers and worse, as if they were as common as a drink of water. He had thrown his lot in with a mad wizard from a foreign kingdom. Yet there was no denying her.

"I will go and tend to my own," he said.

"'Tis well that you should. How many do you have?"

"Three. Two boys and a girl."

"Are they smart?"

"Smarter than I, I fear," Menshun said with a wry laugh.

"And the girl, is she as beautiful as her mother and are the boys as wise and strong as their father?"

Menshun squatted and selected two clubs from the pile. "Hearing you ask that makes me glad of them."

"I look forward to meeting them soon." Verdor was smiling.

"I pray that they stay alive for you to meet them." Menshun stood again. A fly had found a droplet of sweat at his temple. He batted it away with his hand. "I have another question," he said.

Verdor met his eyes.

"Can the Pokers cross your magic ring?" he asked.

"A dung beetle couldn't cross the ring. It will hold. But the Pokers may try to dig under it."

"Is that possible?"

"Yes, but it would be difficult. Putris Darkin's power or any wizard's power is greatly diminished underground. The dirt below our feet belongs to The Earth Mother. She brooks very little magic, nor would any good wizard practice in her home without a very good reason. Darkin will not go deep but he may send the Pokers to dig for him."

"It is what I would do."

"And I, but the tactic has a problem."

"What's that?"

"Once deep in the ground they could easily lose their way. Finding direction under ground is near impossible. They would need a signal from within my ring."

Menshun considered her answer for a moment. "A traitor?" His countenance darkened. "No Giant would ever betray his race. There would be no reason. We can gain little from other kingdoms. I think you speak hastily, Senchai Verdor."

"Perhaps not."

"If you know something, tell it."

"I suspect that Flen has met with Putris Darkin."

Menshun lowered the two clubs he had lifted to his shoulder and balanced their narrow ends on the ground between his feet. He leaned over them toward Verdor.

"Flen is a fool," he said.

"The worst kind of fool," Verdor replied. "The fool who fancies himself more intelligent than all others. The kind of fool easily manipulated."

"We agree on that. Do you have any proof?"

"Walk with me a moment, good Menshun, and I will tell you what I know. I promised to break the fast with Lorca this morning, I won't keep her waiting. Nor should you be delayed in seeing your family."

The two left the wall and the slightly diminished pile of clubs for the center of the city. The sun felt warm on their shoulders and their two shadows, one tall and one short, marched closely in front of them like familiar friends.

"Two days ago," Verdor began, "I spent the night in the fields between here and Flen's home."

Menshun slowed his pace so as not to tax his smaller companion.

"In the morning, while still a distance from the pathway," she continued, "I saw Flen setting out toward Burba. He was on his way to press the Troca with Lorca. He gained some distance on me since I still hadn't completed my prayers and even more because I stopped along the way. I was sure there was no one else on the path that morning except for Flen. His scent lingered on the air long after he passed.

"I came upon a tree that had been destroyed. An old hickory whose trunk your own arms could not encircle. The tree had been violently uprooted. There was dirt and dust and sand scattered over a good distance across the forest floor. Its roots were torn and its trunk and branches were sheared across the grain in ways you would have to see to believe possible."

"Was the tree a dead one? Perhaps what you saw was a display of anger for which Flen is noted."

"The tree was alive, Menshun, and as old as this valley. This was not a display of anger, but a warning to me. I tell you, Menshun, there was not a piece of that tree that would not fit in your pocket. I have seen much, but I was frightened by the power of what destroyed it."

Menshun stopped walking and stared down at the wizard. "Then it could not have been Flen who did so."

"No. At least, not without help."

"That is not proof of Flen's guilt."

"No, but Flen's smell was everywhere in that glade. He was there. He may well have seen it happen."

The two walked on in silence. They were nearing Lorca's house where they would part.

"Have you told Lorca about this?" Menshun asked.

"Not yet. She had her battle with Flen to think about. I have told Hisash that Flen should be watched. But if we are vulnerable in any way, I believe that it would be through Flen."

"Where is Flen now?" Menshun wondered aloud.

"I was told that he went home after the Troca in great distress. He is likely still there."

They had arrived at Lorca's house. Verdor stepped into the governor's doorway and then turned toward Menshun.

"You must go to your family, Menshun. Tell the Giants that when the attack begins, they should leave their homes. I will help them where I can, but they must not stay indoors without guards."

"I'll tell the others. I will see to my family, then I'll see to Flen. I know two Fiercers who would escort him with great tenderness from his home."

"No one should leave this city. It is too late for that. Flen will be able to pass the ring. If Flen cannot find his way back here, he has made his choice. Leave him."

Menshun looked down at the wizard. Her eyes were confident. He had rarely seen such composure even in the most skilled of his woodsmen. *What could describe this absence of doubt,* he wondered.

He had seen similar before, years ago. He and his friend Zapotec were new Fiercers then. They had studied the tree, the way it leaned against another. Their judgment in its path of descent was lacking and instead of the giant ash falling to the ground it balanced about head height, forked around a standing oak. The two youth decided not to seek help. Zap died because of it.

Menshun had relived the scene a hundred times since that day. There was no side pressure on the felled tree. There couldn't have been. It lay like it would finish its descent if they place the cut right there. They would take it slowly. If there were pressure it would show before the cut was too deep.

Menshun told Zap to stay on the uphill side of the tree and watch it for any shivering while Menshun slowly made his cut. If it were under stress the tree would fall toward Menshun, he was sure. He would be ready.

The tree snapped before Menshun was a third through its girth. Even the experienced Fiercers had never seen an ash tree behave in that way. A willow, they said, but not an ash. The tree struck Zap across his abdomen, pinning him against a nearby elm. Menshun stood opposite Zap. The ancient fell separated them. Menshun turned his friend's hands, swollen and bright red, away from embracing the bowl of the tree and held them in his own. The bark was hard and rough beneath his wrists. There was the unmistakable smell of heartwood, fresh and alive like raindrops on a fern leaf. Zap's hands were damp. Menshun stared into his friend's eyes. This was a last time, as only life can give them, without fanfare or circumstance.

Zap's lips had cracked a feeble smile. Crimson drooled from their edges and wordlessly he told his friend that there was no fault. His brown eyes consoled the last eyes they would ever see. In them, Menshun saw inevitability, then nothing.

Verdor's eyes were like that now. *This is what it means to be a Senchai wizard,* he told himself. He was intimidated by her. He turned his head before she could sense his discomfiture. He nodded in her direction, turned from the doorway and strode away, covering the cobbled streets in a stride that only another giant could match.

Thirty-Two

THE POKERS ARRIVED almost in the way Verdor said they would. And with them came a prolonged shading of the sun, as if a large black cloud had passed over it. The accompanying odor was so strong and sour that the Giants' eyes watered and they feared to draw breath.

The pile of clubs that had been largely ignored, rapidly disappeared into the hands of every able giant. The city streets filled with quiet apprehension. No one had yet seen a Poker. No one doubted they were near, even within the city. Many of the Giants stripped their jerkins and tied them over their noses or pressed their hats against their faces. Still, there was little relief from the putrid smell.

In her bedroom, Lindy Hae's eyes popped open.

She was usually an early riser. Most mornings she would have Padar's tea hot before he was done with his ablutions and always before the sun peeked above her windowsill. But she had retired late last evening because of the work at the wall. The morning was old, but why wasn't the room brighter? And why hadn't SeSe awakened her?

Her head stayed on the pillow but her mind barked for the attention of her senses. She hadn't heard a noise; no one touched her bed. "Oh, my bones," she muttered, "what is that smell?"

"Padar," she called when she came to her feet. Padar did not answer. She then remembered that he had spent the night at Menshun's wall with some of the other Fiercers. Silly work, that wall, but it had taken on a festive atmosphere, with the whole valley working. There was no music but there were the bawdy jokes and the occasional teasing flash of an upper thigh by some of the maidens to the delight of the sweaty Fiercers. No one worried about an attack.

Lindy stubbed her toe on her cedar chest at the foot of the bed when she rounded toward her bedroom door. The stench multiplied with every step and when she opened her door she nearly gagged. Something rotten was upstairs.

"Padar Se!" She screamed her son's name, running toward his bedroom. "It's the smell of death, sure."

She ran the hall like a man would, with a full stretching gait, at her child's door instantly. "He's to be fit, so. He's to be fit, so, my darling."

The stink clung to her nightgown. She could feel its weight. Her eyes stung, tears running to drip from her chin.

She didn't unlatch the infant's door, but slammed through it, splintering the stop jamb and exploding the strike-side casing away from the frame with a loud crack.

"Aggh!" The air inside Padar Se's room burned her skin. She nearly lost her balance.

Something in Padar Se's crib. An animal! She tore at her eyes to remove the searing tears, rubbing the watery blindness from them.

The child's neck looked broken. The creature held the boy's limp head in its mouth, lifting it from the mattress. The shiny-wet skin pulsing at the flanks, the animal appeared to be sucking on her son's head. Feral eyes turned upward and fixed on her, watching her confidently. It didn't interrupt its work. The blue flanks pumped in and out like a billows reversed.

Lindy leapt through the air, crashing down on the bed with her outstretched body. She seized the creature just below its head and tore it from her baby, flinging the animal against the wall behind her.

She stood with the infant cradled in her arms. The boy was coated in sticky goo and naked to the waist. His little head lolled to one side grotesquely. Her eyes refused to rest on the round bloody hole in the middle of the crown of his head.

"Wake thee, Padar Se, wake thee, SeSe," she cried, sprinkling the baby with her tears. "Ye'll break the fast now, so you will. And momma has your favorite pease porridge you love, so. But first I'll see a smile on those lovely lips."

She didn't feel the slashing blow to the back of her heels. She didn't care that her legs had simply buckled beneath her, her knees dropped to the broken crib parts that lay around her.

When the Poker broke her neck she was still crooning to the dead child. "And won't we visit your Da at the wall?" she said. "And you can ride about on his shoulders." She gave no heed to the dark ooze pumping from the side of her throat. She fell forward on top of her baby, joyful to be holding the child the way she always had. Joyful that she had saved her Padar Se like a momma should.

Out on the streets, Giants began to search doorways and alleys, looking behind rain barrels, and woodpiles. Women gathered their children close.

It seemed impossible to Menshun that the smell could be so strong and yet nothing had been seen. *They're here,* he thought, *but where are they?* Then he heard a scream. A woman stood not far down the street, pointing upward. Even at the distance he could see that her mouth gaped, she stood frozen in her shoes, just pointing. He followed the direction of her finger.

"Sweet Deddimus." His legs nearly buckled under him. A long moment passed before he could realize what he was looking at.

"Mind the children to the armory," he bellowed at last. No one moved. "Now!"

Giants pushed the children ahead of them. Most were confused, still not having looked up. Parents covered the eyes of many. They herded them forward, in a controlled stampede.

"Hold!" Menshun yelled. The Giants stopped just before the massive doorways to the great building. He turned toward one of his Fiercers.

"Take five men and go inside first. Be sure none of those animals are in there. Then get the children within and stay with them."

Menshun again turned his eyes upward. The creatures had gained advantage on the Giants. *How had they done so, and so quickly?*

Pokers had climbed the peaks of the houses and perched there, shoulder to shoulder, along each ridge from gable to gable. Their opal eyes, gleaming at the Giants below, seemed like lights in the darkened city. They sat, some jostling for position, packing themselves, some shitting on the roof slates so that the offal oozed down the pitch, dropping off the eaves to the streets below. Other than the pushing for space and some subdued chattering, they were quiet.

When one peak was filled, more Pokers streamed up the back roofs, appearing over the ridges on the next and then the next house. Once gaining the peak they merely sat, as if waiting for further instructions. Their heads moved side to side, watching the hurried activities below. Their tongues darted out from their long snouts giving the impression that they were hungry.

"They look like blackbirds on a clothes line, eh, good Menshun?" a nervous voice inquired.

Menshun made no reply. He just stared at the bizarre spectacle playing out on their homes.

"Do you think they can jump from up there?" the nervous voice persisted.

Again, Menshun ignored the intrusion. "Go find the wizard," he told the voice. "Tell her that her Coveret has been breached."

Verdor was already aware. She smelled the Pokers and witnessed the darkening sky with everyone else. Like the others, she too was aware of the roof sitters. They were unnerving to be sure, but her real concern was with Darkin himself. He had figured a way in, at least for his minions, but she knew this was likely a terror tactic. He would show himself soon, but in what way?

She didn't need to wait long. The sky, already diminished, grew lower and even darker. The Giants walking the wall had changed their focus from outside the timber fence to within the city. They were nearest the rooftops and therefore closest to the Pokers who lined the roof peaks. The Giants backed away as far as they could safely go without being too close to another adjacent roof. They stood with clubs, huddled together in groups of eight or ten.

A ripping, tearing sound turned their heads toward the woods again. At first, a single tree, a massive fir over one hundred feet tall and as big around as a silo, uprooted itself from the edge of the distant firewall. The tree flew at them like a spear. Its roots were bent back toward its branches, leaving a tracer of leaves behind it. Terrified, a group of Giants directly in the tree's path, jumped from the parapet amidst the hollering of those further down the walkway. Several of those who leapt lay unconscious on the ground below; others writhed about holding broken arms or legs.

The tree struck the wall like a battering ram. Vibrations from the boom shook the wall for some distance, causing the Giants still on the catwalk to grab the nearest projection for fear of being shaken off. Then the trees came in rapid succession. Each ripped from the earth, each hurtling toward the wall. Faster and faster they came like a rainstorm of huge arrows, crashing against Verdor's ring. The noise was deafening. Giants cowered, covering their heads under their arms. Children burrowed into their mother's laps or clamped their hands over their ears. Their screams couldn't be heard. The Giants had forgotten the threat that watched placidly from the rooftops.

The fusillade continued for an hour. Even the most hardened Fiercers moaned in fear. Then, suddenly, it stopped. No sound now, not even the chirping of a cricket. The quiet smothered the city and was as near maddening as the noise it replaced

But the ring held. The Giants lifted their heads. The children in the armory had stopped their wailing and stared about them wide eyed, holding an apron string or a hand with two of their own. The wall had grown to five times its height on the south side of the city. Trees from the forest, stacked like cordwood against the wall then projecting over it to a height that made the Giants feel intimidated.

"Hold yourselves steady!" Verdor yelled from her position near the wellhead. "It is not yet over. He is trying to panic you into running from the city."

The fire came next. The sky formed it, crafted it into a vortex so thick and hot that it appeared to be an orange liquid. Again the noise, louder now, screaming as if fire could be enraged. A thousand Giants fell to their faces, covering their heads with their arms. Those still on the wall quickly leapt to the ground.

The river of fire dropped on the timbers piled high over the wall. Those Giants who dared to look saw flames soar back up into the sky to an impossible height. The heat was intense. Breathing was a torment. The hot air burned the Giants' lungs. They cupped their hands over their mouths, pressing their heads against the cooler ground. Many lay terrified beneath the conflagration, forgetting their clubs, forgetting the danger within the city walls.

The Pokers attacked. They descended from the roof like a swarm of berserk black ants. Roof after roof emptied its burden, dropping Pokers from the eaves like rats from a burning vessel. With the efficiency of reapers, the Pokers went to work, slashing and tearing. The streets began to trickle and then flow blood rivulets to their gutters.

Not only the Giants were being slaughtered.

Verdor, staff in hand, was cleaving in broad strokes. A blue light ray crackled from the end of her staff. To her right and left, Pokers were sliced in half, their greedy mouths grimacing, their heads laying about her, separate from their bodies.

"Fight!" Verdor screamed.

The Fiercers were the first to respond. They seized their clubs and began bashing the animals in a flurry of motion. They formed a ring, keeping the attackers at bay long enough for Verdor to turn back around with her weapon, and slice through the Pokers. Their cleaved torsos lay smoldering, their flesh still boiling long after they were dead.

The dying about them was dreamlike to the point that the Giants could almost ignore it. But not so the smell. The hot air and the stink of the burning Pokers made it impossible to breathe. Giants were gasping, drowning in foul air.

Verdor saw that many giants were dropping to their knees, clutching their throats. Never stopping her staff in its deadly work, she balled her left fist and then opened it. The wind swirling from her hand was cool, even wet with water drops. She broadcast the fresh air like a farmer sowing seed on a field. From her, relief pushed outward, up and down city streets. Giants soon revived, took up their clubs, and began to fight in deadly earnest. The clubs worked well. They began to make headway into the hordes of Pokers. With Verdor's help the tide of battle began to turn until the Giants were now hunting down Pokers fleeing before them.

Verdor moved quickly from street to street, cutting down the creatures without thought or mercy. Even the fire that raged against the wall began to lessen and the howling noise decreased. She heard shouted curses, warnings, and threats: "Look to your right!" or "Here's one for the filth that spawned ye!"

The despair of defeat soon changed to the optimism of attack. The anger was on the Giants now and even the most timid of them waded into a throng of the beasts, clubs whirring and thumping. The Pokers tried to flee, but they were within Verdor's ring now. Escape was impossible. More and more they were separated and then cut down.

Soon no Pokers remained alive. The fire outside the wall had died to embers. Verdor's cooling wind had cleansed the air of heat. The stink became tolerable.

Menshun looked about him. A breeze tickled a sweat-soaked tendril of hair that fell over his forehead. The streets were quiet now, but gore was everywhere. The blood of his brethren flowed and intermingled with the green ooze of the Pokers. He walked about recognizing old friends, pierced and broken, laying in contorted positions that only violent death could design. He knelt beside a dead friend. "Ah, Forthy," he shook his head, "never mind your wife and children, I'll take care of them as my own."

Many of the Giants stood about in the blood soaked streets, leaning against their clubs, exhausted, mutely surveying the carnage about them. A cry arose here and there. Voices gave note to sorrow or anger.

Menshun made his way to the armory. His wife Maric was there, guarding the young. His daughter was in her mother's lap. The child was staring at the wall, looking at nothing and rocking back and forth. He approached the child and knelt, grazing her cheek with one finger, but his daughter did not respond. She was four years old, one of the last children born in the Valley since their troubles began.

Looking up, he found his wife's eyes staring intently into his own. She began to tremble then, with the child still between them, she lurched forward, throwing her arms around his neck. The sobs came quietly. After a while Menshun reached up and grasped her hands, pulling them from him and looking into her tear-filled eyes.

"Why us?" she pleaded.

Menshun said nothing.

"Meglein?"

Maric shook her head sadly.

"As is Forthy. We'll take their children as our own."

Maric nodded.

"I must go to the wall now. Keep the children here. It may be some time before we get things," here he paused searching for the right words, "cleaned up out there."

Maric nodded again. "Is it over?"

"I don't know. Verdor says there is an evil one named Putris Darkin still out there. I don't know what he wants."

Maric shuddered. Menshun rose to his feet and, bending, placed a palm on his daughter's head. He leaned down and kissed her forehead. Still she made no response.

"Where are the boys?"

"Out there somewhere, I couldn't stop them. They went to fight the Pokers." Maric's lower lip began to tremble again.

"I'll find them. I'll send food and water in to all of you." Glancing again at his daughter, Menshun turned and left the armory.

Thirty-Three

MENSHUN MET LORCA ON the street. The tear in her jerkin at the upper right arm exposed a gash seeping red down to her sleeve. She still carried a club. She was indifferent to her wound.

"I am thankful that you are alive, good Menshun. Are you coming from the armory? I am bound for there myself. How are the children?"

"Some better than others, but alive. They need food and water."

"I have already seen to that, it is on the way. Have you seen Hisash?"

"Not since yesterday."

"Nor have I. She was due to break the fast with Nakus, Verdor, and me, but she never came to us."

Menshun felt Lorca's concern and said, "I'll watch for her."

"Where are you going now?"

"I search for my sons. Then I will go to the wall. I would see the damage to our valley."

"Your sons are well, good Menshun. The youngsters fought bravely not far from me. You will find them down Cook's street, near the tinker's shop. I'm afraid they are in need of a rest."

"Be so kind and tell Maric, would you?"

"Certainly."

"What of the wizard, where is she?"

"She is healing the wounded."

"And the dead? How many did we lose?"

"We don't know yet. Some hid and are still in hiding, I suspect. It may be a while before we know how many we lost. Be ready for the worst, Menshun"

"I will find men to bury them. What do we do with the Pokers?"

"Verdor said to throw them over the wall and she would deal with them."

"Did she say if there will be another attack?"

"She said there will be no more of the Pokers, but there is one out there that seeks our destruction."

"Ours or hers?"

Lorca looked at Menshun. "What do you mean?"

"Never mind, Governor. I must go now and see my sons. I will be at the north wall if you need me."

"I can always count on you, good Menshun. Go well. I'll see you soon."

Clean up work had already begun. Men and women carried buckets from the well and others were sweeping the streets. Still others were collecting bodies and piling them into oxcarts. Few words passed between the workers. Some had sharpened their clubs and were spearing the dead Pokers or scooping them up with hayforks and piling them on other wagons. Most had tied kerchiefs about their faces for the gruesome work.

Menshun found himself pondering the day. It seemed unreal. He could not imagine Pokers before today, and now the hideous creatures were dead all about him. *Why would they attack and kill us? What manner of world have I been blind to? And yet there is another threat. Putris Darkin.*

From what Menshun had seen at the wall the evil one was terrible in his power. Could they withstand him? Would Verdor be able to kill him? He dared not think of how their lives had been changed by what happened today and he had yet to survey the damage to the Valley outside Verdor's ring. He walked on. What his wife asked him kept returning to his mind.

"Why us?" He guessed that there was little advantage in trying to figure that out now.

He passed an alley and saw Flen hovering over a body. It appeared that he was dabbing blood from the pavement stones and wiping the blood onto his clothes. He then saw Flen tear his own jerkin. *Our Flen is a coward,* Menshun thought. But he passed on without comment.

Menshun found his sons where Lorca had said they would be. The two boys sat quietly side by side on the railing of the tinker's porch. Their clubs were propped beside them and they were drinking from a gourd being passed around. Both looked too tired to stand.

"You gave your mother a fright, the two of you."

The two looked at their father. The moment their eyes locked on his, he resolved to let the matter rest. What he saw told him that they no longer belonged to him. Older eyes appraised their father, with understanding. He sensed their aloofness. Not born from arrogance, he was sure, but from a new acceptance, not of Menshun the man, but of themselves. In a way, he liked what he saw. Yet, in another way, it saddened him deeply.

"I go to the wall, will you accompany me?"

The two stood, gathered their clubs and walked alongside their father.

Thirty-Four

GENDAU WAS BEHIND Lord Pater Nos when the old wizard forgot to duck and bumped his head on the low arch above his attic door. "Ouchka wouchka, cried the old bobcat!"

Pater Nos' gnarled hands rubbed the bruise, burying his long fingers into his unruly crown of white hair.

Gendau, who was accompanying him to the pigeon loft, had heard his master refer to the "old bobcat" before, most recently when he bumped his head on these very stairs.

"What happened to the 'old bobcat'?" Gendau asked, settling into a slow ascent of the steps. The wizard's plodding progress was a penance to him.

"Hmmn? The old bobcat? What 'old bobcat'?"

"The one that cried 'Ouchka wouchka'?"

"Hmmm?" The robed form ahead of him hesitated. Gendau almost regretted asking the question, since it slowed them even more. "Oh, that 'old bobcat.' Hmmn! I don't know."

"He must have hurt himself somehow," Gendau said.

"Yes, he must have hurt himself in a very famous way, I would guess."

Pater Nos had now stopped their climb, Gendau impatiently queued behind him in the narrow stairwell. Pater Nos hadn't turned to look back, but Gendau guessed that he was somewhere else in his thoughts. Since Verdor had left the school, he had taken to these "times of wondering," in Gendau's words. Lately, the normally daydreaming Gendau brought his master back to the present rather than the other way around.

Pater Nos abruptly shook his head and continued up the stairs to the roof door.

"Funny, that I never asked him myself about the 'old bob cat.'"

"Asked who, Lord Pater Nos?"

"My father. He used to say that whenever he hit his fingers with a hammer. He was a carpenter. He hit himself often. So I can't say how skilled he was, but I do remember him saying that about the 'old bobcat'."

"You had a father, Lord Pater Nos?" Gendau was truly surprised.

"Why, of course, boy, and a mother. Did you think I fell from the moon?"

"But you're so old. I never thought that you had a father or a mother. I never thought about it."

"Old? I'm a hundred and forty seven. Many wizards live thrice that."

"Well, I'm most apologetic, I never—."

"Oh, never mind that. I'll forgive a curious mind many times. But a lazy mind? Hah, no forgiveness there."

The two passed through the door onto the bright sunlit roof. The sky overhead was brilliant and dazzled their eyes for a few moments. Pater Nos paused at the door to the pigeon cage, as if enjoying the warmth on his shoulders.

"I'm wondering now why I never asked him, young Gendau. That was so unlike me."

"You mean your father about the bobcat?"

"Yes, and now you ask me. Let that be a lesson to you, sir."

"A lesson, good Master? My ignorance astounds me, my lord, but I don't see the lesson there."

"The lesson is that ignorance can be passed on for generations unless someone puts a stop to it with a simple question. I commend you, boy, for your curiosity. If I had your nature I would have asked my father back then. Now we both might never know how the old bobcat hurt himself."

Gendau hugged his teacher's legs. Pater Nos was a demanding instructor, but he had a way of making Gendau feel very good about many things, especially himself. Gendau hungered to excel for the wizard. Pater Nos placed a loving hand on the boy's head.

"Now," Pater Nos said, "I need your skill in choosing birds for all kingdoms and regions, including the Giants. It is dangerous in their Valley now and it may be cruel to send any there but we have no choice. Choose wisely, lad. I need the best flyers."

"All regions, Lord?"

"Yes, I will convene a Vertex."

A Vertex! Gendau let the word stoke his imagination. His hands trembled with excitement. Fumbling with the cage door, he opened it and entered. Pigeons fluttered about him, dusting him with old feathers. He had heard of these special meetings. But he had never seen one. Thomar had once told him about a Vertex called when Thomar himself was a small boy.

"Amazing," Thomar had said to Gendau. "All of the wizards who pledged to the Mosaic came from all corners of the world. One of them was black, dark as the night. He would laugh like this." And then Thomar demonstrated a deep and booming laughter that rattled Gendau's ears. "And his teeth were beautiful to see, for they had gold in them."

"Gold in his teeth? But why?"

"Yes, gold that shone like the sun itself. Not just a few teeth either, but many teeth. All across here." Thomar traced a finger over his upper teeth indicating all of them. "But I don't know why he had gold in them. I never asked him. I was afraid of being rude. But to see him laugh or smile was an event, each time."

Gendau determined that he would ask if he ever met the black wizard.

"And there were others," Thomar's eyes widened, "just as wonderful. Chen Chow Yen, now there's a wizard. He has a crop of black hair that sprouts out from top of his head and falls to the middle of his back like a horse's tail. He never sleeps."

"Never?"

"Not that I could tell. He stands with his arms folded across his chest like this. He doesn't eat. And he wears the most fearsome scowl on his face. He hardly ever talks, but when he does say something, he sounds like he is giving orders to soldiers." Thomar demonstrated to the amusement of Gendau. "But he is very kind. See what he gave me."

Thomar reached under his bed and pulled out a small wood box. "It's called teak," Thomar said. The two looked at the ornate carvings on the box lid. "They are Egrets. They live in Chen Chow Yen's land. They are magnificent birds, tall, up to your knees. They have white feathers and see the crown there? It is bright yellow. And look how spindly their legs are."

Gendau looked down at the lid and the two egrets depicted there. One sat on a nest. The other stood guard. He could even see an egg under the female.

"'Tis truly a wonder,"

"But that's not all. Look inside."

Gendau lifted the lid with his two thumbs. It fit the box seamlessly yet slid open with little effort. Inside there was an egg-shaped stone.

"It is called Jade." Thomar plucked the egg from the box and handed it to Gendau. "What do you think of it?"

Gendau rolled the stone in his hand. "It is hard, yet it feels warm and soft. I have never seen anything like it. It makes me feel good just holding it. Is it a magic stone, Thomar?"

"No, its only Magic is in its beauty."

"Why did he give it to you?"

"I don't know for sure, but he said everyone should have something of beauty near him at all times. But he said it like this." Again, to Gendau's joy, Thomar demonstrated the commanding orders of the wizard.

Gendau made his first selection from the pigeons. He examined its primaries and then flipped it over, feeling its abdomen, then feeling the pulse of its heart against his fingertips.

"Will Chen Chow Yen be coming to the Vertex?"

"So you've heard about our Grand Chen. Yes, he will come. They will all come. Even Thomar and Verdor will be there."

"I would make bold, and ask why you summon a Vertex, Lord Pater Nos."

"There are changes needed, young Gendau. But you must be patient. You will be at each meeting and find out with the others."

Pater Nos selected tiny cylinders and inserted small notes in each. There were only three words "Vertex, eighth moon."

There was no need to sign his name. All would know that only Pater Nos would call such a meeting.

Thirty-Five

"THERE IS A MAN OUTSIDE the wall. He says you know him. Lex Verd, Grand Wizard of the Mosaic, but he carries no staff."

Verdor's hands hesitated imperceptibly, then she continued her healing ministrations on a giant whose leg had been lacerated to the bone. The leg was near whole again; the only sign that he had been wounded was a pink weal where the cut had been mended. Verdor knelt next to him. "You can get up now, Leown, your leg is fine."

Leown sat erect and tested the leg with his fingers. He rubbed it gently at first, then more vigorously. " May the blessings of Deddimus abide with you, Senchai Verdor. You have saved my life"

Though he could have survived without the leg, he was a Fiercer. If he couldn't work, his loss of pride would have ended him as surely as his wound, thanks to Verdor, had failed to do.

"Thank you Leown. I am blessed that I can help you. Now go home to your wife."

Leown stood, tested his weight, and left.

"Excuse me, Senchai," Lorca said, "did you not hear me?"

***

Lorca had come from the wall where she had been presiding over burials. The funerals were a problem. With so many dead and so little space, she decided to use the narrow walkway between the houses and the wall that encircled the city for graves. Many homes now had graves in their back yards. Perhaps they would move the bodies at a future time, perhaps not.

The job of internment was a depressing one, made more so by the prospects of the Giants' future. The fire outside the wall had scorched everything to cinders and dry ash. None of their industries remained except for the oxen which had been corralled within the city. The forests were gone. The river was little more than a serpentine depression in a meadow of soot. The fields were black. Wisps of breeze swirled across the open spaces like miniature dust tornadoes with nothing in their path to hinder them.

The soap works had disappeared, leaving only the large clodding cauldrons looking like they had been birthed from the white ash. They were setting there, still in rows, but tilted this way and that. Lorca dismissed any thoughts about their future. She wouldn't think of that now.

***

The Giants had erected an incline from the ground up to the ramparts, then positioned themselves on scaffolding along the side of the ramp and pushed the stinking lumps of Poker flesh upwards and over with the same clubs that had been used to kill. During this time, Verdor healed the wounded.

True to her word, she had already dealt with the thousands of dead Pokers the Giants had piled outside the wall. Their corpses had made a hill as high as any building in the city. The carrion formed a parallel outer ring nearly the height of Menshun's wall. Disposal of the Poker's bodies was a difficult detail. The smell ached in the Giant's noses. Those that moved the dead creatures would not touch them for fear of never ridding themselves of the stench.

When the Giants were done, Verdor left her healing place and climbed to the catwalk. She waved her hand toward the steaming pile as though swatting an annoying horsefly. There was a brilliant, white flash, as if the sun had descended on the mountain of dead Pokers. Giants nearby covered their eyes. When they dared look again, moments later, the dead Pokers had been reduced to ash, white and deep like powdery snow.

"She'd have fried us all if she did that on this side of the wall," one of the sentries murmured.

"It's a rare power she has," said another.

The darkness had fled. A bright sun took an imposing command of an azure sky, its brilliance doubled over the vast, ashen tundra. It was quiet out beyond the wall. Not a chirp or a buzz was heard, hardly a breeze could be felt now.

Some of the Giants stacked the last of the doors they had removed from their homes to use them for pallets on which to carry the wounded to Verdor. They placed them row on row in the streets and up against the houses. When word passed through their ranks that they would soon be healed, the moaning of the wounded gave way to banter and even boasting at the severity of the wounds they suffered. Verdor walked down the middle of them stopping at each makeshift pallet.

"Are there any wounded yet to be healed?" she asked.

"No, Senchai," Lorca answered from behind.

"Then I will attend to our caller."

Verdor wiped her forehead on her cloak sleeve. Her face was drained of color. Her hair hung in blond rope like cords over her shoulders. Exhaustion pulled at the lids of her eyes. She needed sleep, but the visitor outside the wall would keep her from that. Either it was Putris Darkin, or it was her lover, Thomar. Her salvation or her destruction. "Take me to him," she said wearily.

"There is other news, Verdor."

Lorca and Verdor were now walking rapidly to the western wall. They passed many empty doors that lay in the streets not yet re-hung.

"What is the news?"

"Thankfully, Hisash is safe. She wishes to speak with you and me. It is about Flen. According to her, Flen is our betrayer."

"Have you spoken to Flen?"

"No, Senchai, I have not seen him."

"I suspect she is right, but if Flen is our betrayer that is something for your laws to deal with. I, too, have something to tell you."

The two stopped on their walk to the wall and Verdor pulled Lorca's sleeve toward an empty house. They now stood just inside a door-less archway. Verdor waited a moment until she was certain that there was no one else present.

"He who awaits outside the wall for me may be my lover, Thomar. His Grand name is Lex Verd."

"May be your lover?"

"Yes. Or he could be the one we have awaited. The very soul of evil, Putris Darkin."

***

Lorca looked around the room they had entered. Hardwood floors and a balustrade to the second floor gleamed with a well cared for sheen. Apart from the door missing, there was no sign of the gruesome battle that had taken place mere hours ago on the very street that passed in front of this house. She drew up a chair and sat.

"What will you do?" she said to Verdor.

"I will let him within my ring, my coveret."

Lorca blinked at this cold betrayal. Fear stabbed her stomach like blunt knives, she fought a swell of nausea, swallowing bile that burned her throat.

"In? Within our city? I can't allow you to do that. If it is Darkin, then we will all be dead."

Verdor looked down at her hands. Lorca realized that Verdor was struggling to summon the best way to say what would come next.

"It is time, Lorca."

"What time, time to die?"

"How many have survived the battle?" Verdor asked.

"I don't know. But the first count is that there are six or seven thousand giants left."

"Hear me, Lorca, much depends on it. Your kingdom is done here. You had a struggling chance before this battle, but your numbers are too low for you to build again. Your industry is gone. There is a hex on the land that cannot be removed. You have no way of starting over here and there are no other kingdoms that can harbor you."

Lorca was stunned by Verdor's words. She stood and crossed the room, gazing out through a front window at the street. Her eyes contemplated a filthy scene. There were still pieces of flesh in the gutters and drying blood belonging to giant and beast alike. She turned back toward Verdor.

"We made a mistake inviting you to our valley. Perhaps it was a mistake to have joined the Mosaic at all."

"I am sorry, Lorca. It has nothing and everything to do with me. Like your valley, I was an unwitting player in a deadly vendetta."

"You? You were a pawn to Darkin?"

"Yes, certainly to Darkin and perhaps even to Lord Pater Nos. I meditated on this for a long time. Pater Nos has a weakness and Putris Darkin has discovered it. I would even guess that Lord Pater Nos imagined this day would come."

"Pater Nos is Grand Lord of the Mosaic, what weakness could he have that the evil one would know about?"

"Lord Pater Nos loves me."

"Lord Pater Nos loves all."

"It's true what you say, but with me, unlike any of his other apprentices, his love is like that of a father to a daughter. It cannot be explained."

"He should not have chosen you to apprentice. He would have served you better and protected your life and ours if he let one of the others train you. He made a mistake."

"Perhaps, Lorca. I'm sure he thought of that. However, he knew that only he could train me well enough. I was chosen for this. It is a paradox. He chose me to be his weakness and he trained me to be his strength."

"So now you must face this evil wizard on your own and to Nye with the rest of us?"

Lorca knew that her outburst stung. Verdor waited a moment before responding.

"When I was a child, Lord Pater Nos told me that your race was doomed. He said that your people will go the way of the Gauldea in the time of the wolf."

"I do not know of the Gauldea. What happened to them?"

"Like your race, they were undone by inbreeding. A pestilence scourged their land and they passed."

"Is there no chance for us?"

"There may be; there is a place you may go. I will consult with Pater Nos, if I live."

"And if you don't live, then we are at the mercy of a monster. What is your plan to defeat him, Senchai?"

Verdor turned and walked across the floor to the stairwell. She placed one arm on top of the newel, leaning heavily against it.

"I betrayed my love, Thomar, to the evil one," she said quietly. "I arranged for his capture by Putris Darkin"

When she turned back toward Lorca, there was a look of distant wonder in the Senchai's eyes, like the visage of a person awakening in a strange place. Verdor appeared stunned by the very words that she had just confided to Lorca.

"Impossible, a wizard of the Senchai cannot perform an evil deed."

"No, it is not impossible. I created evil to defeat it. It is the only thing that Putris Darkin would never suspect. Or if he does suspect me, as he might, it is the only thing that would bring him close enough to me. The downfall of a Senchai would be a particular delight to him. He could not stay away."

There was hesitation in Verdor's voice. She looked into Lorca's eyes.

"My greatest dread," she continued, "is that the man out there is Putris Darkin, yet I tremble with fear that it isn't. For I will try to take his life. For now, I have lost my innocence and that troubles me. I have betrayed not only my love, but also the Mosaic. Yet, I have little time to consider the consequences."

Lorca saw the pained expression on the wizard's face. She felt sorry for her. What tremendous burdens to bear for one so young.

"So you guessed that if your lover were captured by Darkin, that Darkin would shape-change into Thomar?"

"Not just shape- change, Lorca, but he will become my love. There will now be two Lex Verds. Each will have the same memories, the same experiences. The only difference is that one is evil."

"How could you know that Putris Darkin wouldn't kill Lex Verd immediately?"

"I didn't know. I only knew that his killing my Thomar would do him no good. He could then no longer duplicate him—Darkin's only chance to get near me. I guessed that he would take that opportunity, even if Darkin guessed what I was up to."

"My spirit grieves your pain, Senchai. But I too have troubles. I must consider my own. You are asking me to betray them."

"You need to trust me as you have in the past. I will not speak of it now, but I have heard of a place for all of you. It may be your only chance."

Lorca sat again in the chair. She looked out a window and pulled her fingers through her hair. There was still blood stuck to it that had dried. She began to pick it out. She wanted to scream. She was now speaking of shape-changers, and Pokers, of the soul of evil. She tried to remember if she had ever used the word evil in her life before this week.

"So, it falls to me. If I let him in, we may be destroyed now. But you say that we are a doomed race."

"Yes, Governor, if you stay here."

Lorca lowered her face into the palms of her hands. Her fingers probed her closed eyes. This was an impossible situation. The wall that had saved them had become their prison. Death would come, slowly within or rapidly without, but it would assuredly arrive. Once the grain, the oxen, the water were gone, what would replace them? There was no way to bring in any kind of crop from the scorched earth.

"You didn't know this all along?" she said.

"No, Lorca. I devised this plan only a short time ago. I realized that Putris Darkin wants me. At first, I believed that he was drawn to the valley because of the rape of Hisash by her father. I was mistaken. I believe that Darkin has planned this from the first days of my apprenticeship to Lord Pater Nos. He could do anything if he defeats me. He may even entomb me alive in some deep cave for hundreds of years. It would not be unlike him. He will do this to destroy Lord Pater Nos, then he will do to the other kingdoms what he has done here."

"Why does he hate you so?"

"It's not me. He is hatred. Hatred sustains him. He is also the reason that the Mosaic exists, why Lord Pater Nos exists. The two give choice to the world. If I am destroyed then there will be a very long period of unimaginable terror."

"Can't the other wizards stop him? Is it to you to keep Lord Pater Nos alive?"

"Yes. I must defeat Putris Darkin." Verdor looked down at her hands. "I am a very powerful wizard. I am the only one who has a chance against Putris Darkin. I blush to say that to you, Lorca, but I am convinced that it is the truth."

"But you don't know for sure."

"I am sure only that I am the one"

Lorca sighed deeply. She searched her palms for an answer and finding none there she stared openly into the Senchai's face.

"You're asking me to risk my people's lives without their knowledge."

Verdor walked over to the sitting giant. She placed a hand on Lorca's arm.

"I know this is difficult. There is no time to include them. But if we survive, there may be hope for the Giants."

"Where?"

"Give me time. There might be a place, suitable for all of you. It is a chance."

"But he could be your lover."

"Yes, he may be. I will try, but it might be impossible for me to tell. I will slay the one who enters my ring. I will have little time to ponder the choice. Each moment that we are together, he will be plotting the same for me. So I have decided already what I will do. But even if he is my Thomar, it will not change your chances for survival."

"Can you kill him? The evil one?"

"I can only take his life from him for a while. I will remove his head and trap it in a box and then hide it. But unlike Senchai wizards, he cannot be killed. He is forever."

Lorca drew a deep breath and let it out slowly. The nightmare would not end. Was it only two days ago that Flen had nearly killed her? That seemed trivial now. Yesterday she couldn't have imagined the horrible monsters that had descended on them with their slashing snouts. Their slime was still on her clothing. The city was defiled and blood spattered. Building the wall itself had stretched her hold on reality, but now the landscape outside the barrier they had built made that great sacrifice seem like a minor inconvenience. Yet to be faced was an unfathomable evil knocking to be let in.

"I have another question, Senchai Verdor."

"Ask."

"Even if we go to this other place, we still have the problem of inbreeding. How will going anywhere else answer that?"

"There are no guarantees, Lorca. I can only say that the Mosaic may be able to help you. We will look carefully at your kinship lines. Your records may indicate a way. Perhaps there will be other Giants where you will go. Hope is all I can offer. The alternative is to die here."

Lorca studied the eyes of Verdor for a long time. *What wouldn't I give,* she thought, *for a single breath of fresh air.*

***

The two left the house. Was the fate of the world standing outside of Menshun's wall? The stockade had served its purpose and would fall in the way that all bastions eventually do. The wizard could see the timber barrier's future, skeletal, protruding from wind-blown sand in a sea of desolation, its history long forgotten, a peculiar landmark to nomads and dingoes. But the present held hope. It glimmered like an unsteady candle flame deep within a darkening fog, beckoning them.

The women walked toward it.

Lorca said, "Let's let him in, and may Deddimus help us."

Thirty-Six

THOMAR REBUKED HIMSELF for giving up so easily. What precious time he had wasted. He had taken some comfort in that he was close to the cave mouth, not deep within. Pater Nos would sense him. That could be days away.

He decided to dig, if only to occupy his hands. That was when he fell through the opening of the cave and to freedom. He had smashed Darkin's table and taken one of the legs as a digging tool. He meant to lean against the invisible barrier, find its base, and start his excavation. The barrier was no longer there.

He tossed the table leg aside and left the cave for the bright light of day. He hadn't walked ten steps when he came upon his clothing strewn in pieces over the ground but all there, even his bag. Thomar dressed quickly. He began a steady jog.

What is the meaning of all this? Darkin doesn't give gifts. Thomar guessed he was being used in some fashion. *To trap Verdor? I must get to the city of the Giants.* If only he wasn't too late. The desolation he met over the next rise led him to fear that he was.

Thomar walked into a bizarre world. The greens and grays of the woodland had disappeared. The trees were gone; the air was clear and clean, too sterile. Not so much as a grain of pollen tickled the hairs in his nose. A light powder ash covered the barren ground. It clung to his clothing and billowed up around his feet at each step. Whatever had happened here, nothing had survived. Only the faint smell of smoke lingered. How long had it been like this? He had been unconscious when carried into the cave.

He raced toward the west and the Giants' city of Burba.

Thirty-Seven

"SHE LIES!"

Flen was standing by his chair in the council room, his forefinger pointing straight at Hisash. Her left eye was a swollen black and blue smudge, partially shut. When she spoke, her words were slurred. She had spoken her piece. Flen would now get his turn.

The Governor's council sat around the table in Lorca's home. The complexion of the council table had changed since the battle with the Pokers. Some of the members had been killed. Lorca had appointed delegates to fill their seats until elections could be held. She surveyed the newest members from her head position. All good and true, she was sure. She was especially comforted by Menshun's presence. His leadership would be most welcome in the decisions they would soon face.

Lorca struck the table with her fist.

"We will determine which of you is lying. You will mind your manners in here, Flen. Is that understood?"

"Yes, good Governor, it is. I am set on edge by her words. All of you know me. All of you know that I have sat among you for years, even at this very table. Long before the Lady Hisash."

Hisash had brought a charge of treason against Flen and though the charge had little bearing on the Giants' present plight, according to Clan law such a charge must be addressed immediately. With the recent devastation, the law seemed to be all that was left of their once prosperous society. Lorca, though reluctant to hold the trial now, saw the value of a distraction, a respite of normalcy most beneficial despite its timing.

At the center of the table lay the sphere. If it were once alive as Hisash claimed, now it was dead. It still shone like a glass apple, but the glow that had first caught her attention was gone.

The globe was passed around the council members. Each in turn rolled it in their hands or put it up to their ears before it was returned to the center of the table.

"It glowed, I swear it," Hisash had testified. "And it had a low hum." No one sitting could detect either.

"Just tell your story, Flen. We know who you are."

"Yes, Governor. Then you'll remember that much of my time over the years has been spent at the Library of Tomes. I go there to study my craft so to make me a better, and I hope, a more compassionate executioner. It is there that I study the quaffing of the nog for the condemned and—."

"Get on with it, Flen," Nakus interjected. "We know of your time at the library, though what there is to study about what you do would make a dolt wonder. Were you there before Hisash arrived, like she said? What do you know of the sphere there?"

She was pointing at the sphere. Her contempt for Flen was ill disguised.

Lorca spoke before Flen had a chance to answer.

"Good Nakus, and all of you. This is a truth find, nothing more. It will remain civil, true to our custom and it will be lawful. It is true that we have suffered much, and the charges brought here are serious, but the law is to be respected. Now, continue with your questioning in pleasant order."

"Thank you good Governor." Flen showed Nakus his algae-colored teeth in a broad smile.

Nakus glowered back at him.

"And," he added, "I would say that I hope there are no hard feelings about the Troca, good Governor. I saw my lawful duty clear. You can't fault a man for seeing his lawful duty. Can you now?"

Lorca's stomach twisted suddenly and she felt a moment of revulsion that threatened to make her sick. "Get on with it, Flen."

"Yes, your worship, as I started to say, I was studying in the library, when I heard noises coming from the basement, loud noises, digging noises. Well, I said to myself, what manner of skullduggery is afoot here, which threatens to disrupt my quietude? So I left my chair and went to the basement."

"What did you see there, good Flen?"

"By my troth, I saw nothing at first, it was rare dark down there, it being early morning. Then methinks I saw the glow of a taper, at the far end, soft-like. Well, herself must have heard me coming because the digging sounds had stopped, sudden like. Of course, I didn't know that Hishash was there then, but my curiosity was nagged upon, so, 'I would investigate this,' I spoke plain to myself. I am," Flen cleared his throat, "or was, a member of this board and doesn't it fall to all of us to look out for—."

"Yes, Flen, continue."

"Of course, Governor. Allow me to quaff, if you'd be so kind, for sure my being is in a sorry state. Like all of you, I have just fought my life's struggle at great peril, and now this." He lifted a hand and proffered it toward Hisash as if to sum up the woman and her testimony and the profound shock of these accusations.

"Quaff, then." Lorca, despite her admonition to everyone else, was having difficulty with her own anger.

Flen lifted the goblet. Greedy lips protruded to meet the rim in anticipation of the governor's wine. He drank deeply, all the while his eyes, peering over the arc of the cup, taking everyone in. His eyes rested momentarily on those of Menshun, who regarded Flen with regal contempt. *There will be trouble there,* Flen's instincts warned. Finally he placed the vessel carefully back on the table in front of him and, shifting his feet, he drew a deep breath, belched behind one hand, and began again.

"Well, 'Who's there?' I called out. But no answer. Now I was standing at the foot of the stairs, waiting for my eyes to adjust to the darkness, when I heard a noise over my right ear. Well, I turned my head just in time to see the face of a shovel. I ducked just so, and smack," Flen slapped his hands together, "she hit the handrail post, just missing my head!"

Flen ducked to his haunches to show a demonstration of his position by the stair rail.

"Well, I near jumped loose of my skin. Then up I come with my fist like this and cuffed her a good one." Flen was looking around the table now. "But by my salt, I didn't know it was the Lady Hisash or I wouldn't have hit her. You all know me on that as sure."

He was standing again by his former chair with an apologetic look on his face, hands spread before him.

"What about the sphere, what do you know about that?" Pusah the grainer asked.

"I've never seen it before in my life, by all I hold by. I swear it's true."

Lorca asked, "So you hit Hisash and then what did you do?"

"Well, I bent over her and tried to revive her. The shame was on me for hitting a woman, but I didn't know, like I said. Then I heard the Pokers. They were digging in to the basement. O course, I didn't know they was Pokers, that's sure, but I heard them coming, digging like tunneling rats. And Maree knows how I hate the rats, don't you now, Maree, I speak the truth there on that, so he'll say, eh, Maree?"

Maree, a new face on the board had been quiet up 'til now. He nodded his head in acquiescence. "He hates the rats," he said, then shrugged his shoulders.

"'Tis true. Well, it sounded like the rats were ready to burst through the wall. Ye'll take yourself out of here now, I said. But, I wouldn't leave her down there with the creatures, no, I wouldn't. So I carried her to the second floor and hid her among the shelves there, so I did. She was breathing hearty sure enough."

"Then what did you do? Why didn't you seek help for Hisash?"

"I left the library with a great cloud over me, good governor. The shame of what I did stung me like a scorpion. So I wandered around the streets of Burba trying to think what to do. But like I said, the shame was on me. I beg the good woman's forgiveness. Then there were Pokers everywhere. And you know what happened next. It's glad I am they never found her. Not that I would take credit for her life or such as that, but the truth is what it is, and may I never breathe a joyful breath if I'm lying. It wasn't I who betrayed us as she says."

Hisash looked at her hands. She said nothing.

"The Pokers came to the same basement that you and Hisash had your disagreement in. Any idea why they might have chosen that basement? How do you account for that, good Flen?"

"I don't know, good Governor, but you all remember it was she and only she, the wizard not counting, who had seen the Pokers before. I would offer my humble opinion, that she was in league with them, but its only opinion. I cannot prove it. What I know is what I told you this day. It wasn't me who betrayed us."

"Does anyone else have any questions?"

Lorca looked around the room. Most eyes were still on Flen who stood near his chair, a chair that once represented his office. He was a giant of standing; he had a position of importance. Now he hulked apologetically, winding his hands around each other as if warming them.

"I would ask a question of Flen."

"Of course, good Menshun." Flen's hands stopped moving. His right eyelid began to twitch. He attacked it vigorously with one fist, rubbing it.

"How did you tear your shirt so, good Flen?"

Flen exhaled. He didn't realize that he was holding his breath.

"'Twas the heat of battle, good Menshun, you know how it was, neh?"

"Ai, I do know. And the blood on your jerkin?"

"The same, sir. Untidy out there. Brothers in arms are we now, neh?" Flen was grinning foppishly.

Menshun said nothing. He fixed the standing giant with steel eyes. Despite being on his feet, Flen felt diminished by the sitting Menshun, who was nodding his head now, slowly, thoughtfully. But Flen wasn't sure if he was agreeing that they were brothers in arms or whether Menshun had made up his mind on Flen's testimony.

Flen continued grinning but his eyes sought out the empty cup that stood on the table before him. He wished someone would fill it.

"If there are no other questions, then the two of you," she nodded toward both Hisash and Flen, "will leave us to our deliberations"

The two left the hall by different doors.

"If there is anything any of you wish to say," Lorca directed them, "then say it now. If not, then we will vote on this matter."

Flen had made his case. Well enough at least. According to the law, unless there was unanimous agreement by the board, in the absence of two witnesses, no charge could be supported. The council largely agreed that Flen was lying, but he had salted the lies with enough truth to cast doubt in some minds.

After all, Hisash couldn't account about how she came to wake up on the second floor of the Library of Tomes. They determined that it must have been Flen who carried her there. And though he was a scoundrel, it didn't seem possible that he, or any Giant, could cause such death and destruction to be brought to their valley. It simply defied all logic. No one of them could be that evil, many concluded. No, not possible.

Lorca could afford no more time on the matter. She had earlier left the wizard, Verdor, at the wall, looking down on her Thomar from the heights of the catwalk. What was occurring now between the two of them was three times more important than who had betrayed them. That damage had been done. Mayhap they could forestall any more. Though not satisfied with the outcome, she was content that the hearing was over.

Soon the hall was empty. No council member had thought to collect the sphere from the center of the table. But Flen thought of it. It belonged to him, a gift from his Bobolink. No, it didn't glow now or hum anymore, but it was from her. He made his way back to the hall and sulked in a side vestibule, unnoticed, until he saw a chance to retrieve it. When the Bobolink returned, she may want an accounting of it. He stuffed the orb in his loincloth. While leaving, he was sure that he felt the object vibrate against him.

***

"Will you accompany me then, good Menshun?"

Lorca was leaving the house and had turned back toward the Fiercer. "I would be near the Senchai in case we can assist her."

On their way, Lorca told Menshun what she knew of Verdor's plans. They found Verdor on the wall where the Governor had left her earlier. The Senchai was frowning. She was no longer looking over the ramparts but was sitting on the catwalk in a cross-legged position. Her eyes were closed and it appeared to Lorca that she was lost in thought or meditating. Verdor opened her eyes when the Governor and Menshun approached.

Lorca shrugged her shoulders and opened her hands. She looked at Verdor affecting a "well, have you let him in yet?" look.

"There are two of them out there," Verdor said.

"Two? Two Lex Verds? Now? Outside our wall?"

"Yes, I was about to drop the ring of protection when I received word that there was another stranger at the east wall. I have been waiting on you to return."

"We are here and ready to help you, Senchai," Menshun said.

"Praise to Deddimus that your Thomar is alive."

"Yes Lorca, my heart leapt at the news, but now I have to decide which one is Putris Darkin."

"Unless," Menshun offered, "your wizard is still captive and there are now three. Could Putris Darkin do that?"

"No, Menshun, he can only duplicate what he sees by becoming that which he wishes to copy. One of them is my Thomar."

"What will you do now, and how can we help you?"

Verdor offered her hand and the giant helped her stand. "I will go to my room above the Library. I will send Nakus to tell you to open the wall and let them in. By then I will have dropped the ring. From that moment on all of you will be vulnerable."

"Will they kill each other out there?" Menshun asked.

"It is unlikely. They will place a coveret around themselves. It would seem Putris Darkin has changed the game he wants to play. He must have released my Thomar, knowing that he would immediately come to my aid. He must be enjoying this gambit."

Verdor was approaching the steep ladder that would take her down from the heights of the wall. "When I send Nakus, the two of you will escort both of them to my room. It has two doors, bring one to each. There you will leave us alone. Do not speak to either of them. Keep them apart so they cannot speak to each other."

Verdor silently descended to the ground. The other two followed.

"One of them is a killer." Menshun said.

"He is. But you needn't worry unless I fail. He will not kill until he captures me first. I will choose the moment, good Menshun. Until then, I too will have a protection."

"Shouldn't we at least bind them?"

"No, there's nothing to be done except what I have already asked you to do."

***

Verdor looked at the two of them, touched by their concern for her, but they could not know the power they would soon have within their city. She turned to leave them.

"Senchai."

Verdor wheeled around to see the Governor standing resolutely. Tears were brimming in her eyes.

"Yes, Lorca?"

"I would know you better."

"And I, you," Verdor responded, nodding in affirmation.

Again, Verdor turned toward her room. The streets were still very busy with cleaners and what Verdor considered their pointless work. None of them would be here for much longer. But it was work. She envied them the comfort they took in it. Their labor helped them put one foot in front of the other, a welcomed purpose, despite its gruesome scope. Each task was done to perfection before the next was started. It seemed that they couldn't allow themselves to think of what they would do when the work stopped.

Verdor had her work to do also. The next hour was already written. Now it became a matter of finishing it. She would do what she had planned.

"Mother Earth, guide me," she prayed quietly.

She thought of her father, Jordan, and how he had taught her to kill the deerfly when she was a child. She could still see him carrying the unsuspecting insect down from the top of his head, giving it a ride on the back of one hand before the other hand killed it in less than an eye blink's time.

"You can't always reason with the one who will harm you," he had told her.

The sky was a deep blue overhead and the sun was warm. A beautiful day. How absurd, it seemed, to be about such work on this day. It should be raining and cold.

The room in which Verdor was staying was larger than a typical giant's bedroom. Meant for the caretaker, it constituted the entire second floor of the library, in part, a home as well as storage for the overflow books and documents from the Library of Tomes. The bulk of what was stored here was the Giants' records of kinship, among other things. The stairs up to the second floor ended at a long hallway. Her bedroom had two doorways so if the need arose, it could be further divided.

The interior had never been finished, the ceiling joists exposed to rafters that slanted to a peak above the room's centerline. Fresh air found its way in at the two vents high up to the gable peaks. A woven screen made from finely cut ash strips kept out the birds and bats, but some mud daubers had found their way through and constructed earthen nests down along the side of a few rafters.

The room was comfortable, but Verdor felt foreign here and had slept outside under the familiar stars at least as many times as she had slept in the large four-post bed. A downy tick mattress covered the bed topped by linen sheets which, she was sure, Lorca had donated to her. The trunk she had requested, with the brass hasp and hinge straps, had been placed at the foot of the bed.

Verdor pulled the sword out from under the mattress. Though old, the weapon was free of rust and very sharp. Verdor pushed it back in place, leaving only the knob of its handle exposed. The trunk lid was opened and rested against the bed. There was nothing more to do but wait. And remember.

***

"Why didn't you kill him, Lord Pater Nos?" she had asked her master when still a small child.

"He cannot be killed, Belinda. Evil is eternal."

"Then what are we to do against him?"

"There is only one thing that can be done, and it is for you and me to be steadfast in the way of the Senchai. You are a warrior for the Good."

"Then why is it that we can be killed and not him?"

"Come here, child."

Belinda went to him and he helped her into his lap. She studied his grizzled face and waited for him to speak. In Pater Nos' lap, she felt safe. He always smoothed her wrinkled brow with patient answers spoken so lovingly and with such certainty that her cares would disappear.

"Everyone meets Putris Darkin at some time in their lives," he said.

"Everyone?"

"Yes, child."

"Even those who aren't wizards?"

"Yes."

"Aren't they afraid of him? I would be so afraid. I would run and hide under my bed until he went away."

Pater Nos chuckled. "Putris Darkin is not always scary. Sometimes he may be quite beautiful. He may look like someone you love or something you desire."

Belinda considered Pater Nos' answer. "He's tricky," she said. She had heard Pater Nos use this word once when they came upon an opossum lying in their path. It appeared dead. Pater Nos told her that it only pretended to be dead until the danger passed. 'Tricky,' he had said about the long-tailed animal.

"Very tricky. So you must be prepared always."

"What do you do to be prepared? I will do the same."

"I just take a few moments each day to say that I am worthy and good just the way I am and that my life is a gift that is meant to be given and not hoarded to myself."

"I don't understand." she said.

"Soon you will."

"But am I worthy? Am I good?"

"You are most worthy, and very, very, very, good." Pater Nos hugged her to him harder each time he said very.

"Do the others know how to be prepared, or just us?"

"Very many know. Some never learn."

Belinda felt better. "Still, it doesn't seem fair that he can kill us and we cannot kill him."

"I will tell you a secret." He had her rapt attention now. Belinda loved Pater Nos' secrets. He whispered in her ear. "He cannot be killed, but he can be captured."

"How?"

"In time you will know, child. You can't be a wizard overnight, as bright as you are."

She had forgotten their little secret for years until she came upon a passage in one of Pater Nos' obscure texts she'd found while snooping in his private library.

Darkin's fear, is Darkin's scare.
Darkness is his resting lair.
The bite of steel
Removes the head
Quickly now, he is not dead.
Close him deep

Close him fast.
Then pray your children's peace will last.

***

The fall of footsteps on stairs snapped Verdor back to the present. She sat at the edge of the bed, her feet just touching the floor. She could face both doors to the bedroom without turning her head from either. Her stomach churned. Her pulse quickened. She raised her eyes to the open rafters and concentrated on subduing the panic that welled within.

The lock of hair. She had given it to Thomar. She had placed a spell on it so that only he could see it. It would be in his possession. Would Darkin see it? Was his magic strong enough to overcome her spell?

The commotion in the hall stopped. The two Lex Verds stood, one at each door. Verdor noted the aura of protection with which they had covered themselves. The air around them shimmered like dry heat.

"Put your bags into the doorway," she commanded them.

She would not look into their eyes.

The two removed the straps from their shoulders and, dropping their bags to the floor, pushed them toward her with a foot. Verdor regarded each bag for a moment, then standing, walked over to them and, careful not to mix them up, dragged them back to the bed. She sat down and placed one of them on her lap. From the bag that came from the door on her right, she found her lock of hair. She did not remove it or even pull it over the lip of Thomar's bag, where it could be seen.

Her pulse pounded in her temples. She could feel and hear the thumping of her heart. She must control her breathing, her being. *I have been trained for this. I will not fail.* She couldn't let the evil one guess how much she wanted to shout for joy. But she dared not think even of happiness. It might show in her bearing, or show even in the movement of her hand, quicker perhaps, or slower. Anything could give her intentions away. The blinking of her eyes must remain steady and even.

"There will be times when you must secret your emotions," Pater Nos had told her. "When you are fearful or in deep stress, or even joyful, the hardest of all emotions to contain, you must die within. Separate your being from your intentions. You can't allow even the pupils of your eyes to change. Your survival may depend on it."

Verdor still had the other bag to look into. Had Putris Darkin discovered her ploy? Suddenly it seemed amateurish, like something a first year apprentice might try.

"The best hidden is sometimes the most obvious," Lord Pater Nos had taught her. She hoped that it were true now.

The second bag also contained her lock of hair. Identical to the first. He had discovered her. Her spirit dropped like the knife of the guillotine, sudden and with the same decisive despair.

She raised her eyes to the two figures at the doors. They stood there, hands at their sides. In their eyes she saw a pleading, a kindness, an emotional love that attached itself to her heart and drew her equally to both. No evil showed in either of them.

The game was over. There was no more use in pretense. It would do no good to even guess. Depending on how Darkin reacted, she might not know for years if she had guessed correctly. Now or in time, at his whim, he could take her, or infiltrate the Mosaic school. With her captured, he could destroy at his leisure. She had no choice but to kill them both.

Tears welled up in her eyes. Could this be all of it? Could this be the culmination of her training? To kill her lover only to capture the evil Putris Darkin? How long could he be held? He would again be free, some day, perhaps next year, or in a hundred years. She was sure that he would have an escape plan if this trial didn't go his way. He would cover all avenues. The heart of evil could not be underestimated.

"Don't say anything," she commanded.

She walked over to them each in turn, searching for any spark of truth.

"I understand."

Their lips did not move but their message came into her, probing her mind. "I understand," they both said as if sympathizing with her dilemma. The real Thomar would think that. She loved him for it. How the imposter must be enjoying this. Twice more she confronted them, staring up into gentle blue eyes. Suddenly, she knew exactly which one was her lover. The knowledge almost buckled her knees. But she was able to maintain her balance or at least disguise her lapse with an abrupt turn toward the bed.

Sitting where she could easily draw the sword, she folded her arms briefly closed her eyes as if praying for guidance. She could not betray her new confidence, her knowledge. She let the tears of her agony flow like before.

"Each of you will kiss me," she said. "It is my last hope and then I will face my destiny. When I point to one of you, he will enter this room unprotected; we will be equally vulnerable. After the kiss he will return to his place outside the room. This, I have ordained, will be the trial. There will be no other." Tears soaked her cheeks and wet the front of her cloak. She pointed first to her lover, Thomar. Her finger trembled.

Without hesitation, Thomar sprang into the room.

***

Putris Darkin watched casually from the other door. He calculated his situation behind blue eyes. *If she chooses her Thomar, there is nothing they could do to us,* he thought. *We are protected and they would both be vulnerable. We could attack now, perhaps take both of them. How would you feel about that, Pater Nos? But what if she eschews her Thomar for us?* The thought of that possibility stayed his hand. He was rewarded and stunned by what he saw next.

Verdor had pointed to her Thomar and he had quickly entered the room like a goat in heat. He crossed the room in four or five quick strides, arms open. The face he presented to her was rapture. She was coming to her feet from her position against the bed. Thomar never saw her extract the blade from below the mattress. In a flash of steel, the room was sprayed in blood. Thomar's head flew toward Verdor, separated from his body. His last word was "Belinda."

His body crumpled at her feet. His heart, unaware of his death, still pumped blood, which pooled quickly about Verdor. The front of her cloak glistened with it. Her face was a mask of red, matted hair and crimson gore.

Darkin watched her catch the head in her free arm and pin it to her chest momentarily, then drop it into the chest at the foot of the bed. She slammed the lid shut and stood, turning toward him.

"Thomar!" she screamed, "Hold me!" She looked as if she would drop to the floor.

Darkin bounded into the room. He had won. His reign had begun with the help of this fool wizard. He ran to her. He would hold her. He would rape her and put her in a box and then bury her alive. *I have beaten you, Pater Nos. Soon you will feel my delight at your torment.* He reached for her.

***

Unlike Thomar, Darkin did see the flash of her sword. His head, like that of the unfortunate Thomar also seemed to spring from his body. A coal-black viscous goo oozed from the headless neck. She held his head by its hair and turned him to face away from her. He saw his body topple over and heard it crumple on the floor.

Quickly she dropped the head into the open trunk. In that second, before she closed the lid, if he had acted, he could have saved himself. But that precious second was used up in confusion. What happened to Thomar's blood? Darkin's arrogance would not allow him to grasp his defeat. He had to ponder why there was only one head in the trunk, his. He needed to recount the seconds before he entered her room to see when, exactly, she opened the trap.

As he heard the clasps fasten the dull click of his fate, he realized that he had fallen for a simple ruse. *Fantechtuhea, a seperation!*

The abject simplicity of it threatened to explode his evil brain with self-loathing.

Sometime in the future, when Putris Darkin's mind would clear, maybe because of the interminable monotony of staring at blackness, when it wouldn't matter if his eyes were open or not, he would recall the sphere, his crystal globe he had given to that idiot Flen. When he did arrive at that point of clarity, he would take a modicum of comfort in knowing that no matter where they put him, no matter how deep the cave or how dark the forest, that globe would lead Flen to him. If not Flen, then someone, sometime, would find him. But those thoughts hadn't occurred to him yet. Now all that he could do was to control his eyes and his mouth. He closed the one and opened the other.

His rage burst in a soundless howl of raw hatred that echoed hollowly within the coffin.

Thirty-Eight

THOMAR HELD BELINDA against him. *She is alive! Alive!* he kept repeating in his thoughts. He pulled away from her briefly to confirm with his eyes what his arms told him was true. He breathed deeply the scent of her.

She smiled at him. "Thomar, Thomar, you must let me breathe."

The two sat next to each other on the bed. The torso of Putris Darkin lay on the floor and was already beginning to smell. The black, oozing, tar-like fluid formed a small puddle beneath his corpse.

Verdor's sword also lay on the floor. The chest, with Putris Darkin's head in it, sat benignly against the foot of the bed. Seeing it there, no one could ever guess the horror within.

"We should be rid of that," Thomar said.

Verdor waved her hand over the corpse of Putris Darkin. It blurred momentarily and then vanished. The locked chest remained.

"We need to talk about this," Thomar said. "It was you who took my 'Cept, then." His staff leaned against the wall at the head of the bed next to Verdor's. He was glad to see it again, but he ignored it for now. He traced his fingers on the glittering tiny star that adorned Verdor's ear, admiring its beauty. How well it complemented the perfectly delicate curve of her earlobe.

"It's very beautiful, " he said. "When did you put it there?"

"The jewel is agift from the Fairy Queen," she said. "It's what saved your life."

Thomar tilted his head, questioning her without words.

"I almost missed it at first," Verdor continued.

The wonder of what had happened still showed in her distant look, as if she were dreaming with her eyes open.

"When I couldn't decide which of you was Putris Darkin, I could only walk back and forth in front of both of you. I was terrified, Thomar, desperate to find some glimmer of truth in your eyes. I was so occupied with my sorrow at not being able to that I almost didn't feel the warmth from it."

"It became warm?"

"Only when I neared you. When I came close to Putris Darkin, it became cool. It is how I knew. Its power was so startling that I nearly fell to my knees. It's almost like the Fairy Queen knew ahead of time the dilemma I would face, even before I planned it."

Thomar looked at her. She was more beautiful than ever, he thought, but different. The nagging anger pushed its way into his belly uninvited. She said nothing for a while, but met his gaze openly.

"I love you," she finally said.

"I know that you do, Belinda, its just that..."

He was ashamed of himself. He wished he could be a stalwart Senchai and admit to himself that she did what she had to do.

"Just that I betrayed you?" Verdor finished his thought

"Yes," he looked down at his hands, "and..."

"That you could never do that to me, could you, my love?"

Thomar thought about it for a long moment. He stood and walked away from the bed over to the window where he looked out, seeing only his dark thoughts.

"No," he said. "I would never have placed you in such danger. You have broken my trust, but not only that, you have broken our code. Where would we be, any of us, if we played so loosely with each other's safety? You left me vulnerable, Belinda, vulnerable to death."

Verdor came to her feet and quickly walked to the window and stood near Thomar.

"Look at me, Thomar."

Thomar turned to face her but his eyes refused to rise from their study of the floor.

"I didn't ask for this problem. I didn't expect to be fighting for the life of the world on my first assignment. Look at me!" Her voice was higher now, louder. Tears were brimming, threatening to spill over. She bit down on her quivering lip. Thomar's gaze shifted warily upward until he was looking at her face.

"Why do you think Lord Pater Nos sent me here?"

"A Senchai was requested," Thomar answered. "He could have sent any of us."

"True, he might have sent you. But why did he send me?"

"I cannot say." Thomar's face was sullen. His eyes fidgeted between the floor and Verdor's chin, only occasionally meeting her angry gaze.

"I came here thinking this was a problem of kinship, or drought or fertility, basic problems that any of the kingdoms might have. But all these things weren't how they first appeared, and I believe Lord Pater Nos suspected such."

"Pater Nos? He would be the last to send you into the arms of Putris Darkin."

"Listen to me, Thomar. He knew what he could never tell me. That Darkin was waiting for me no matter where Pater Nos sent me. Pater Nos knew that, Thomar, don't you see that?"

"That makes no sense. Pater Nos loves you like you were his own flesh."

"That is exactly why, no matter where he sent me, that unless he trained me only to keep me safe within the walls of the Mosaic, that Darkin would be waiting to capture me, yes, even on my first assignment. Pater Nos knew this could happen. Perhaps not here, but somewhere. Don't you see, Thomar? I was Pater Nos' vulnerability. His love for me might be his undoing. But he had to risk me. Now, Thomar, how do you think I felt once I realized that the one I knew and loved as my father, could use me so?"

"He didn't betray you, Belinda. He sent you on a mission like he would send anyone."

"Oh Thomar, you don't see it, do you? Why do you think that he didn't let Master Singh train me, or one of the others?"

Thomar made no response.

"Lord Pater Nos saw something in me. He trained me personally because he wanted to give me my best chance against an evil that he knew would someday exact revenge on him. Thomar, without ever saying it, Pater Nos taught me that codes and rules are only ideals. They are tools like our staffs or our potions. They can be bartered and broken. In the end, evil must lose."

Thomar brought one hand to his face and stroked the fine stubble of his unshaven face. He saw the difference in her now, the difference between them. He would have adhered rigidly to a high moral reason if put in her situation and would not have been creative enough to set these things aside. He had lived by honor; it would limit him.

Verdor reached toward him and took his other hand. She drew a deep breath and began again.

"When I first crossed the Mohrs into this Valley, Thomar, I smelled an odor that I had never smelled before. It turned out to be Pokers. But I had no way of knowing that. So though the smell bothered me, I set it aside for a while. I stayed busy studying the tomes at the Library, looking at the Giant's marriages and births. I was not sure what I was looking for. Everything seemed to be as I expected. There was no evident reason why the Giants and their oxen were suffering the way they were. There have been no live births here in almost two years. Nothing made any sense. During my investigation, I became aware of a law called the Troca, which would have unsettled the Government."

Thomar frowned, but Verdor continued.

"The Troca is an ancient law whereby anyone can challenge the governor's position to death by combat. The Troca was forgotten about until the governor's assistant, Hisash, discovered it. It was she who, at first, pressed the old law for reasons I won't talk about now.

"By then I was thinking that the Valley was under some kind of attack. I felt the Giants to be in immediate danger and told the governor so. This was no time for internal bickering. I visited Hisash. She and Flen, the kingdom's executioner conspired together. I expected to talk Hisash and Flen out of their plans. At the house of Hisash I met a Poker."

"Why would a Poker go to her house?"

"The Poker claimed to have been invited by the evil that happened there."

"Evil?"

"Yes, it seemed believable. Her father often raped Hisash when she was still young. Hisash killed him and hid his body. No one ever knew that he was murdered. However, what the Poker said was a lie. I was the reason for its presence. Seeing the Poker confirmed my suspicion of an evil being in the Valley. Who else could it be but Putris Darkin? He poisoned the air so that the women and oxen would become infertile, a problem that would bring a Senchai wizard. Darkin was nearby, I could feel his presence. I was in fear for this Kingdom. I placed protection around the city. But still the Pokers invaded us. There was a great slaughter, with death on both sides. But as you see, we prevailed."

Thomar could imagine the energy she had spent protecting an entire city of this size, against the onslaught of Putris Darkin, and to heal the wounded besides. His anger began to diminish. *How very tired she must be now,* he thought. He could see that she was shaken in the telling of it.

"Stop," he said, "You need not explain to me."

"What I need is to protect our love, Thomar, please let me finish." She paused again for a deep breath, and continued.

"There was little chance that Darkin could get near me, nor I near him. I had to make him vulnerable, somehow, and that is when I thought to involve you, Thomar. Our love is no secret to the world. I guessed that he knew about us. I guessed that you would be captured and that he would duplicate you to get within my circle. That is why I sent the lock of hair. I placed a spell on it so only you could see it. But that worked against me."

"How could you be sure that he wouldn't arrive without me?"

"I was surprised that the two of you came. I expected only him. The one hope I held on to was that you would be worth more to him alive and so you would be safe. If I prevailed, I would come and find you. If I failed, then neither you nor I, nor the Mosaic would matter anymore. Yes, Thomar, I gambled with your life, but I also gambled with my own. Forgive me, Thomar, it was the hardest…"

Her voice broke off. Tears ran freely down her cheeks. She swallowed twice, squeezing her eyelids shut.

"The fairies were watching the cave where Darkin kept you prisoner. I did not abandon you entirely, Thomar."

Her words came faster now; in earnest, as if she must finish soon or her courage would fail her altogether.

Saying nothing, Thomar pulled her toward the bed and the two sat once again on the edge of the mattress. He would not interrupt her again, afraid that if she stopped something would break inside her.

"His plan was simple, I thought." She was speaking now of Putris Darkin. "He would duplicate you and come to capture me. He would use me to torture Lord Pater Nos. His motive was pure revenge. Revenge to him was like strong wine. In the end it fouled his judgment. He thought he had won. His arrogance wouldn't let him believe anything else."

Verdor was squeezing Thomar's arm; her eyes and cheeks were wet. "I knew that I couldn't be captured, no matter the cost. Not for me, but for the sake of what is good. Sending for you and making you weak was the only thing that I could think of that would put Darkin out in the open. Thomar," her voice quivered, "I sent for you in the same way and with the same sorrow that Pater Nos sent me out here. My fear was almost unbearable. Lord Pater Nos had no choice. I had no choice."

Still she continued, telling him of her first meeting with the Poker, of her inability to stop Flen from challenging Lorca and how Lorca almost died then. She told him about the horrible war with the Pokers and how so many good Giants had been killed. She described Menshun and the wall built on faith by his Fiercers. Her grief at the destruction of their industry by Darkin's firestorm was complete. She told him of her plan to ask Lord Pater Nos for his help in moving the Giants to a place where they could start over. She left nothing out, the hope, joy, despair and doubt. Then she stopped.

She was staring at Thomar's face as if her eyes were fingers. With them she touched every tiny wrinkle, every line. She probed the blueness of his eyes, the fullness of his lips, as if to coax from his face understanding, if not forgiveness.

"I admire you, Belinda," Thomar said finally. "I am ashamed to confess that the wizard that I am tells me you did exactly the right thing. But the man that I am is very deeply hurt."

"Did he hurt you? Did Darkin hurt you?"

"A trifle. I found it harder to reconcile the abandonment, the loss of trust. I felt so lost."

"Sometimes I feel lost now too, Thomar. I have become calculating. I had to do evil to fight evil. It is difficult to admit that. My acts must seem treacherous and I grieve what they have done to my soul as much as to you. But Thomar, by my oath, I would do the same again. Darkin had to be stopped. Everything we have done, everything Lord Pater Nos has done, would have been destroyed. Please trust me when I tell you that I will always love you."

Thomar looked steadily into Verdor's face now. "I need time to think about things, Belinda. You are a far better wizard than I am. I'm not jealous of that, in fact, I rejoice in it. It's the first time that I have had to confront my weaknesses." He kissed her lightly on her lips.

"But you are still innocent," she said. "I would rather your innocence. It is true that I have trapped Putris Darkin, but I have also trapped myself. I, too, will need time to heal from this."

"You are so very strong, Belinda."

"That was mostly fear and resignation, Thomar. There was no way to fool Darkin except to do the unthinkable. Even then he discovered my plan. I expect that he was playing along to see how, or if, it would turn to his advantage."

Belinda would say no more on the matter.

The humming of a mud dauber somewhere in the rafters gave the only sound to the room. For a time, nearness was enough. The two fell against each other. Thomar began to realize what he had always been taught. Being a wizard of the Mosaic was not about him or Verdor, but about fighting evil. Verdor was helping him understand that. He would need some time, he knew, time to find stillness and harmony again. But that would come.

Verdor pulled away from him. "We still have work to do," she said, "and there are some friends I would like you to meet."

Verdor stood and called out to the room. "Mona!"

Mona was on a windowsill toward the back of the house. Thomar never saw her arrive, she simply appeared.

"Thomar," Verdor said, "this is Mona of the fairies. Mona, this is my love, Thomar."

Thomar bowed his head. The little creature fascinated him. He always knew that Verdor had communion with the fairies, that was a part of her that he had never seen until now.

"Ah," Thomar smiled broadly, "you must be the Fairy Queen."

Mona was folding her wings. She smiled up at Thomar.

"No Thomar," Verdor interjected, "Mona is not the queen, but the King and Queen sent her to help me."

Thomar was still smiling. He thought about what had recently happened, but all he could remember, and none too clearly, was seeing himself moving quickly into the room while he was still standing at the door. He had watched his evil double, Putris Darkin, watching him also, when he moved toward Verdor. It is a spell, he quickly realized. He saw himself beheaded by Verdor, saw the blood, and then his love call out to the wrong Thomar.

And so he observed from the doorway as events took their course, ending with Putris Darkin's head locked within the trunk.

How easily Darkin was fooled after all, he thought. Yet another lesson taught at the Mosaic: the avaricious are easily beguiled.

"My eternal gratitude to you, Mona, and to your Queen. I must allow that I am still awestruck about what just happened, or how you helped."

Mona bowed. "I can only express the joy of the King and Queen, and of all the Fairy Kingdom, at your love for the Savior." When she said Savior she looked at Verdor. "We have watched you for a long time, Thomar. We find you suitable for her."

"We," the term Putris Darkin used when referring to himself.

"Savior?" Thomar glanced at Verdor. She didn't notice and was still watching Mona. When he looked back at Mona he understood what "we" meant this time.

The floorboards were set alive in a wave of motion. The light from the window began to shimmer and in seconds the floor was covered with thousands of fairies. Many took to flight and were tittering about his head, flying close, touching him gently. Their tinkling voices reminded Thomar of crystalline wind chimes, but he could understand nothing of their language. Some of the fairies were sitting in Verdor's tresses. In their colorful clothing they looked to Thomar like a loosely contrived wreath of living flowers.

Mona said, "We are here to complete your request, Savior. The trunk is ready?"

"Yes, Mona. It must be well hidden. Can you carry it?"

"Of course. And where we hide it, it will stay hidden. My wings on that promise."

With that she raised her hands, unfolded her wings and then flew up from the windowsill. "Blessings on you, Thomar," she said with a smile. Mona left through the open window without a backward glance.

The other fairies swarmed around the box like honeybees on comb. They produced silken strings, no bigger around than spider webs and began to encase the chest with them. Each fairy tied an individual harness to it until the box disappeared, appearing now to be the silken cocoon of a giant moth. When this was done they simply raised it from the floor and flew it out the window unseen by anyone below, and only minutes behind Mona.

"You must meet the Giants," Verdor said to Thomar when all the fairies were gone.

They gathered their staffs. Then, hand in hand, the two passed through the bedroom door, down the stairs and outside to where Lorca and Menshun were waiting.

"The name Savior suits you, Belinda," Thomar remarked on their way down the stairs.

Verdor's face flushed. "Their love for me blinds them to my faults," she said.

"That, my dear… " Thomar raised an index finger, the gesture a parody of Pater Nos when he was instructing them as children and Belinda smiled, "…is a frailty of love, for which I have reason to be truly grateful."

Thirty-Nine

VERDOR AND THOMAR LEFT the Library she had called home. Governor Lorca and Menshun were waiting for them. The reassuring smile of Verdor told the Giants that what they had desperately awaited was good news.

After the introductions, Lorca sent a youngster running to find Nakus at the governor's house. "Tell her to expect two more guests for midday repast. Tell her only the very best of our wine and the best of what she can find in the pantry will do."

The four of them walked the cobbled streets of Burba toward the governor's house with Thomar and Verdor just behind the two Giants. Thomar's attention had shifted to his stomach. Lorca overheard him tell Verdor that he had not eaten in three days, and that the promise of imminent food was welcome. "My appetite," he said, "will do well among this race. It's a giant one." Verdor chuckled.

Despite the grim circumstances surrounding them, Lorca smiled at their joviality. It had been too long since these streets had heard the sound of laughter. Lorca liked Thomar. Verdor looked happy in his presence, though there was no denying that she was tired. It had been an ordeal for her that would have sapped ten Fiercers. How remarkable that Verdor had borne the burden alone. And yet her job wasn't done.

There is the problem of what is to be done with us. We have food and water in store to last a half-year. Something will have to be done soon if we are to move before winter. It will take planning. More trials to come, she thought, but they will wait a few hours. Lorca was elated and curious about how Verdor had defeated Putris Darkin, but she would not trouble her with questions now.

A pigeon had arrived from the Mosaic while they were fearfully awaiting Verdor's outcome with Putris Darkin. She would say nothing of that now. There would be time for that after bellies were full and hearts were rested. There was one thing though, that needed Verdor's attention, Hisash's eye. But Lorca had no doubt that Verdor would tend to that straightaway. So what could the tidings be from Lord Pater Nos? It must be good news.

She glanced at Menshun who quietly walked beside her. He seemed to be enjoying the gaiety of the two behind them. But he said nothing.

The streets were clean again. *We will leave this city in good shape.* She was thankful that the Giants were such good and industrious people. Lorca was pleased to be their leader. *But yes,* she hoped, again thinking of the pigeon, *everyone of us could use some good news.*

Forty

THE MESSAGE BROUGHT by pigeon from the Mosaic, was historic news. A Vertex, a meeting of wizards, it said, would be held in the Valley of the Giants. Such a gathering of power, Lorca was told, had never before been assembled outside the Mosaic School. Pater Nos was, the message said, on his way to the Valley with his apprentice, Gendau, Master Singh and his apprentice, a young girl named Ruta and a large number of wizards.

"Andera?"

"Yes Lorca," Verdor said. "Andera is what Pater Nos calls it."

"And no one has ever been there and returned?"

"None that we know of."

Lorca shifted in her seat at the head of the conference table. Her gaze roamed around its gleaming surface, taking in all of her council. Her concern about their future as a race was renewed. Since the war with the Pokers, and the destruction wrought by Putris Darkin she had never felt so powerless. Relinquishing such control to the wizard Verdor, even though she trusted her, was troubling to a woman used to leading. But isn't that what she had done since these troubles started? The battle with the Pokers, more horrible than she could have ever imagined, was, in ways unaccounted for 'til now, a relief. The Giants were doing something about their survival. Fighting. Now the surrender of their future would be complete if they followed Verdor's plan. The uncertainty was staggering.

"What do you think, Menshun?"

Everyone turned to hear Menshun's opinion. He had been listening in his customary silence. Now he scratched his chin with a callused hand.

"I am one who considered only what he can see, touch, smell or taste. In all my years, I have never given one thought to any of the mysteries that all of us now accept and with no more question than we would question the setting sun. In the last week, creatures that were once only fables or children's stories have invaded us.

"Now we have a different knowledge. Many of our friends are dead. All of us would be dead if it were not for The Senchai." His eyes shifted to where Verdor sat diagonally across from him. Verdor returned his gaze comfortably. Lorca thought that she looked rested today. Quite a change from yesterday when after their midday repast, she had collapsed at the dining table and was carried to bed by the Senchai, Lex Verd.

"There is no difference now," Menshun continued. "Our lives are still in her hands. But, you asked me my opinion. Then I say that we trust her as we have. What choice do we have in any case?"

Several of the Giants were nodding. Hisash spoke.

"I don't understand. Where is this place? Will there be forests? If no one has ever been there, how does anyone guess what might be there?"

Verdor spoke. "Lord Pater Nos has seen glimpses of it. He has his ways. And yes, there will be Forests and a river, one that you can name. It is similar to what this valley used to be, only there will be no desolation or poisoned air. You will have a chance to reestablish yourselves as the proud race you once were."

Hisash didn't look convinced. "But where is it?" she demanded. Lex Verd answered her.

"Good Hisash, if there was a road to Andera, which there is none yet, it would take you about thirty days travel by ox cart. Think of Andera as a reflection of this valley at the edge of all the kingdoms."

Thomar had her attention now.

"What is it that you see when you look into a pool of water or on the surface of a quiet eddy of the Grune?" he asked.

Hisash took a moment to consider his question. "If the water is clear, I see the bottom. I see stones or fallen leaves. I see sticks fallen in or washed down from someplace else."

"Surely you have looked into the water to comb your beautiful hair?"

Lex Verd's smile was disarming. Hisash, noticeably warmed by it, appeared to relax. She answered him quietly. "Yes, Senchai Verd, that is my reflection."

"True," Verd said. "Andera can be called the reflection of this valley. Your reflection is always present, even when there is no place to see it, like the pool you look into while you comb your hair."

The other giants at the table were rapt, listening to the new Senchai. He spoke with such authority in a voice like music. Lorca guessed that their best storytellers would be envious of his skill. Most now sitting at the table seemed convinced that no more need be said.

"Good Senchai," Nakus said, "I, too, comb my beautiful hair in the pools of the Grune," Here, everyone laughed at the chunky Nakus who was pulling at the mop of gnarled red curls tangled about her head. "If I should go to Andera, would I have a refection there also?"

"Yes Nakus," Lex Verd was grinning, "you will have a refection in Andera."

Nakus shrugged. "I will go there," she said with no more concern than if she were selecting mushrooms at market.

"And before you do, good Nakus," Lex Verd added, "with your permission, I will fix your hair so to make your new reflection jealous of your beauty."

Again, there was laughter. Lorca brought them back to the seriousness of the moment.

"Can we get there without death or harm?" she asked.

"We of the Mosaic School believe that you will go there as if waking from sleep. You will not remember traveling."

"What of our dead? What do we tell the orphaned children about their parents who lie buried here?"

"The dead will go with you. Their graves will be placed outside the city which we will also move. Andera is not a place without grief or sorrow. Those things will be the same. The loved ones will be mourned and missed."

"Will you come with us, Senchai Verdor?" Lorca asked.

"Not now, but someday soon. Lord Pater Nos has found a trade route, but it must be cleared. A road must be built."

"There is no chance that we can stay here?"

"If you could, we would use our power to fix your valley, but the curse lies deep and cannot be uprooted."

"Why do you help us so?"

"It is because of your circumstances, not the least of which is your demise if you should stay here. Because of your size, there is no other kingdom that can take you in. What happened here was not your fault. You were pawns in Darkin's revenge against Lord Pater Nos. The Mosaic owes you this. You need a kingdom of your own. Pater Nos has found one for you."

The discussion went on all afternoon and well into the evening. Questions were asked and patiently answered. Supper was called for and served at the Council table. Later, when the sun tilted toward the mountaintops that bordered their desolate valley, Lorca's council voted. All were in favor and agreed to leave the decision to the choice of every individual in the kingdom.

Lorca accompanied Verdor while she said her goodbyes. Verdor thanked Menshun for his help. Menshun was about to turn away but he suddenly reached out and touched the Senchai's cheek with a thick finger. He grunted, obviously embarrassed at his own forwardness, and abruptly withdrew his hand. He nodded his head once as if trying to shake a tear or a drop of sweat from the end of his nose. He turned and walked toward his home and family.

Would that there be trees in Andera, Lorca wished, *forests full of them.* She hoped the trees would be unruly with branches sprouting from massive trunks every which way and in sore need of the discipline from Menshun's axe. *He needs very hard work,* she thought.

Like Menshun, Hisash also could find no words for goodbye, but her eyes confirmed deep gratitude, eyes that bore no trace of the damage inflicted just days ago by Flen's fist.

"I expect that you will be governor some day, Hisash," Verdor said. Hisash stood biting her lip or pursing them tightly until Verdor moved on to Nakus.

Verdor hugged the oversized frame of Nakus, careful not to disturb Nakus' new hairdo, a gift from Lex Verd, which she flaunted regally in front of the other women. Nakus pressed a small loaf of oat bread into Verdor's hand, still warm from the oven. "For your journey back," she said. "And there will be no need to share with your man there, I've taken care of him." Nakus smiled at Senchai Lex Verd.

Indeed, she had taken care of him, Lorca noticed. Thomar's carrying bag showed the the outline of not only a loaf, but also of a plump sausage that bulged against the leather confines of his bag, the end protruding out the opening.

"Now be off with you," Nakus scolded. "It isn't seemly for a woman of my stature to be crying like an undone maiden." Her hand smoothed the side of her new coif. "And good on you as you go." She abruptly showed Verdor her back and, clutching her ever present apron in front of her, strode toward the Governor's house and what Lorca knew would be the comforting surrounds of her scullery where tears would be blamed on the onions she would soon be peeling.

When the goodbyes were over, Lorca said to Verdor, "I would know you better, Senchai Verdor." In repeating the words she had said when Verdor left her to face the evil Putris Darkin, Lorca wondered again if she would ever see the Senchai again.

"And I you, Lorca."

The two women held each other's hands. "Is there a kingdom where good-byes are not ever said?" Lorca asked.

"Perhaps," Verdor answered.

"And what do you think the women wear there?"

"Their clothes there would be the height of high fashion, I'm sure. The women would paint themselves to please the men and never do any work. And of course, chickens would never need to be plucked." Verdor smiled and wiped aside a tear. "But maybe Andera is such a place."

Lorca was studying Verdor's face so she might never forget her. "Tell me, Verdor, though it's none of my business, do wizard's marry?"

"Yes, Governor," Verdor's grin was mischievous, "but only after they retire."

"Go on with that, Senchai. Wizards never retire. Do they?"

"None that I have ever heard of, but who knows what the future will bring."

"Indeed. Who would ever know if a wizard wouldn't?" They traded smiles. "Blessings on you, Verdor. I would leave you with one request."

"Speak it."

"None of the other kingdoms understood us. We are different, no doubt. I don't know what we are facing, but I will miss this valley. There may never be a trace of our feet ever imprinting the ground here. I would not like us to be forgotten. We are a noble race. Will you tell them that?"

"Ah, Lorca, in a short time we will all be trading with you. Do you think that the other kingdoms can go without soap? You are going far, but you will not disappear. You will have an emissary to the Mosaic like before. I have not given up hope that the Mosaic can help you with your kinship difficulties. You may yet become a thriving race again. There is always hope, good Lorca. We will be there for you. You will see."

All the Giants decided to go to Andera—all but one. Flen would stay. He would not face a life of servitude, of drawing hay or slopping the dung of oxen. He would live in the woods here. His Bobolink would come back for him. He was as sure of that as he was certain that the rest of them were fools for going so far away. *Madness. Let them go.* His hand stroked the crystalline sphere in his pocket.

Feeling watched, he looked up from a ruck sack he was preparing for his own move. Senchai Verdor stood near. She seemed to tower over him, despite her smaller stature. The setting sun was now behind her causing her to appear enveloped within a halo of brilliant light, she was a Giant and he no more than a child. He squinted up at her under bushy eyebrows .

"Flen!" She said. "You do not want to go where that will lead you."

Flen trembled. The fear that she might take the sphere from him slammed against him as if it were his old hammer. He looked at her timidly, cowering. He felt very heavy. His own bulk became onerous. He wondered if he could move. Her unseen eyes skewered his soul. But she did nothing nor said anything more. Flen slunk away, finding shadow where he could, until he disappeared around a near corner.

One hundred and seven wizards descended on the Valley from places never seen by most present and referred to only by storytellers. The black wizard with his gold teeth and easy smile and Chen Chow Yen who never smiled, and who, Thomar once told Gendau, never slept, was among them.

Young Gendau was thrilled. What would be asked of these wizards would require their combined power. What they would do had never been done before.

The time was now. The Giants had, as agreed, gone to their homes for the night. When they awoke, they would be in Andera. They would awake in their beds, under familiar roofs. A cicada's harping would promise a hot day under a cloudless sky. The ubiquitous smell of wood smoke from the soap works would celebrate accustomed normalcy.

A sleepy Fiercer would sit at the edge of his bed and stretch away the drowsiness from sleep, twice interrupted by infant twins. From the kitchen would arise the smells of hens' eggs and spiced tongue and pan fried bread and the sounds of iron against hearthstone.

A river, yet unnamed, still high from recent rains would nurture the hay fields while oxen lowed in the open firebreaks, their tails chasing away summer flies. The work of survival would continue. Some would go to the woods with Menshun, others to the clodding fires or the brackering ring. Some would go to work on the road already well underway through the mountains. Soon, bars of soap would be traded to the other kingdoms the way they always had been.

In the evening, Giants would gather to sing the old songs while some banged on hollowed log drums with no regard to measure or cadence, sounds so dear to their ears and traditions. The songs would remind their young of a glorious history, of loves lost and battles won. Some songs would set the Giants to dancing and others would bring a wistful tear.

There would be some sadness at their departure from their former home because sorrow comes from memory. Some things, they would remember well. Their history books would make detailed records of this journey. Some things would be left behind. Some, maybe two or three would recall a giant named Flen. But had they dreamed of him or had his name been mentioned by one of the ancient storytellers? If they looked, they would not find his name in the Tomes. There would be no file or heading for executioners. The word Troca would not appear there.

The Giants would thrive in Andera.

All of the Grand Wizards stood in position outside the city, facing toward it from all points of direction. At Pater Nos' signal, they extended their hands out against the night sky. When their work was done, the city of Burba was gone.

The night moved on. A brilliant moon navigated steadily across a starry sky drawing behind it tomorrow's promise. Only Verdor, Thomar, Gendau and Ruta, Master Singh's new apprentice, remained. Ruta's red curls appeared black in the silvered darkness. The four stood at the edge of what was once the basement to the Library of Tomes. Not even a rock from its foundation was left behind.

Verdor leaned against Thomar, holding his hand.

"'Tis a wonderment, Senchai Verdor," young Ruta said.

"'Tis all of that, Ruta," Verdor replied.

About the Author:

Joseph A. Callan is the father of four children. He has been a carpenter in Upstate New York for almost forty years, where he lives with his wife, Mary Eileen. When he's not working or writing, he's probably fly fishing his favorite stream.

Visit him on the Web at **www.josephacallan.com**

CPSIA information can be obtained at www.ICGtesting.com
Printed in the USA
BVOW040856111111

275875BV00002B/5/P